BEARER OF MASKS

BEARER OF MASKS

ISBN: 978-1-9168887-6-0 (Kindle)
ISBN: 978-1-9168887-7-7 (Paperback)

Cover Design: Franziska Stern – Instagram: @coverdungeonrabbit
Editing: Sydney Hawthorn
Book Design and Typesetting: Enchanted Ink Publishing

First printing, 2022.

Hannah, this book is for you, bestie.

You're a true superhero in your own right.

Other books by Lauren Jade Case

The Creature Chronicles:

The Starlight Trilogy:

Starlight

Starfall

The Abnormal Spies Series:

Bearer of Masks

My intent with this book and this story is never to harm and I don't want to risk someone's health by not disclosing that which may cause such things. While some triggers may appear in one chapter, in one line, in large or small quantities, I never want or mean to hurt another person. And while warnings aren't required, I don't want to compromise anyone with anything.

Below is a list of what the following book does contain and so now please be aware that these things are present in the story of BEARER OF MASKS to some degree.

This book contains the following content warnings:

Adult language
Injuries/ injury detail
Blood/ Gore
Violence
Prejudice
Mentions of drugs
Scenes of a sexual nature
Mental abuse

BEARER OF MASKS

LAUREN JADE CASE

Case File: **#492**
Written by: PRAXIS [redacted]
Date: 36th Day of Autumn 2406
Location: [redacted]

Log type: MISSION
Status: CLOSED/ COMPLETE
If Complete, to what level: [redacted]

Due to the extenuating circumstances after the last case, 2 new entries were taken on the 22nd day of the autumn season. [**Information of who, fully redacted from document**]

They settled into [redacted] rather well [redacted].

Quickly they came to be tested. They were charged with finding and retrieving the [redacted]. The artefact had been lost for near one hundred years. Its creator had beset it with magic, [redacted]. The creator had been gifted with being able to present inanimate objects power – that was his entire anomaly – and mostly he chose to offer things [redacted]. Except this [redacted]. This [redacted] he had gifted [redacted], so the [redacted] then [redacted] to [redacted].

The creators family wanted it back in their custody because once the creator came to pass, the world began to remember what [redacted] – how good and bad of a thing it was. And they decided they wanted it safe.

[redacted] were set aside for the mission.

Providing each member gave an accurate account, this file is to document the proceedings of case number #492.

CHAPTER ONE
CHANDLER

22nd Day of Autumn 2406

Water droplets hung in the air and Chandler could sense them without having to touch, just like she always could. They danced in their own current, invisible to the eye, but always ready for the taking. Always ready for *her*.

Instead of plucking one out of the air, she cracked her knuckles and clutched her bag strap tightly to stop it falling off her shoulder.

She had bigger things to focus on.

Today was the day. The day of the big job interview. She'd even dressed in her repurposed black and white pin-stripe suit for the occasion. Her hazel eyes were lined on top with black to sharpen them and her shapeless brown hair was stuck into a ponytail. Her shoes had an edged heel, not so much that she couldn't walk, but enough to showcase her presence when she walked.

This interview *had* to count. *Normals* struggled to get seen, let alone *Abnormals*. Chandler's last chance had been six months ago.

Luckily, she did have a bar-maid job back home. She worked in a youth nightclub and it wasn't a bad place. Her boss and co-workers were lovely. Nothing got out of hand because everyone entering was offered the same amount of alcohol – two tokens each, one per drink – and the rest was soft drinks.

But it wasn't what she wanted.

A voice rattled over the overhead tannoy. "*To the people aboard this shuttle, you next stop is New London*."

Chandler elbowed her way to the doors. Stacks of people were ahead of her, already in position to leap off when the shuttle stopped. Most wore the same sorts of suits and skirts, clutched briefcases and bags, whispered into earpieces or stared at the latest model watches. As she stopped among them, she tried to quieten her breathing. She hoped that if they glanced at her right now, she'd look like she was one of them.

The shuttle eased to a stop. Chandler was pulled out by the crowd and managed to find her footing just as they all got to the stairs that descended onto the streets below.

Currently it was the third season of the year, and the city it was warmer then back home but the wind was still abrasive. It lifted hair and trash, brushed cheeks and legs, made goose-bumps rise and forced people to cover. Chandler gripped her bag tighter.

She marched down one street, turned right onto the next, and followed round that one's curve. She didn't know the name of anything here – she hadn't grown up anywhere near New London. All she had was a printed out map and lines she'd drawn over it for the directions she needed to take. She'd also marked up some odd shops for reassurance, ways of double-checking she was heading in the right direction if she looked up.

She kept going until she found the grey building she'd been searching for.

From what Chandler knew, this part of the city was known as the business sector. Despite that, not many people had followed her off the shuttle to come this way. It suited her fine, but she had expected more hustle and bustle for a supposed reputable area.

A carved golden sign on the front of the building glinted in the low light that broke round corners of buildings to shine upon it. *Eichner Grand*. Chandler grimaced inwardly but pointed her chin up. Taking in a lungful of air, she walked inside.

Typing away on a gold plated computer system at the front desk was a greying male. He kept looking between four stacked screens at his left and then at something below the desk's top on the right, probably at a small screen or something on a shelf. Chandler strolled right up to him and he looked up immediately.

"May I offer assistance?" he asked.

"I have an interview with Mr Ulgg," she answered.

The man raised an extremely bushy eyebrow. "Mr Ulgg you say?"

Chandler fought the urge to crack her knuckles. "May the grey skies brighten up and let fish swim through rainbows again."

She honestly had no idea what the saying meant, only that she'd been given the instruction to repeat it upon arrival. It seemed strange. *Beyond* strange really. At no other interview had she been made to repeat a passphrase. She'd never heard of it happening anywhere. But every process was different. Maybe it was a way of showing who could follow instructions, despite how ridiculous they may be.

They man nodded and got up from his chair, scurrying round her side of the counter. His little yellow bow-tie was slightly askew yet otherwise he was dressed immaculately in a black suit.

In one motion he swooped his arm in a gesture of her to follow and walked off. Chandler was forced into a quick-march to catch up.

They trudged down so many twisting corridors Chandler was convinced they'd gone to the back of the building. Who knew an interview for an office position at a hotel would mean so much walking? They eventually stopped and the person she'd been following knocked on a blank wooden door.

Immediately, the door swung open. A tall and muscular man stood on the other side. His shirt was tight at his neck and long trousers didn't quite cover the fact he wore heavy duty boots. His ginger hair was rough around the edges, like he'd cut it himself, and a slight shadow of a beard formed on his jaw.

"Miss Burdess, I assume?" the man asked. His tone was calm, his voice less gruff that what Chandler would've assumed from his size. She nodded. "Come in."

He moved back but Chandler still had to duck under his arm to enter.

The room was clean and sparse. Only a solid wood desk, a green rug over wooden flooring, three chairs facing the desk, and one lopsided chandelier occupied the space.

"Welcome, Miss Burdess," the man said, taking a seat behind the desk. "What would you like me to call you?"

"Chandler is fine," she answered as she sat in the chair opposite.

"Chandler," he repeated. "It's a pretty name. Not one I've heard in a while."

"It was apparently my dad's name."

"I see." The man grabbed some papers stacked nearby. "Twenty-two years young, aren't you?"

"I am right now, yes Sir." She'd always been told to address people with respect, especially hopeful employers.

"You're a little shorter than I was expecting."

Chandler stood at barely above five foot three; though wearing heels helped boost her height a little most days. The urge to crack her knuckles at the comment spread across her brain but she resisted, settling for rubbing the skin on her fingers instead.

"And, you applied for a job with us recently," he continued.

"Yes, Sir."

He set the papers back down. "My name's Praxis. A little uncommon, I know. But you are too, aren't you?"

She blinked, slightly taken aback. "If you're referring to my Abnormality—"

"I am," he cut in. "I'm sure you've had lots of comments about it over the years."

"Yes, I have."

"And I'm sure you've been turned away from places and jobs before."

"I have," she repeated, a little blunter.

"People in the big wide world don't like things they can't understand, cannot control, or do not belong in." Praxis sat forwards, mashing his fingers together. "But that's *exactly* what we're looking for."

Chandler blanched, unsure she heard correctly. Usually people would send her packing at the first mention of her Abnormality. No one saw them as a bonus, as something they wanted. Either she was dreaming or Praxis was being cruel.

"What are you saying?" she asked carefully.

He stood. "You're hired."

"I'm..."

Perhaps there could be a third version of events: that this *was* real and the man in front of her was giving her a fighting chance. This was no dream and Praxis wasn't being cruel. That this was really *it*.

"Hired," he repeated.

Chandler looked around the office. Was this to be her room? Or was she going to be placed somewhere else in the hotel? Would she sit below in a basement room, at a desk, with a whole computer of her own? It wasn't a career, but it was a start for her, a possible chance at the new life she wanted. A stepping stone. All of it was much better than what she'd had before.

"But the job isn't what you think."

The world came crashing back down around her. She stared at Praxis, all hope melting away. The water in the air around her stirred and she focused on her breathing for control.

"It's not like you think at all," he continued. "You applied for a position that isn't real."

Anger and confusion bubbled up inside Chandler in a cold, swirling spiral. She'd had enough. "Then why am I here? How can I be hired for a job that doesn't exist?"

"There is still a job for you, just not at this hotel."

He stood and moved to the far wall. There must've been a keypad or lever that Chandler missed because Praxis did something and the entire panel slid away, revealing a lit grey corridor.

"I know how hard life can be in this world," Praxis said, turning back to face Chandler. "Especially for people like you, like *us*. But if you come with me, I will explain everything and I will tell you exactly how, in reality, the world relies on people like us without even knowing about it."

Chandler finally gave in and crackled her knuckles; the *pop*s were satisfying to her ears.

She was fed up being played for a fool. She wondered if she could trust this man and his mysteries. A hidden corridor wasn't the best way to start. Plenty of Abnormals had gone missing over the years – no one Normal was overly upset by it, the disappearances actually helped them worry about one less thing. She could almost hear her mother's snide remarks about trust, how she was being foolish to even consider the potential.

Chandler wiped her mother from her mind. She was fed up being played the fool by her own mother. She couldn't trust her most of all. *That* was the real problem.

Praxis stepped into the corridor, his back to her.

Just this once, instead of cracking her knuckles, Chandler held out her hand and let a droplet of water solidify to ice on the tip of her finger. To prove she could. To know she had it waiting in case.

She gripped her bag and stood, trusting herself and that she was making the right decision.

CHAPTER TWO
ZIVA

22nd Day of Autumn 2406

Ignoring the guard blocking part of the doorway, the shuttle cart was empty. It didn't matter that the entire shuttle consisted of only one cart instead of many strung together. What mattered to Ziva was the space and quiet that came with it.

Back home, she barely got anything to herself. Living with both parents, five siblings, and one grandmother all crammed into a six bedroom complex in Old London really took things away. It didn't matter who was the oldest or youngest, everyone had to do their bit. Ziva had to share with the twins – the next oldest siblings – and they took up the most room with their bunk-beds and toys.

Ziva relaxed into the red leather chair. She sipped at the water she'd been offered and put it down on the table in front of her.

Most shuttles ran over-ground, whizzing way above towns and cities in the air. It was a way to save space and to free up the underground tunnels – some had begun to collapse and now all sat empty. Except Ziva was currently underground, in an abandoned tunnel, aboard a small one carriage shuttle. Apparently it wasn't all empty down here as suspected.

The guard at the door had been the one to escort her this way but he hadn't conducted the initial interview that had paved the way for whatever this was. Another man had done that; he'd called himself Praxis. He'd stayed behind to interview someone else, apparently. Ziva didn't mind. She was comfy and mostly mentally free.

She glanced around the spacious carriage. Normal shuttles consisted of at least three carriages stuck together. This entire shuttle was one thing, and was much larger than a usual compartment. Ziva wondered if this was what luxury looked like, what money could buy.

Red wasn't the best colour – Ziva wanted to change it, make it a sleek black or stunning gold – but it worked with the white of everything else. The windows were tinted and there was no latch to open them. The guard had at least left the entrance door open for air. Down here, the air was indeed crisp, probably from being so far underground and away from the smog of the city.

In the centre of the carriage a table and six chairs were all nailed to the floor. Spotlights on the ceilings and under seats illuminated the space without it being unbearable.

"Miss?"

Ziva glanced up. The guard from the doorway approached her, his little beret tilted further than it should've been, just like his smile. He appeared young, maybe only a few years older than Ziva's twenty-one. Ivory skin accompanied rich green eyes and short brown hair.

"Are you hungry?" he asked, his voice a level of monotone Ziva hadn't heard before. "Do you want a snack?"

Ziva's stomach grumbled and she smiled weakly. "Anything orange, please?"

His right eyebrow quirked, elongating the scar that ran through it and past his right eye. "Would a real orange suffice?" He offered out his hand, showing the fruit in his palm.

"Where did you get that from?" she asked, staring.

"I brought two with me today, but I'm not going to eat it. It's yours."

She took it, thanked him, and peeled the skin. The guard slunk back to the doorway and Ziva watched him out the corner of her eye as she popped a segment of orange into her mouth.

Rotating the pieces in her hand, she smiled. For as long as she could remember, Ziva had been obsessed with colour. Every week she'd loved a different one. All were exciting.

Until that childish excitement morphed into a terrifying realisation.

The world itself had changed quite a long time ago, but Ziva's world had changed only a few years back. Her love of colour had sunk away when she realised she could *change* colour. Blues could become yellows, reds could be greys, and whites could be pinks. It didn't discriminate. She could make them all dance whenever she touched an item and thought about its colour shift.

At first, her family had marvelled in amazement. But then she created a white so bright that it blinded and a black so dark it stole light.

At the front of the shuttle the guard shifted, straightening his back. Ziva sat up to see why.

Praxis, the man who'd interviewed her, was climbing aboard. But he wasn't alone. A girl followed him in. The guard shut the door immediately after and walked to where the starting room at the front of the shuttle probably was.

Ziva hid her orange below the table, fiddling with it in her lap, and sneaking in another bit when no one watched. Praxis then sat opposite her and directed the other guest to the chair at her right.

The shuttle rumbled softly and sprang to life – the lights momentarily flickered. Shuttles ran smoothly along their path so it was hard to tell when they were actually moving or when they were stationary. Ziva assumed they'd set off on their journey though, on their way to wherever these tracks ended.

"Ziva," Praxis said, drawing in her attention. He waved his hand at the other occupant. "This is Chandler."

She looked at the girl and smiled. "Morning."

Chandler nodded. "Hi." She cracked her knuckles, leaving sounds like thunder echoing in such a hollow space.

They had to be around the same age, Ziva was sure. She was young and the other girl appeared to be also. Chandler's pale white skin illuminated pinkish under the shuttle light while Ziva's smooth russet brown skin remained the same. Both had brown hair, though Ziva's verged on being black, and it hung down to her waist, cut with full fringe to give it some life. Both also seemed to have brown eyes, though the other girls were more hazel. Ziva was angles and lines, skin and bone; Chandler had curves. Chandler wore a suit and wore it well, but Ziva was dressed in her mother's hand-me-down denim skirt and a white t-shirt.

"Now you're acquainted..." Praxis sat back, throwing his feet onto the table and tucking his hands behind his head. "You've both got a lot in common. You're both new recruits, for starters."

"New recruits?" Ziva questioned. She'd applied for a receptionist position.

Chandler looked at her. "So he didn't explain anything to you beforehand either?"

"You're both *Abnormals*," Praxis continued. Chandler didn't flinch but Ziva did. She could feel the ghosts of all the needles that had been stuck into her by doctors during their rigorous testing period. "You both have a power, an Abnormality.

And you both are needed *because* of that power and because of yourselves in general, really."

Ziva's heart-rate spiked; the organ threatened to pound so hard it would cut itself by squeezing through her ribs.

She shifted to look at Chandler, who stared blankly, but crackled her knuckles.

How could they be needed? How could Ziva's "power" be of use? It was colour related – the most boring kind of power she'd heard of, even if she could manipulate light and dark itself through it.

Still, Praxis looked unfazed. "The jobs you applied for don't exist."

"We're getting that," Chandler mumbled.

He shrugged and sat upright suddenly; Ziva gasped at the bolt of movement. "I told you both that I'd explain how the world relies on us, which it *does*, and it doesn't even know." He paused, allowing his words to sink in, and Ziva shuddered at the anticipation. "Our power is the answer. We hide in the shadows, ride the storms, and stalk in the night. While the world thinks our governments and royalties run the world with its services, really it is *us* that keep it turning. *We* are the shadows. *We* create the storms. And we are known only to ourselves. That means no government or royalty or body of power knows of us. We are dead and hidden to them."

Ziva swallowed thickly. "Dead?"

Praxis nodded. "From here on out, if you choose to stay, your old life is gone. To the outside world, you vanished. Not completely. You may still keep contact with your family and friends, but they can never know what you do or where that may take you."

Chandler sat forwards, her suit sleeves pulling up her arms to reveal a pattern against her skin on her left forearm – it looked like winding vines with roses, and a snake burrowing through it all, its head at her wrist. "But what do we do?" she asked simply.

"We do whatever is needed of us," Praxis answered.

"What does that even mean? And what do you mean *if* we choose to stay?"

Ziva slipped another piece of orange into her mouth, hiding the motion in a fake cough, hoping the tang would calm her. But it didn't. She only felt growing apprehension.

"You need to complete one mission before your choice on staying can be made." He looked between them both carefully. "One mission. Then you may stay or leave. After that, you may leave at *any* point, but once the decision to go is made then it is kept. As for the missions, they can be anything. From capturing a person, to hiding an artefact, to rewriting a document. Anything that may disrupt the world's turning, we must stop. We must keep the world progressing towards the new dawn. Our powers allow us and *only* us to do that. That is our job. Our life."

The powers he referred too mostly came from mutations. Virus' had spread, caused some science and genes to shift, and people years later were born with powers. No one knew exactly *when* the shift had happened, just that every-so-often people had a new ability wake within them. Some estimated things had changed over one hundred years ago but it was too hard to tell. It didn't entirely matter to a lot of people.

But maybe a mutation *could* be a good thing after all if this was the offering afterwards.

Ziva tried to focus. She'd never heard of such an organisation before, yet Praxis had basically said that was the entire point.

"Not everyone who has an Abnormality is part of our organisation," he added. "Even though I know we're rare, we can't recruit *everyone*. There's still too many to have you all, sadly. But everyone here *is* Abnormal."

The shuttle lights flickered and then turned off. Quickly, a softer glow illuminated the carriage. The guard returned; Ziva noticed his beret was a little straighter now.

Praxis left his seat first. Ziva was slow to follow and Chandler even slower.

The guard unhooked the giant metal bar that stretched across the door, clearly there as a lock. The door fell away at a small kick, revealing steps – Ziva didn't remembered climbing any on the way in, but she had been a little distracted.

"So we have a choice," Chandler spoke, and Ziva whirled round to face her.

Praxis took his time to answer. He scratched the underside of his chin, the sound of his nails catching on stubble was gentle yet somehow loud in the enclosed space. "You do," he said. "You just have to complete one mission first. That's the arrangement and there's no changing it."

The guard led the way out and Praxis followed. Ziva stuffed the final pieces of orange in her mouth and stepped out, too.

Looking up, she realised they were still underground. She blinked. She didn't know why but she'd expected to come out above it. The white tiles of the walls flickered in her gaze, a few shifting to a tulip yellow before resting again. She glanced away.

Praxis marched to the front of the very small group. "Are you ready to go to where you'll be staying until your mission is over?"

It wasn't much of a question since there wasn't much choice. They'd been plucked up, brought in with a fake promise of a real job, and were being forced to go somewhere to complete some dubious-sounding mission that could literally be *anything* imaginable.

Ziva might've asked for peace and quiet and space, but this isn't what she'd meant. She hadn't intended to be picked up and carted off in a way to test her abilities. She bit her bottom lip nervously. Her mother had always warned her to be careful in what she wished for.

CHAPTER THREE
QUINTON

22nd Day of Autumn 2406

Redwing was alive with activity.

Quinton stood on the first floor indoor balcony, arms balancing him on the railing, one ankle crossed behind the other. Gretchen, his best friend, was beside him. He flipped between looking at those running around – staff and others on the stairs – and watching the front door.

People were buzzing for two reasons today: supposedly there were *two* new missions beginning *and* two new recruits being brought in.

Gretchen nudged him as she leant back against the railing, her arms awkwardly folding back over it for balance. He raised an eyebrow at her, noting the duffel bag at her feet. "Who'd ya think the big P is bringin' in?"

Quinton shifted his gaze back to the door. "Could be any two."

"Is it *definitely* two? Last I heard, the word was three."

"As long as they have powers."

"We *all* have powers so that's not a hard thing to aim for." She twisted back round, leaning on her elbows, her gaze back on the door. "Seamus was betting one would have a fire power. Bet Doug ten pieces on it."

Quinton felt himself smile. "What did Doug bet in return?"

"Ten pieces that it one was a water power."

"And what did you bet?"

"I don't do that."

"You're an idiot if you think I believe that," Quinton muttered. "I *know* you can never leave a Grittal bet alone."

"The twins are dumb."

He laughed. "They might be, but my point still stands."

Gretchen raised a hand in surrender. "Fine. You've got me," she huffed. "I bet ten that one has earth."

"And what happens if two of you win?" The front door opened and closed, and Quinton's eyes zoned in on it. But it was only the third Grittal brother, Wane, leaving. Quinton turned back to his friend. "What has you all so uptight that any of them will have an elemental power?"

She shrugged non-committally and didn't respond.

Word in this place spread like air. Quinton knew that wasn't always the case. Secrets could be kept well-hidden, even here, but they had to be halfway buried.

Quinton stood up properly, his back aching, and smoothed out the front of his shirt. Gretchen's neatly-drawn eyebrows rose as he did, only for him to realise she was staring at his crystal necklace.

The clear quartz lay against the centre of his chest, dangling from a delicate silver chain. It wasn't cold against his skin whenever the two things touched, but if someone else held it they would complain about the low temperature. Quinton never understood why, but then again he couldn't use his powers on himself.

Gretchen stared at the necklace; her thickly lined blue eyes were glued onto it. He understood that stare. He'd seen it from plenty of people over the course of his life. There was no ill intent behind the look, just basic curiosity. His whole power was controlled and determined by the crystal. Others had to hold it for him to *see*.

He pinched the small crystal between his finger and thumb. "Do you want to know?"

She shook her head, causing several strands of blonde hair to fall free to her shoulders from its clasp. She had dared once, and then never since. That was *before*. Before a future he'd seen that hadn't changed. Before he'd seen that she'd break her own leg and she wouldn't be able to heal it.

The cast and crutches had disappeared several weeks ago, but Gretchen was still overly cautious on stairs. Thankfully Redwing had many.

Quinton let the crystal rest against his skin again.

Few people resisted the urge to know their futures – those who'd learnt and accepted that while futures might change, not all could or would, were the ones that left Quinton's power alone. Nearly everyone here had tried at some point though. They had to touch the crystal, and then Quinton had to touch it after. He would then relay what he saw. Not all visions were good, and not all were bad. It was a matter of *seeing*.

"Are you ready?" he asked, finally nodding and acknowledging her bag. "Wane left a few minutes ago."

Gretchen snorted. "He's over-eager and young."

Quinton raised an eyebrow. "He's twenty, that's one year younger than you. Actually, won't he *be* your age in like ten days?"

"All that matters is that I'm still younger than you."

He rolled his eyes. Quinton was two years older – almost exactly to the day – than her.

She laughed and lifted her bag onto one shoulder. "For a duo mission, I really could've ended up with someone worse," she said. "I ain't mad."

"Yeah, you could've been stuck with me as your partner."

She elbowed him in the ribs. "You know that ain't a bad thing! I would've gladly had you beside me."

He rubbed his side. "Too bad I wasn't chosen."

"Yeah," she agreed, sighing. "Maybe next time you can help dig up an old, crusty person."

Missions came and went, and the people picked to carry them out were either decided amongst themselves or by their leaders. A person's power usually came into account when choosing. If it was a non-specific task, the leaders left it up to everyone else.

The leaders of Redwing – Praxis Ulgg, who was top dog, Maggie, the ancient kind lady, and Violette, the young and bitchy woman – ultimately had the final say on anything, however, even if they did leave a lot up to the recruits. At any moment they could over-rule or change something.

Gretchen had been picked for her mission by the leaders. The other party that was heading out on another mission had too.

To collect broken bones from an unmarked grave that could potentially rewrite Ancient Egyptian history, it was best to send along a girl who had the power to mend or break bones and then a boy who could lift anything above his head as if it weighed the same as feathers to carry them out.

Quinton looked back at the unmoving door. "Not a damn chance, Gritty."

A new voice cut in before Gretchen could respond. "Hey, Bony!"

The Grittal twins, Seamus and Doug, raced towards Quinton and Gretchen. They stopped right beside her, wrapping an arm each over her shoulders. She made a face at Quinton for help, but all he offered was a smile as he folded his arms over his chest and leant back.

Everyone at Redwing knew the twins were trouble. They made no secret of it either.

All three brothers had flaming ginger hair, though the twins' was curled in tight ringlets and stuck out in all angles. Their dark blue eyes sparked with constant mischief. And while Wane was actually both the tallest and biggest built despite being the youngest, the twins were still well stocked themselves.

"Hey, Bony," cooed Seamus. "You better look after our tiny brother."

"If you don't," Doug took over, "we'll have to reward you."

Gretchen rolled her eyes. "I ain't leaving him behind."

"Not even if we pay you?"

"Not even if we let you off the bet?" Seamus added.

"We'll *both* be back before you know it," Gretchen said. "Then you can go about stuffing him in a bin, or locking him in the attic, or whatever small torture you've cooked up next."

Doug pointed at his twin. "They all sound like good ideas."

Seamus nodded firmly. "A bin in the attack?"

The twins let Gretchen go, grinning from ear to ear, and walked away chatting in whispers. It wasn't until they'd slunk down the stairs and around a corner that Gretchen visibly relaxed; her shoulders lowered and her breathing audibly softened.

"I thought you didn't bet," Quinton mocked. She shot him a fierce glare.

Just as she was clearly about to swear, the bell at the front door rang.

Gretchen ran to the banister, dropping her bag in the process, and leaned over. Quinton shuffled after her slowly. Though he'd been interested in what was to come – why the sudden need for new recruits? Why was everything being kept so hush-hush?

– he was in no way going to show it or give the leaders the satisfaction of knowing. At least it looked better that everyone else was here too.

New recruits changed things. They were *interesting*. Dynamics shifted. Potential was stirred. More ground was given to walk on.

Night had fallen outside. Dark and coldness wafted in as the grand double doors opened, hitting Quinton even up on the first floor.

Redwing stopped. There were no footsteps, no shouts, and no laughs.

Until the stomps came.

First came Abel Rickter. He was the main guard and followed Praxis whenever he left Redwing on a "selecting mission". Normally he would patrol the grounds with a few others, not that anyone could get inside Redwing without knowing of its existence first.

Redwing wasn't the only base out in the world. Every recruit knew there were more places, but most didn't know of any besides their "home" one. The leaders knew more, of course, but it still wasn't clear how much *they* knew. Keeping information like that close to the chest was paramount in this line of work where secrets were the highest valued thing. Even if that meant keeping secrets from each other. Quinton had always wondered how many other places there were, how many more recruits in other places there were.

Praxis followed behind Abel. His boots caused of most of the disturbance as he marched to his own tune, the noise echoing around the entryway.

A girl in a denim skirt walked behind him. She wore a smile, like she was thoroughly blown away by what she saw and didn't know how else to react. Her walk was swift, the way she moved elegant. When she stopped, she stood straight.

Another girl brought up the rear, with shoes that clicked and a suit that looked like it wasn't quite made for her. She clasped her bag tightly as she peered around, not quiet seeming to make eye-contact with anyone. Her shoulders appeared tight, and she was shorter than the other girl but carried herself just as well.

"I think," Gretchen whispered, "from looking at them, I'd guess we *all* lost the bet."

Praxis led the girls around the foyer, past everyone who was ogling, and into his office. "I wouldn't assume too early," Quinton said, watching as the door closed.

"You think we stand a chance?"

"Hard to say. Wait. What do you mean, *we*?" He looked sideways at her.

Gretchen picked up her bag again and hoisted it onto her shoulders, smiling. "Now I'm kind of mad I was picked for this mission. Who wants to dig up some dusty bones and smuggle them out of a country when there's new recruits? The excitement levels in this building just went up a million percent."

"You are not wrong."

There hadn't been many new recruits in the last few years, and certainly no females; not since Gretchen eight years ago. But it didn't matter what gender anyone was.

What mattered was that things had just become *fascinating*.

CHAPTER FOUR
CHANDLER

22nd Day of Autumn 2406

"Take a seat."

Praxis signalled to the two blue worn and partly ruined blue suede chairs. The other girl, Ziva, took up the offer. Chandler causiously sat in the other seat.

The guard who'd been with them in the shuttle had disappeared at some point. Replacing him behind Praxis were two women – one old, one young. They'd been stationed in the office when they'd arrived.

"Redwing is where you'll be staying for the foreseeable future," Praxis said. "This place will be your home and refuge, so use it as such. You will each have a room of your own as well as an attached bathroom. Helpers will come every morning to clean and to assist in nearly any duty you ask of them. They will also prepare all meals of the day and clean your laundry. Your rooms will be on the third floor. I will take you there in a few minutes so you can see for yourselves. The second floor is for staff rooms. The first is an open space, meant for games and lounging and moving. Lastly is the ground floor. That's this room – my office – the kitchen, and the dining area and small library room. Of course, the more you move around, the more you'll figure this out yourselves."

When he raised his eyebrows in question, Chandler nodded back.

Praxis continued. "While I run Redwing now, behind me stands my second in commands. Maggie," the old woman tilted her head, sending grey curls tumbling over her face, "has been with us for years, and was the original owner of this building and runner of this section of our society. Violette," the younger woman smiled, but it didn't reach her eyes, "transferred here from another branch a few years back but knows the ins and outs here as well as anyone. Together we take charge, sort the missions, send you out, and look after you too. You can come to us with any needs, and we'll sort them out. Remember, you're here because of your powers. They make you special and we need them. The *world* needs them. And that's the end of my little speech." His smile wobbled. "Do you have any questions?"

Chandler played with the back of her knuckles. She had many questions, but some were clearer than others.

However, Ziva jumped in first. "What about our stuff from home?"

Praxis nodded several times. "You will each be given one hundred and fifty pieces to spend on new clothing and things you may need. As for other sentimental items... well, they depend on whether you stay or go."

Chandler didn't have time to stop the words from flying out her mouth. "Nothing is given for free. Not jobs and not money." Her heart thudded with agitation and she fought harder to not crack her knuckles. "*And* our decision on whether we stay or go depends on getting a mission because you say we have to complete one first. For all we know, you could hold out on giving us one. Fine, we have to do one. But when will it come? You could keep us from making a decision about leaving for *years*!

Violette continued to stare like she didn't care to be here at all. Maggie, however, gave Chandler an appraising look, like she'd just said the exactly right thing.

Praxis leant back in his chair. "Those who go on missions are mostly determined by those of us in this room. Usually those selected to go have the right skill, whether that's by power or personality. Yet, when we get new recruits, because we know we cannot keep them, whatever mission comes in next, it is nearly always theirs. Only extreme circumstances would make that not true. So that means whatever mission comes in next will likely be yours."

"When it that going to be?" Ziva asked.

Praxis' eyebrows scrunched up. "It could come in tomorrow or years down the line, though the latter isn't likely compared to the former."

"And the money?" Chandler pressed. She squeezed her forefinger and it cracked, mostly by accident, but it fizzled away some of the anxiety that'd wound up inside her.

"Let's call these pieces an advancement."

"Advancement?" Ziva asked. "Do we get *paid* here?"

He nodded again. "Like any other job."

Chandler let go of her hands completely. "We get a salary?"

"Like any other job," he repeated. "It's a weekly wage. You started earning it the minute you crossed into this building. Two hundred pieces each. Count the one-fifty as an extra, welcome bonus. But it's what you're worth here, and what you deserve to earn. We have indirect, unknowing investors that keep up going by adding into our normal appearing ventures."

"People who don't know we're Abnormals are funding us?"

"They do. We then have Abnormals on the outside process and send those invested pieces to us here. We have people everywhere, doing everything."

Chandler tried to keep her face neutral as hope filled her insides. This really could be the chance she needed. Lack of beginning consent and lies at joining aside, she could worry about the choice on staying later. At least, for now, she was here, away from *her mother*, being treated like a person, earning a wage. Depending on how long she stayed, even between now and just her first mission, she could earn enough to live on whatever the choice after.

If she dared to think about it, it might make her actually *happy*.

Chandler shook her head. She wouldn't let herself get that far.

Letting out a steady breath, she asked, "How will we get these new things?"

Suddenly Praxis launched to his feet. "Your Helpers can go into the nearby town to get them for you."

"They can go themselves, Ulgg." It took Chandler a second to register that it'd been Maggie who'd spoken. Her voice was deep and raspy, scratchy like it'd been used too much in the past and had never recovered. Her piercing, dark eyes cut through her scraggly hair to focus between Chandler and Ziva. "The nearby town has all you might need," she said. "And some other exciting things too. It's a growing place."

"We'll go together, in the morning," Chandler decided aloud. Ziva turned to her in her seat, looking shocked, but didn't say anything outwardly *against* the idea.

"If that's all settled..." Praxis looked over their heads to the door. "Shall I take you to your rooms?"

The girls stood in unison and Praxis took that as answer, leading out.

On the way in, there hadn't been time to examine what they were walking in to. Now, as they strolled from the office, they could do what they wanted. Praxis moved slowly as if expecting them to stare at everything.

Grand front doors opened into a giant, clean and wooden entryway. At the far end was a massive staircase that split in two halfway up. Two ends of a long table and a few chairs stuck out from behind the staircase were it seemed to be tucked away.

They climbed the stairs and when Praxis went ahead, Ziva touched Chandler's elbow gently. Chandler looked at her. "You said we'd go together into town tomorrow," Ziva said. "Why?"

Chandler stopped. "I just think its best we stick together. If that's ok with you?"

Together, they were in the same boat. Both new and both unsure of anything to come. It made sense for them to keep each other close.

Ziva smiled and nodded.

In a quiet decision, they carried on following Praxis.

Staircase after staircase they climbed until they reached the third floor.

Deep red walls were lined with wooden doors set. Grey carpet ran the long length and the ceiling followed in white. Hanging lampshades softened the glow of the bulbs, muted yellow illuminating the space. In a few places between doorways sat paintings nails to the walls, all with tarnished gold frames. It was as if whoever had decorated had done so years ago and had never looked back.

Praxis stopped at the first two rooms on the left. "Here we are," he announced. "Take whichever you like. They're both the same. There aren't any locks on the door but no one will come in without knocking and waiting for permission, that's one of the few firm rules we have here." He started off back the way he'd come but turned back round at the last second. "One last thing. Every day, there is some training taking place for whoever is here at the time. We meet in the foyer at eight every morning. It's the only thing that's required of you while you stay. Rule two, if you will."

"Training?" Ziva questioned.

"It's usually running laps or defence training or even just wall climbing. You never know the situation you may find yourselves in while on a mission."

Chandler watched Ziva's eyes bug out. "Situations?" the girl asked.

"You will be let off tomorrow," Praxis told them. "But from the day after, if you're still here, you'll be required to attend."

"If we don't?" Chandler asked.

Praxis grinned and walked off without answering.

Ziva stepped up to the second door since she was closest to it already. "I'll see you in the morning?"

Chandler nodded. "What time would be best for you?"

"Shall we say, maybe, eight?"

"Want to meet out here? Then we can get lost in this stupidly big place together before leaving."

A new voice chimed in. "It's only stupidly big until you find all the hidden passageways."

Both girls looked in the direction of the voice. It'd come from where Praxis had gone.

In the leader's place was a tall guy with blazing dyed red hair that'd been tied back into a mini ponytail at the nape of his neck.

"When you find *those*," they continued, "then this place becomes impossibly *massive*."

Ziva moved up to Chandler's side, looking excited. "Secret passages?"

The male shrugged. "There might be some, there might not be any. This place is old. Built when passageways would've been a thing." He strode forwards, showing off a smile. "I'm Quinton, by the way, and you're the new recruits I'm guessing?"

Chandler looked up at him, thinking he looked familiar. A moment later she realised why. "You were on the first floor watching us when we came in."

Quite a few people had been staring when her and Ziva had entered. Chandler had avoided looking back, but it was the red hair that had given him away then and now.

He flashed his smile directly at her, stormy blue eyes dancing with amusement. "What are your names? Or are we to call you *Abbies*?"

Chandler immediately disliked whatever "*Abbies*" was. She assumed it was a combination of "newbies" and "Abnormals". Being called the first name was bad enough. The second one haunted her every waking moment. The combination left a sour taste on her tongue.

"I'm Ziva," the other girl answered. She held out her hand and Quinton took it.

Chandler inwardly sighed. "Chandler."

Quinton nodded once. "Well, welcome aboard this ship, Ziva and Chandler," he said. "A few of us are headed into town tomorrow, just like you are." The look on his face made Chandler think his decision to go into town had been made moments ago after learning that she and Ziva were going. "There will be people to ask for answers if you have any questions. I'm sure you have some."

"A few," Ziva confirmed.

"I'm sure it's been a long day and you're tired. Maybe I'll see you tomorrow?" Quinton smiled and walked down the hallway.

Ziva shrugged and opened the door to her new room. With a final smile, she went in.

Chandler waited a moment longer, gripping her bag's strap until her fingers ached. The air chilled around her but she quickly shook it off and went into her new room. The door closed quietly behind her and she put her forehead against it as she cracked her fingers one by one to release the tension stacked up inside her bones.

This was where things were going to change for her. They had to. And she let herself begin to hope – just a tiny sliver opening inside her chest like a bud of a plant flowering – that actually, at last, it might.

CHAPTER FIVE
QUINTON

23nd Day of Autumn 2406

Quinton stared up at the ceiling, one hand below his pillow and the other on his lower stomach.

For the past nine years he'd woken up in this same room. It was smaller than the one he'd grown up in, but there was something *better* about here. Maybe it was something to do with not having to leave if he didn't want. Or maybe it was because he could make this place truly his own.

He'd added thick green curtains that tied back to the posts of his bed in the last year. Posters of rock bands were haphazardly stuck on the walls, and a threadbare rug was half scrunched in the middle of the room. Cushions lined the window-seat – this side of the building only had seats, no balconies.

Knowing sleep wouldn't claim him again, Quinton rolled out of bed and into the shower. Water rolled down him in streams, taking drips of hair colour with it. He tried to not make a mess, the red was new, but with dyed hair it was easy to get run-off everywhere accidently.

When he was done, he wrapped a towel around his waist and grabbed some dark jeans and a white t-shit from his wardrobe.

Birds had originally woken him this morning. They were still chirping now, tweeting outside his window. It hadn't been a late rise but still late enough that he planned on missing training for the day. Praxis could come and find him later to complain and dish out consequences.

He dressed, tugged on his sturdy boots, towel-dried his hair and stuck it in a band as he walked out into the hall. He touched the gem that rested just below his throat, wondering what the day would bring.

Plenty of Helpers passed him on the main stairs. Most no longer tipped their head in a half-bow type move – it'd taken years for them to break *that* habit – but a few still insisted. He briefly nodded back and moved on.

Chatter grew louder the lower he sank down the stairs. When he rounded to behind them, he found the dining table half occupied. The remaining recruits of Redwing had begun to dig into breakfast. All kinds of flavours and textures were spread across the surface for all, including Violette who had graced the morning with her presence for a change. She scowled at Quinton when she spotted him.

He ignored her as he sat down.

Wide windows ran up this side of the building, touching the floor above, and the drapes had been pulled back to bring the light in. Quinton sat with his back to them, facing the front door.

Violette threw down her napkin and stood, leaving with two tight fists visible. Quinton didn't care; they tried to avoid each other these days. Relatively few good memories mixed with bad history. As if any of that was his fault...

It wasn't until he reached for the jam that he realised there was *fresh* company at the table. The new *abbies* sat with spare seats on either side of them.

He lathered his toast and took a bite, watching them out the corner of his eye. While the rest of the table had a lower-than-normal volume, the girls were barely talking.

It seemed they were planning to stick together, which made sense. Most recruits had come one at a time. These girls had something precious to be able to go through this with each other.

Echoing laughter came from somewhere overhead and then Seamus stepped into view from around the main staircase, followed by his twin.

At once the twins locked sights with the new recruits, smacking each other's chests in excitement. Quinton chewed the last of his toast as the twins slumped on either side of the *abbies*.

"So, what are your powers then?" Doug asked with little caution or tact.

Ziva loudly gasped. Chandler scowled at her plate. Quinton shook his head at it all. *He* knew the twins were just trying to win a bet, not meaning to be disrespectful or prying into secrets. He also told himself that he wasn't tuning it out to see if Gretchen had won her ten pieces and not because he was also interested.

Quinton picked up his mug of tea and added three sugars.

"Come on *abbies*," Seamus prompted. "There's no need to be shy."

"Is that any of your business?" Chandler replied.

Quinton smiled into his cup as the twins roared with furious laughter. "This one!" Doug cried. "Oh, this is going to be so much fun."

"We just have a bet on you, is all," Seamus explained, barely able to talk through his laughter.

Ziva's eyebrows scrunched together. "You bet on our powers?"

Doug shrugged, grinning widely. "Why not? We've done it to everyone who has come in since us."

Chandler put her fork down and sat back. "And what exactly were the parameters of the bet?"

"Parameters!" the twins yelled together in excitement.

Seamus took over to answer a moment later. "That one of you is some kind of traditional elemental. Earth, fire, water, air, you know?"

"Well, I'm not," Ziva announced, sounding both proud and not all at once. Quinton raised an eyebrow, wondering what could illicit such a mixed reaction.

Everyone here lived with their powers on full display, proud and flaunting. Most coming into their own once they'd realised it was safe here. They could be as free as they wanted. But it wasn't surprising the new recruits weren't so forthcoming and open with their powers. They'd come from somewhere, had lives elsewhere. And if those lives hadn't been safe they were likely still feeling unsafe and untrusting. Maybe with time they'd come to claim themselves, but there was no expectation, no obligation too.

As interested as Quinton was, he couldn't blame them for being guarded and nor would he force them to open up.

"How much are the winnings?" Chandler asked next.

Seamus perked up further. "Ten pieces."

"Then I'm happy to say no one won." Chandler scraped her chair and walked off. Ziva didn't take one look at the boys before racing off to join her new friend.

The twins watched them go with equal parts interest and loss. The chatter around the table resumed to a normal level, close to yelling.

Quinton lowered his mug and scooted over a seat. "Better luck next bet," he said casually.

"Oh whatever, Queenie," Seamus dismissed sourly.

Quinton got up and clapped the boys on the back. Doug

shook his head. Seamus did nothing. Grinning, Quinton walked off. Despite now knowing Gretchen had lost the bet too, Quinton hadn't. He hadn't bet on anything.

Interesting.

Thinking of Gretchen, he pulled his phone out to message her just as it buzzed. The message was from the woman herself, saying that she and Wane had landed in Old Cairo safely. Quinton typed a quick response to say "be safe" and pocketed the phone again.

In the main foyer, Maggie and Praxis brushed past him, moving into the drawing room where the walls were thicker, making it easier to hide noise. The soft click of the door and the audible turn of the lock said they didn't want to be disturbed.

Interesting again, he thought.

By the smaller clusters of people joining in the hallway, it seemed others were planning on missing the morning training, too. They looked like they were preparing for a trip into town. Seemed Quinton hadn't entirely lied to the girls last night when he'd claimed as much after all. Plus, with Gretchen gone and the twins now sulking, he had nothing better to do here anyway.

Tugging at jacket on from the cloak-room, he thought of his old life, the one from before here.

It'd been stimulating and tough and even downright vicious at times. But the business world was serious above all else. His dad had taught him that. If you wanted to be at the top, you had to work the hardest, be the best, and look like the strongest. It was a game made of power.

For a lot of people, it would've been enough. But Quinton had never felt fulfilled there. That was how he'd come to be where he was now, at Redwing, with a job that gave him everything – excitement, intrigue, chances, opportunities, power, and *freedom*. Everything and anything he'd been missing before, he had it now.

He touched his crystal and looked at the group who were leaving.

Flora zipped up her yellow raincoat. Aleema's dark grey hijab matched her jeans today. Dalton unclasped one strap of his denim dungarees, the same attire that had caught Quinton's eye in the past but made him laugh now.

Quinton shrugged. Any company was better than none, and this group were always welcoming.

He wandered over and Aleema was quick to pull him into a conversation about video games. She was the top player at Redwing, nearly always beating anyone who dared to challenge her. She could master anything as long as she could read the controls.

As a group of four, they left Redwing for the nearby town.

Quinton clutched his crystal the entire way.

CHAPTER SIX
ZIVA

23rd Day of Autumn 2406

What are we supposed to be getting anyway?" Ziva asked, shoving the caramel coloured coat back on the rack.

She glanced over at Chandler, who was holding up a deep green cardigan dotted with tiny red-capped mushrooms. Personally, Ziva would never choose something like that. But Ziva could see how Chandler could make it work.

Last night, the Helpers – it was basically the polite way of saying maids and servants – had given them both an old fashioned nightgown to wear to sleep. This morning they'd been handed some plain blue jeans and a white top.

Ziva hadn't minded. Everything had been comfy and it was only temporary until they could get their own things. Chandler, however, seemed to have taken some scissors to the bottom of her jeans, fraying them dramatically.

Just like Praxis had promised, they'd both been given some advancement money to spend. They'd walked their way into town. Shops lined the streets in small towers. Some places had passages to another in walls or several flights of stairs needed climbing first. Fashion and furniture and *things* were everywhere.

But Ziva was lost.

Chandler turned to her, slipping the cardigan into the crook of her elbow. "What's your style?" she asked.

Ziva tried not to outwardly wince. "I don't know. I've never really had one." Her style had been whatever clothes her mother had given her that fit.

"Well," Chandler swung her arms wide, indicating to the charity shop they stood in and the window, at the other shops outside, "now's your chance to find out."

"How do I do that?"

"Is there anything you're feeling? Anything you've wanted to try out before, anything you've suspected you might look good in?"

Ziva thought for a moment. "I suit the autumn and winter tones," she said.

"Ok." Chandler nodded. "That's a good start. What else?"

She glanced at the odd cardigan Chandler held. "Maybe simple things?"

"Well, how about you start there? Pick up unpatterned pieces, some simple items like tops and trousers, and then you can always build things up later? You can try *anything*. Even if you know you'll hate it. It's all about trying."

Chandler went to the counter, paid for her item, and they left.

Ziva walked into the next store with Chandler's voice quietly muttering in her head, looking around the racks a little on her own. She could try simple things. Simple items she could blend or build upon. She could do that.

A bright cobalt blue turtle-neck caught her attention first. She then found a ribbed white one. They were both lightweight and simple, but Ziva liked them. She smiled to herself right as Chandler's head appeared round a clothing corner. Chandler's smile encouraged her to keep going.

Ziva wandered a bit longer before stumbling across a pair of white boots, a pair of dark blue jeans with little golden accents at the bottom, and a long, copper coat.

Happy that these items were "simple" yet finding comfort in that, she paid for them and then the girls moved on again, this time to an underwear store. Ziva still went plain again except for a rust-coloured set Chandler insisted she buy.

Soon, they stood outside with plenty of bags each, breathing in the chill of autumn air. Chandler seemed unbothered by it. Ziva felt the bite on the back of her neck and the tips of her ears.

"Are you hungry?" Ziva suggested, pointing to the nearby diner.

Chandler nodded. "Why not, yeah."

Once inside, they were seen into a small booth. The seats were worn but padded enough. The red leather worked well with the black and white flooring, and soft white lights. Above the bar at the back were little glasses hanging upside-down in neat rows.

"Want to share a giant milkshake?" Chandler asked, showing Ziva a picture of one on the menu she'd acquired.

"Bloody skies above," Ziva whispered.

The milkshake really *was* giant. A full bucket of ice-cream with whipped cream, sprinkles, and syrup on top. It was the sort of thing that was built for a minimum of two people to share.

"I'll take that as a yes?" Chandler laughed.

"It does look lovely, but aren't we going to be sick?"

"I'm sure we'll be fine." She smiled kindly. "That expression you just said? I've never heard it before."

Ziva's face heated. "My grandmother says it all the time."

"And you picked it up, too?" Chandler guessed.

"I spend a lot of time with her."

A waitress came and took their order: one giant strawberry milkshake to share, one cheeseburger and chips for Chandler, and one large bowl of curly fries for Ziva. The woman nodded before disappearing.

Chandler gazed out the window, squinting at the sunlight. "How come you don't know what your style is?"

Ziva touched the bottom edge of her t-shirt. "Erm..." How could she explain it? "I've never been given a chance to find it."

Her new companion's stare caught hers. "Why?"

"We weren't poor!" Ziva closed her eyes when she heard how high pitched and defensive her voice had become. She sighed and opened her brown eyes again. "I live with my entire family. There's nine of us in one house."

"*Nine*?"

"We had to be careful with money. If I wanted gymnastic lessons, then there had to be a compromise."

"And the compromise was clothes."

"Sort of," Ziva nodded. "My grandmother's clothes went to my mother, and then me. Sometimes I got one of my dad's old shirts but they were tired. And because my parents wanted to keep everything fair, they gave all of us kids gymnastic lessons so my siblings didn't feel left out if I had them. To pay for all that, we couldn't afford other things. So if clothes were good enough to pass down and we didn't have to buy new ones..."

The words came out harsh and the tone she used had a hint of venom attached. Ziva didn't mean to sound like she resented what her parents did. She understood that they wanted to keep things fair, but was one new top too much to ask for if it was for a birthday or Christmas or Hanukkah? Was it really too much to ask for an actual gift, for something personal that only she had, something she didn't have to share?

She flinched at her own thoughts. She hadn't realised so many things had burrowed deep inside her chest that way, like a slow-eating heartworm.

"Everything I had, I had to get myself," Chandler said then. Her gaze went back out the window. Her hair glistened in the sunlight, turning it a honey colour.

"What about your family?" Ziva asked.

The waitress reappeared, putting down plates and bowls and an over-sized glass. Chandler picked up a chip and dunked it down past the cream to the milkshake itself before eating it.

"Let me put it this way," she said, chewing. "At my last job, I asked to be paid in physical pieces each time and not to have the money transferred into my account."

Ziva stared, her hand paused above her own chips. "What?"

"My *mother* thought that whatever money *I* made was hers as well. I didn't know she was stealing it at first. Then one day I couldn't afford the shuttle ride because my card declined. Actually, I think I'd always known but hadn't realised how *bad* it was."

"What did you do?"

"That's when I switched to the real form of the money. I hid the coins in a little pocket I sewed into the inside corner of my mattress. I put the bare minimum I could into my account too, just enough to make it look like I was getting money. Whatever I didn't take or put away, I asked my boss to keep a hold of. Just as a second back-up. I trusted her at least."

Chandler sighed as she dipped another chip and ate it. She said nothing else.

Not wanting to stare despite being so absorbed in what Chandler had said, about the implications of her words, Ziva tucked into her own chips and took the first real sips of their shared bucket shake. Her head buzzed immediately.

She clutched it. "Ugh. It's good, but I'm not sure if I have brain freeze or a sugar rush already."

Chandler grinned and tried it too, clearly glad for the change in conversation. Quickly she held her head. "Both," she groaned. "Definitely both."

They laughed together, and something between them. A shift of something like *trust*.

Chandler sat back first. Quietly, she asked, "What about your Abnormality?"

Ziva's cheeks warmed. "I thought you said it was no one's business?"

"Back there, it wasn't."

"Did you lie to those boys about your Abnormality? So they wouldn't win the bet? And what do you mean by 'back there'?"

"I meant back at *that place*. At Redwing," she whispered as the corners of her mouth lifted. "And technically I didn't lie?"

"Technically?"

"My power isn't a main elemental one, though I suppose it's a derivative of one if you want to be pedantic."

"What one are we talking about?"

Chandler glanced over her shoulder. The diner had a few other guests, but they were on the far side of the place. She sighed and fixed her sights on Ziva. "I can control ice."

Ziva sucked in a sharp breath. "*Ice*?"

Again Chandler looked around. Then swirled her finger above the table.

The same chill from outside swept into the air. Suddenly, tiny flecks of snow fell an inch from Ziva's face. She went to reach for a snowflake and they grew more solid in form. All at once, they fell and shattered against the table, small shards flinging everywhere. The air settled back again and the little shards melted into nothing.

"Ice," Chandler reaffirmed.

Ziva shivered as the returned warmth rushed her. "Mine's not nearly as impressive or even as good as yours."

"I don't believe that."

"You should," Ziva said.

"Try me."

Reaching out, Ziva grasped the edge of the milkshake glass. As she willed it, the contents changed from pink to blue to black. "It'll still taste like strawberry," she promised, pushing it away from herself.

Chandler cautiously took a sip and her whole face changed; a look of astonishment flooded her features. Ziva had never thought her power was impressive, certainly not warranting that kind of reaction. It was a simple trick, nothing more.

"Damn," Chandler whistled.

Ziva shrugged. "I can change the colours of things."

"You don't sound impressed."

"It's hardly what you have."

"Maybe it's not the same, but it's still impressive. I bet you can confuse a lot of people. A good yet simple mind-fuck is always appreciated and can be *very* powerful. The simpler the magic the better."

Ziva laughed and Chandler smiled back.

Once more the atmosphere between them shifted, becoming both tighter and looser. Ziva could almost picture a piece of ribbon or string tying their wrists at either end. It connected their pasts, in acknowledgement, and now their futures together. They'd shared with each other one, if not their *most*, prized secret. Their power.

They had originally stuck together because they were new. But perhaps that wouldn't be the only reason they hung around each other anymore.

CHAPTER SEVEN
ZIVA

24th Day of Autumn 2406

Gardens of endless possibilities lay outside in the dark. Ziva pressed on the doors cautiously, and they opened with ease. She'd never expected to find one in the kitchen that led outside, or for it to be so easy to move, but clearly, she'd been wrong. It clicked shut behind her, and she wondered if it had locked. She'd seen no key in the lock. Her hand half strayed back to check but she stopped herself halfway. If she was locked out, she might as well make the most of it. And if she wasn't, then she was where she wanted to be.

A brisk breeze tickled her face. She drew her new coat around her tighter.

The dipping temperatures weren't unexpected for early autumn. In olden calendar terms – Ziva remembered learning about them in history lessons in school – it would've been the month they used to refer to as September. Times had changed though, bringing the end to months and having the world go by the four seasons instead, each ruling with ninety-two days, except winter which had eighty-nine. Yet this weather was cooler than average. Setting the anti-global-warming measures in place did *sometimes* have other effects, but the world would've been a lot worse off if they hadn't been implemented.

Ziva walked into the gardens, her feet tapping against the stone path. She hadn't been able to rest since coming back from town. They'd missed dinner, but Ziva hadn't minded. She hadn't been hungry and still wasn't. She was sure the milkshake from lunch was the cause of her restlessness too.

She'd thought a walk might do her good as nothing else had worked. Even though it *was* past midnight already.

Lamps lit the dark garden and pathway, all bent near the top this way and that. It was impossible to see what ran beyond them. A buzz of insects were living their lives somewhere nearby and a soft splashing of water told Ziva to stick to the path.

"Miss?"

Ziva gasped and swung round.

In her panic, she'd pulled her arms up through her sleeves, leaving the material empty, to her chest as if to protect it – she thought of a turtle popping its head back into its hard shell to protect itself. The sleeves of her coat lifted in the wind as it picked up and it sounded like they hit something.

The guard from the shuttle, the one who'd given her the orange, stepped into the light. He stood only a step away.

She unfolded her arms and tucked herself back into her clothes properly. "I'm so sorry!"

The guard touched his jaw. "Never in all my years here have I been slapped by a *coat sleeve*," he commented. His voice was gruffer than before.

"Sorry," she murmured again as her insides squirmed.

"It didn't hurt. I'm just a little stunned it happened." He removed his hand from his face and smiled. From how awkward it appeared, Ziva wondered how often he did so. "I was hit with an umbrella once, but I deserved that."

Ziva let out an unexpected laugh. "What did you do?"

"Hit someone with a painting first."

She laughed again and his smile grew more relaxed, more comfortable. Despite the dark, she could still see the depth of the green in his eyes. A juniper green.

Ziva tore her gaze away. "I really am sorry."

"I know, and all is forgiven. Your laugh settled it."

Her face flushed. "What's your name?"

"What's *your* name, Miss?"

"Not Miss. Just Ziva."

"Alright, not Miss just Ziva. I'm Abel." He looked over her head; it was easy for him to do so since he was at least a foot taller. "Why are you outside? We're in the new morning. Shouldn't you be sleeping?"

"What about you?" she asked back. The wind wafted through her hair so it tickled her back of her neck and moved the edges of her coat again.

"I'm on patrol, Miss. My shift just started."

"Ziva," she mumbled. "Shift? There are other guards?"

Abel nodded. "You probably haven't seen them yet."

Ziva considered that. She hadn't really met many people here yet. Chandler had been the first and they'd stuck together since. She'd seen the boy with the red hair, Quinton, last night. But otherwise, she didn't know anyone else's name besides the leaders. She also bet that she hadn't glimpsed everyone's face either.

"What are you doing out here so late?" Abel asked again.

"I came for a walk," she answered honestly.

He nodded briskly once. "I have to make my rounds, but I wouldn't mind the company if you wanted to join?"

Abel moved on without waiting for an answer. His heavy boots crunched the path, though the noise started to fade.

Ziva gave herself a moment to think. She wasn't against the idea of knowing more people, even though she wasn't sure how much she wanted to know or how long she'd stay to become more than acquaintances with those here. Abel didn't seem bad though. He'd been nice on the shuttle.

The darkness crept closer and that made her decide quickly.

Ziva half ran down the path until Abel's form came into view. She tried to quieten her breathing as she ease to his strides, trying to match his pace.

"You came?" he said, sounding genuinely surprised.

"You were the one that extended your company to me." She smiled up at him just as he turned to gaze down at her, one eyebrow raised. Ziva gulped and forced her eyes forwards. "How many guards are there here?"

"Seven," he answered. "We take three hour shifts throughout the day to patrol the grounds, though some of us leave to accompany missions from time to time so we have to put in extra here and there."

"Missions," she whispered.

"Some require guards in travel or for practicality sake. Sometimes it's just our power that's required."

She gawked up at him. "You're like us?"

His mouth quirked up into an unexpected smile. "We have a gift, yes." His hands guided her before she missed a turning in the bending path and fell over the edge to what lay off the path – she didn't want to find out why she'd been directed away from whatever was there. "Just because we guard does not mean we are without an Abnormality. If anything, most times, our gifts make what our job easier. Your job is to protect the world. Ours it to protect the protectors at home."

A shiver ran down Ziva's spine but it wasn't from the cold. "And sometimes you look after us elsewhere."

"Sometimes, yes. We guard this mansion *and* you. Our gifts

determine how we can help. Yours helps the world reach a new dawn, and ours means we get you there."

He spoke with devotion, a power that he truly believed in the words he chose to speak.

Ziva stole another glance at him. The night's breeze lifted the edges of his hair, though most of it was tucked underneath his beret. His eyes were focused on the path ahead but she had the sneaking suspicion he was watching her, too.

Abel had a *gift*, as he'd called it. So while everyone's waking moments were to make sure the world didn't get in trouble, his was to make sure they themselves didn't fall. It was a job within a job for him. A gift to secure the safety of those with gifts.

Ziva loved how he'd called their Abnormalities *gifts*.

"I never thanked you properly for the orange," Ziva blurted. She hoped the dark hid her flaming cheeks.

He stopped and fully peered down at her. "I don't usually offer my food so easily."

"But you did to me?"

Abel's third smile to Ziva was the most relaxed one he'd managed but then his eyebrows screwed together and he set off marching again. Ziva breathed out, a buzzing in the air she hadn't noticed simmering.

She gave them both a moment. She had no idea what was happening as she'd never had much interaction with anyone outside her family, but it hadn't been like this with Quinton last night, though that meeting had been brief. Yet there was just something *different* in this interaction and she wasn't sure if she liked it or not.

Taking another breath, she decided that whatever was happening, Abel had been kind to her. He'd shown her friendship despite having no obligation to.

"How long have you been here?" she asked when she caught up again.

He turned them round a sharp bend with an outstretched hand, slowing his pace to allow her to go first. "Nearly twelve years."

"*Twelve*?"

"I arrived when I was thirteen. That's a lot less than some."

"Really?" she asked. Who had been here the longest? Why did they choose to stay?

They turned again. "A young girl, around your age? She was the last female to arrive," he said. "That was nearly eight years ago now. Besides her? Two males arrived a year after, months apart. That's it. Most who appear between our ages," a lamp flickered above them, "came here when they were a lot younger."

"Are there not many who are older?"

Abel stopped and then walked off. He never answered. Ziva thought then not to ask again. Clearly something had happened and it wasn't good.

The path winded more and all too soon the mansion drew up ahead. Abel pulled out a stack of keys from inside his uniform jacket, and shoved one into the kitchen door she'd come out from. He raised an eyebrow, almost in amusement, when Ziva sighed – apparently she *had* locked herself out after all, though she was curious as to how he knew where she'd come from.

"Thank you," she said, though unsure as to what specifically. Abel bobbed his head in acknowledgement. "Do you always work the same shifts?"

"Not always, no. The three hour intervals don't always match up."

"And you really do things around the mansion? Even go on missions? Have a power?"

He reached around her side to open the door. "I do." He dropped his hand from the door but caught the edge of her coat sleeve, holding it, and subsequently her arm, up in front of them. "Try to keep these to yourself? I don't want to be called in for an accident."

She laughed nervously. "I'll try."

"And whatever you're thinking my power is, it probably isn't that." Ziva hadn't been thinking about his Abnormality, but now she was. Abel dropped her coat and arm. "Go to sleep." He turned away and called back when he was a few paces away. "Miss?"

"Mm?" she said, looking at him from half inside the house.

"Thank you for you company tonight."

"Thank you for the walk! I hope you won't get too cold out here."

"I'm wrapped up pretty well. I'm used to it."

"Well, just yell if I can repay the favour of the orange with some soup?"

He bowed his head. "I hope I see you around, Ziva," he said, almost like a whisper, and slipped into the darkness of the garden.

CHAPTER EIGHT

CHANDLER

24th Day of Autumn 2406

Music drifted through the walls.

Chandler tip-toed down the stairs to the first floor. It was past three in the morning but she just couldn't sleep. Her first idea had been to have a bath, hoping to soothe her muscles and mind. Her second idea had been to start reading. Her third idea was to investigate the piano music.

Currently she was on her final idea: investigate this *mansion*.

Lights in the open spaces and stairwells had been left on, but they weren't blaring. The soft glow made it easy to navigate the space without hurting the eyes.

The sheer size of Redwing was unreal. Despite all the cities in the world, all the big and small places, there was something about this place that felt *different*. It wasn't specifically one thing. Not the wooden stairs or the weird decorating styles. Not the looming paintings of knights or the large dining table.

Not the vast rooms or the grand entryway. It was a collection of everything together that made it *something*. And Chandler didn't think, even if she spent all the time in the world here, she'd be able to place what that something was.

The first floor was empty. Unsurprising since it was early morning. Plenty of scattered and upturned seats ran at the back of this space.

Chandler moved towards the full wall window that drew down past the floor to the space below. She could glimpse nothing but faint yellow glowing of dotted lights. Her own reflection stared back from the glass, the light behind her illuminating her shape in the glass.

For the first time since leaving, she thought of her mother. What was she doing right now? Was she sleeping? Had she even noticed Chandler was gone?

Chandler turned from the darkness. Her mother had probably only noticed the money was gone, though Chandler hadn't managed to secure *every* last piece before leaving. She sighed and headed down to the ground floor.

During the day, the maids and cooks and cleaners – the Helpers – had bustled around, almost invisibly. They wore black clothing, keep their hair neat and shoes shined. Chandler had bumped into a few after arriving back from town.

But now they must've gone to their rooms, too. It left Redwing feeling empty and vast.

In the night, the world whispered with opportunities and secrets.

She edged away from the stairs, the music slipping away behind her – it must've come from a higher room – and went towards an unknown room.

Pulling at the handle, Chandler held her breath. It opened to reveal rows of coats and shoes.

She mumbled to herself and closed the door again.

A flicker of annoyance curdled in her gut. The whole mansion was bigger than the entire apartment complex she'd lived in. That one cloakroom was bigger than half her shared living space. But then, places like this were built *years ago* for the very wealthy. They weren't brick boxes built into spaces to house a growing population.

Moving on, she tried not to get her hopes up. She crackled her forefinger before touching the brass handle on the door, finding it mildly warm.

Red and gold wallpaper walls matched with dark wooden floors. A thick rug nestled comfortably under cream sofas and a high-back red armchair was angled from the roaring fire. A large painting hung over the hearth, depicting the mansion and an oddly dressed couple with their two children in the forefront. Raggedy curtains had been closed over tall windows on either side of the fire, and two cream lamps sat on little tables in the corners of the room had been switched on. Fresh flowers were cut and arranged in an ornate vase on top of a small designated wooden table.

Chandler loved it. It was cosy and quaint and comforting.

She cracked her knuckles and shuffled round to see that the red high-back chair was one of a pair, and its twin was faced away from the door. The person sitting in it shuffled it and themselves round.

Quinton sat there, eyebrow-raised, white shirt open at the top, black cotton trousers hanging down to his bare feet. A notepad was open in his lap, a pen tucked between his fingers. Another pen was stashed inside his tied-back red hair, though a few strands had been pulled loose and hung around his face.

"I thought I was the only one awake," she said.

He closed the notepad and stashed his pen with the other. "I'd thought the same. Apparently we were both wrong."

Chandler hummed in agreement and moved further into the room, letting the door gently shut behind her. "This room looks so old."

"This *house* is old," he told her. "But I can assure you the lamps are new."

"The lamps?" She looked at him.

Quinton grinned in response. "Yes. The funny things that are letting out the light right now?"

"I know what lamps are."

"Just checking."

She rolled her eyes. "How new are they? They look bloody old to me."

"Well…" He rubbed his chin like he was thinking. "About three years old? There was an *incident*, so Mags ordered new ones. They just look old to keep up with the theme. I think the only new thing around here is the pool table upstairs."

Her eyes drifted over the painting again. The people captured there were all blond.

"And you, and your friend," Quinton added.

Chandler flopped onto a sofa and rubbed the backs of her hands, careful to control her urges. "I forgot we were spectacles and betting pieces around here."

"The twins are still quite sour about losing that bet you know."

"Good. They can stay that way."

"Oh, they will for a while. Then they'll make new bets on you."

"Maybe I should bet on myself?"

"We've *all* been spectacles a few times and bets have been made on us for a few different reasons."

Chandler looked over at him, and found him already watching her. "What are you doing in here? Is your room not quiet enough?"

"Not always." He sat back and untied his hair which fell in rich crimson waves to his shoulders. The pens slid through it to his awaiting hand. "Aleema's playing the old piano in the attic. It sits right above my room."

"Couldn't you have asked her to stop?"

"She gets nightmares," he said, like it explained everything. "And what about you? You're also not in your room."

"I couldn't sleep, but not because of the music."

"I didn't see you in town today."

Chandler raised her eyebrows at him. "I didn't realise you were looking for me."

"Not specifically." He shrugged carelessly. "I just thought you might have questions."

"I do."

They were silent, an old clock in the room tracking how long for. However, the *tick-tick-tick* of every second felt like it counted something more than time.

Quinton broke the silence first. "Did you lie to the twins?"

"Did I lie?" she questioned.

"About your powers."

She scoffed. "Why does everyone think I lied?" she asked. "And what is everyone's obsession with knowing powers?"

"You didn't answer the question," he replied, smiling slightly.

She stared back. "You didn't answer mine."

He laughed, loud and unrestrained, and held his hands up in mock surrender. "We'll call it a stalemate and come back to that," he suggested. Chandler didn't want to cycle back, but figured at some point she'd have no choice, so stayed silent and hoped he'd forget. "Ask one of your other questions."

"This place is under some kind of glamour, isn't it?"

On the way here, Chandler couldn't remember seeing the mansion until it had sprung up in front of her. It was like she'd crossed over some line and it'd suddenly appeared once she had.

A place like this should've been visible for miles. Only when they were a little ways out however had she and Ziva spotted it – they'd commented on it at the same time.

Quinton blinked, seeming genuinely surprised. "It is. The original owner of the house had the power of glamours. The house was stuck inside the bubble and then Maggie got the same power later on."

"What happens when..."

"She isn't around? There's a little added *kick* to her power. The glamour around this house is one glamour, right? It acts like a doorway. Well, Maggie can pass the keys to that doorway on without weakening or breaking anything, and did. To both Praxis and Violette. They can control it as well as her. So, because now this glamour works differently to others, if and when the time comes, the keys can be passed on and on again without breaking anything."

"To keep this place hidden."

He nodded and she sighed. That explained one thing. It almost made her relax. No one would be able to find her here if she stayed.

"Don't look too impressed," he teased.

"Oh, I'm not," she quipped back.

"I might have something that *can* impress you?"

"That doesn't sound entirely sketchy."

Quinton laughed again. "Trust me, I meant nothing salacious."

"Was the impressive thing big words?"

He grinned but left his chair and sat down beside her. This close, she could smell a hint of cherry on him – it wasn't overpowering or sweet, just *there*. "My *power* is what I was referring to."

She shifted to face him properly, their knees nearly touching. She was conscious not to move. "Are we back to that already?

"Doesn't everything come back to that? And while I'm sure yours won't impress me, since it's not an elemental—"

"It's not," she cut in. Like she'd told Ziva, technically her power was a by-product.

As if even thinking about drew it out, the air around her grew colder. The water droplets she could feel began to slowly shift their vibrations.

Chandler cracked her knuckles to dissipate the energy.

Quinton picked up the small crystal that hung around his neck on a chain and held it out in his palm like he'd felt nothing in the air. "I can read the future," he told her simply. "Though, I will warn you, that futures can fluctuate. What I see may happen, may half happen, or might not at all. It's a finicky thing dealing with time."

"Alright," she nodded. "What do I need to do?"

"Hold the crystal."

"That's it?"

Quinton nodded. "That's it."

Chandler had never believed in fates. One time, when her mother had actually pretended to care, when Chandler had been younger, they'd gone to the circus. The fortune teller there and her crystal ball had told Chandler she'd grow to find success in her work. How unspecific. She'd probably dished out that future to every kid who'd come by that day.

"Fine, I'll play," she said, taking the crystal in hand.

It was warm to the touch. She didn't let go until Quinton tapped on the back of her hand, the *tick-tick-ticks* of the same clock as before counting for him.

Gently, she lowered her hand into his and dropped the crystal. He touched his spare hand over it and his eyes clouded slightly, the colour muting just a shade. Chandler cracked her knuckles in anticipation, unable to stop herself now.

The whole experience lasted maybe a minute.

Quinton's eyes normalised in colour, a stormy blue settling in. She waited for what he was going to say, though not enthusiastically. Quinton, however, looked amused and confused all at once. He opened his mouth to share what he'd seen.

"I—"

Chandler yelled and clutched the side of her head as a deafening sound blared relentlessly through the entire building.

CHAPTER NINE
QUINTON

24TH Day of Autumn 2406

Quinton stared at Chandler for the few moments the alarm blared until it shut off. Then he just blinked. He was used to the ugly noise after so many years.

"What the bloody hell was that?" she asked.

He slipped a pen between his fingers and twiddled with it. "It's a calling for your first mission."

Chandler went to speak but was cut off by the door opening.

Ziva barrelled into the room, eyes wide and alert in panic. A white streak now ran through the front of her hair which was tied up into a sloppy ponytail, a streak Quinton hadn't noticed the last time they'd met.

"What's going on?" Ziva half-yelled; clearly the alarm had obscured her level of hearing.

Before Quinton could answer with the same vague words he'd given Chandler, he was stalled by another intruder. This one he was less than pleased to see.

Violette's heart-shaped face popped round the door. Her expression was soft until she spotted Quinton, and then it turned stony and sharp. She wore a familiar black, silk robe. Quinton hated the sight of it.

"Why are you still standing here?" Violette snipped. Quinton remembered a time when her voice had had a nice chirp to it. That was lost now.

"Because we don't know what's going on?" Chandler said back, aiming it like a question.

Violette shot Quinton a venom-filled glare and then gave the girls a softer, yet still disgruntled, stare. "Follow me."

Ziva and Chandler filed out behind Violette after one shared, silent glance at each other.

Quinton sighed, plucking up his notebook and tucking it beneath his arm. He liked to keep it close because it was where he drew, a place where he kept his fleeting memories or dreams. Or flashes of things he'd seen.

Every time he had a vision, he'd either write or draw about it so he couldn't forget it. It didn't matter if that future changed or never happened. What he saw, he captured and recreated on paper.

And now, thanks to Chandler, he had one more to add.

But never before had an image involved *him*.

He left the room and hurried across the entryway to catch up, and was met with a door to the face. He sighed again. The rules said that any new initiates would get the newest mission after their arrival as a test, as a way to decide if they wanted the job and were qualified for it, unless for specific other reasons they couldn't be chosen.

That was what the alarm had meant. It was a call to all that there was a new mission.

It was why Violette had come for the girls and had taken them, because this would be *their* mission.

Quinton was almost annoyed. The girls had been here

barely two days and yet they were getting their chance. During his time, Quinton had waited for nearly a month – by which time, he'd already settled in.

Just as he went to press his ear to the door, it swung open.

Praxis stared at him in a way that said he was unsurprised to find Quinton there.

"Don't just stand there," Praxis said. "I'd rather have you inside than standing at the door."

Quinton didn't bother hiding his grin as he slipped round Praxis' frame.

The office was in its usual state of disarray but now seemed even smaller with all the people crowded into it. Quinton wanted to text Gretchen about the whole thing. So while Praxis slunk over to his chair, Quinton slipped his pen into his pocket and dug out his phone – thank everything that phones went back to having physical buttons.

He hung back and typed as everyone talked.

Quinton:
I hope you're good and getting lots of sleep

Wane isn't keeping you up all night is he?

"The alarm sounded a new mission," Praxis started. "As we explained when you first arrived, this mission is yours. By the end, you'll be able to choose if you want to stay or leave. This is your opportunity. But that's not all the mission is. It's also a means to discover yourselves."

"Gritty":
Shut the fuck up, you arse. You're the one keeping me awake! What do you want?

"What *is* the mission?" Ziva asked. Quinton watched as she ran a hand up her face and into her hair, dislodging the white strand.

Quinton:
Arse? Bit rude

A new missions landed

Praxis held up an orange file – clearly he'd had time to organise this one particular thing if nothing else. He opened it and drew out a single slip of paper. "The world changed some of us a long time ago. To one male, one of these changes was the ability to give inanimate objects a *gift*. To most, he gave life. Except once. To one object he created he gifted freedom. So in turn that object gifted freedom to the wearer."

"Gritty":
Already? Damn. We just left.

Quinton:
I think its going to be a good one

"Gritty":
I guess the new gals will get to try themselves out, right? & how do you know itll be good?

Praxis prattled on. "The object was a Mask. It's been lost for over one hundred years and was apparently made somewhere near the time of the 'first changed'."

The 'first changed' referred to the first known generation

who had suffered through the Abnormalities. It'd happened nearly one hundred and eighty years ago.

While a virus, or several – scientists were still debating – caused the mutations in the genes, not everyone born with a mutation got a power and not everyone born who ended up with a power had one right from the start. Families didn't all have a power, either; some did and some didn't. Father's with power might never pass one on to their children but Mother's might. It redefined what lucky meant and if that luck was good or bad.

Quinton:
Im in the office with them

But thats not why Im interrupting your pleasant day

A new mission so soon isnt the weirdest bit about today at all

"Did this Mask have a name?" Ziva asked. Chandler kept quiet.

"The Lost Mask of Iris," Praxis answered.

Quinton whistled lowly and Violette looked at him with a sneer. He wanted pull a face back. His insides squirmed at the idea, an energy buzzing around his body. But she'd just grow *worse*, choosing to physical charge herself up somehow.

Ziva fidgeted. "I've heard of it."

"A lot of people have," Violette said, calming her tone just enough to seem respectable. "The whole mysterious air around it has heightened its fame."

Praxis slid his sheet of paper away. "Well, now the Creator's family want it back in their possession," he announced.

"What?" Quinton spluttered. He blinked as all three leaders stared at him with varying degrees of confusion. "You *can't* be serious?"

"I am."

"That thing is called the *lost* Mask for a reason!"

"Very clever," Violette muttered. Quinton ground his teeth together.

Praxis ignored the tension. "Because the Mask can create an illusion around the person wearing it, changing them into whomever they want to be, it can be seen as a good *or* bad thing. That's why the family want it back, so it can't be used for the bad."

"Is there even a starting point?" Chandler asked, finally speaking up. The leader's eyes shifted to her. "If it's been lost for this long..."

"The last anyone knew, it was on display in a museum in Snowdonne."

Quinton groaned inwardly. Snowdonne was the new country founded when Greenland split itself in two – really the Island itself came apart; land separated by a large storm. He'd been there with his family years ago. Nice place, average company, boring hotel rooms, and dead reasons for being there.

"Gritty":
Spill the bloody juice!

Dont keep your gal waiting here!

"When was it last known to have been there?" Ziva asked.

"Records are within the last few years," Praxis said.

"So the family want a lost Mask safe and in their company?" Ziva turned to Chandler. "Doesn't seem *so* bad."

Violette's grin wasn't pleasant. "What's the times-scale?"

"Ten days," Praxis answered coolly.

Chandler looked like she wanted to choke. "We have to do all this, in *ten days*?"

Praxis nodded. "You need to locate the Mask, take it, and deliver it safely to the family."

"What happens if we don't?"

"Then it gets passed on to a more competent team," Violette told them.

It was Quinton's turn to grimace. He hated how harsh Violette sounded, but in this one instant he hated more that she was *right*.

"Not every mission comes with a time-scale," Praxis explained. "Just some. The one here is an *optimal* time-scale. But as Violette said, if you can't fulfil it, then another team will be sent out. In other cases, if something isn't complete, that's the end of the run for that mission. There would be no crew after. They tend to be for the more immediate life-threatening missions. One and done types where failure for one team is the end of the line."

"Right," Ziva sighed.

Chandler folded her arms. "And then we decide if we stay or go? Once the mission is over by completion or time?"

Praxis nodded slowly. "There's something else." Quinton revelled at the face Violette pulled which said that she no longer knew what was happening. "I know I told you that you could still be yourselves, and you can. It wasn't a complete lie. However, you will need some aliases. You can still be yourself here and to your family, but to everyone else, that *you* is gone. You need a cover."

"In case we're ever caught," Ziva said aloud, seeming to piece it together well enough. Eyes flicked to her and she appeared to shrink. "Right? If we're caught by someone or something while on a mission, a cover is a way to protect ourselves and each other."

"It is," Violette confirmed.

Quinton:
I managed to get one of the new *abbies* to touch my crystal

"Quinton?" Praxis called. Quinton looked up from his phone. "You'll be going with the girls."

He blinked. "What?"

"You're a long-standing member, and you're here now. You've heard the brief. It's a high-quality case and they'll need back-up."

"I agree," Maggie said, speaking for the first time. Quinton had almost forgotten she was in the room. Her soft smile reached him; it was the smile of a mother, of a grandmother, of a woman who cared for all that were under her care.

He typed into the keys on his phone quickly without having to look down.

Quinton:
Guess who is also now going to Snowdonne?

He only looked down when a reply pinged through as the group in the office went back over the new mission details.

"Gritty":
Fuck Snowdonne. Fuck sleep. Your crystal? What did you see?

Quinton:
I saw myself

"Gritty":
Quinton! What the fuck?!?!?!?!

That's never happened before, right? You're not joking, are you?

Bloody ground beneath me.

Quinton smiled at the old saying. Gretchen said it all the time in bad situations; and then he remembered the situation she was using it for now revolved around him. He stopped smiling.

"Ten days," Violette's voice carried. Quinton looked up to see her reaching up to tap her nails against the clock on the wall.

Whether it was the tone in her voice or the final piece dropping into place in their brains, everyone kicked into gear. Ziva practically ran from the room, her slippers squeaking against the floor. Chandler brushed past Quinton calmly, but didn't look up. Violette purposely barged into his shoulder. Praxis stacked the file on top of his others on the desk and left.

Maggie tapped him on the shoulder, gesturing for him to move out, then locked the office behind her. She gave him a small smile and stumbled off to the kitchen, her left leg slightly staggering as her old injury plagued her.

He watched to make sure she got there alright, then bounded up the stairs two at a time.

Back in his room, he dragged out his suitcase and began throwing things into it, notebook and pens included.

Thinking of the notebook reminded him of the new image he needed to add. He was now going on a mission, to find the Lost Mask of Iris, an Abnormal artefact that had been lost for over one hundred years, and had ten days to do it. All with someone his new vision had included. A vision he somehow *knew* was connected to the mission, though it didn't quite make sense yet.

Once packed and back out on the landing, he drew out his phone again.

Quinton:
Its very real. I saw myself and I think its linked to the case.

It has to be

"Gritty":
I swear if you don't tell me what you saw. . .

As best he could, he typed his vision out to his best friend. The whole time he was aware that Chandler would likely ask him to share what he'd seen and he wouldn't lie when she did.

He had one rule when it came to his gift: *always share what you see.* He would always tell the person whose possible future he saw what it was.

And so he would have to tell Chandler that he saw them together, with a marriage ring on her finger made of silver and emeralds.

CHAPTER TEN
CHANDLER

24th Day of Autumn 2406

The higher the air-shuttle climbed, the more Chandler became aware of the water around her.

Drops became crystals. Clouds became heavy. Rain became sleet.

But only in her mind.

To stop herself from touching and potentially destroying the air-shuttle, she sat in the middle seat. Ziva took the window, gawking out of it, and Quinton was by the aisle, legs stuck out until someone passed and he respectfully withdrew them.

As much as she wanted to be near the window, felt drawn to touch the sky and turn it into ice, this was as close as she'd allow herself to be.

Ziva pulled back from the window and smiled at Chandler. "I like your outfit."

Chandler half laughed. "Thanks."

Having not had long to pack up and dress, she'd simply

thrown on the best thing she could find that was both cosy and quick; her self-made frayed jeans from the day before and the green cardigan with the mushrooms on. Everything else she'd owned – which really wasn't a lot – had been shoved into a decent sized bag she'd found under her bed in her temporary room and was now in the holder above her.

"It's adorable," Quinton commented.

Chandler rolled her eyes. Ziva clearly hadn't been as quiet as she'd thought but it wasn't her fault. Early morning flights meant people slept and so the noise level was down.

Quinton leant across her to Ziva. "And you look lovely too."

Ziva positively beamed. "Thank you!"

It was true. Both of them *did* look well put-together, as if they'd had all the time in the world to pick up outfits and pack the rest of their fashions.

Really, they'd thrown everything together in about fifteen minutes and had met each other in the foyer without original coordination. Praxis had driven them into town to the nearest shuttle tracks. From there, it'd been a direct transfer to the air-shuttle port. The whole ride to the port, Quinton had been booking their seats for the flight – he'd claimed to know what he was doing and where was best to sit. Ziva and Chandler had let him get on with it. Chandler had been too stunned that she was actually getting to *fly* to suggest or do anything.

Chandler gazed out of the small window to the clouds she couldn't touch with her fingers. "How much longer have we got?"

"Another few hours before we land in Snowdonne," Quinton answered, tapping on the screen that was built into the seat in front of him. "A snowstorm near the island means we have to take a slight detour."

"Great," she mumbled.

"But there's food," Ziva reminded her.

Moments ago a stewardess had come along with trays of

food for every passenger. Chandler had picked crackers, which she'd tucked away in her cardigan pockets for later, and then a tray of seasoned, roasted vegetables with a slice of buttered toast. But she hadn't touched them yet.

She was worried. About the travel. About this mission. And, worst of all, about her mother.

The concern wasn't about her mother's welfare exactly – why should she worry about a woman who'd barely shown an ounce of care herself. It was more about what her mother was going to do. Whatever Chandler had left behind, it wasn't that important to her – she always took her most important bits in her bag with her each day. But would her mother go to the authorities to get her back somehow? What about the access she still had to one bank account under Chandler's name where there was a little still left? Chandler worried if her salary from this job would go in there, or could she get help opening a new, *secret* one?

Could I cut her off for good now?

For years Chandler had dreamed about the day when she'd finally get away. But never had she truly believed it might happen. She'd never given herself the room to hope. Even working a longer shift at work had been trouble. At best, in later life, she'd thought she might be able to move apartments, to have her own space, as long as she stayed within the same block.

Now she was sat in an air-shuttle well on her way to Snowdonne.

Will I ever go back?

From the sounds of it, she didn't have to if things went well. So she needed them to go brilliantly. If this whole thing gave her the chance to run away, wouldn't she take it with a handshake and a scream at the skies?

Yet, unbidden, her mind conjured up images of her mother, full of life and laughter, pressing a birthday cake under Chandler's chin.

Why am I thinking of that? I want out! I want to run!

"You going to eat that?"

With a plastic spork in hand, Quinton leant way to close to Chandler, eagerly waiting to steal her piece of toast. His question had brought her mind back to the present. To stop him, she snatched it up and shoved it in her mouth all at once. She chewed and swallowed, then quickly added the second piece for good measure.

"Yes," she mumbled round the warm bread.

Quinton backed off slightly, grinning. "You could've just answered."

Ziva closed the gap between the three of them from her side. When she spoke, she lowered her voice. "So what are we looking for when we land?"

"Our bags?" Quinton said unhelpfully.

Ziva glared, though there wasn't much weight behind it. "You know what I mean."

"He just has to be a little bitch about everything," Chandler whispered.

Quinton snorted. "*Little* bitch?"

"Alright, if you prefer to be called a big bitch." She shrugged.

He shook his head, grinning. "And I did know what you meant," he said, going back on topic. He dropped his voice further. "We go to the museum. First, we'll stop at the hotel and dump our stuff." He touched his crystal, wrapping the chain around his fingers. "Then we'll go."

Chandler knew he couldn't say much more, not here, not when anyone could be listening. They'd discuss a better plan in the privacy of the hotel.

Quinton twisted the chain more and she narrowed her eyes on it. "Are you going to tell me what you saw?" she whispered carefully.

"Saw?" Ziva asked, eyes flicking between Chandler and Quinton. "Did you touch it?"

"Because that doesn't sound dirty," Quinton commented.

Ziva ignored his comment. "What does it do?"

Someone behind them started snoring loudly.

"*It* doesn't do anything. I do." Quinton's eyebrows rose. "But neither of *you* told me *yours*," he huffed quietly.

"Colour," Ziva blurted. "What did you see?"

He let go of his necklace. "Not here."

"Ooh," Chandler cooed. "Must be *juicy*!"

Quinton looked at her curiously before an amused expression took over, but he said nothing more. Ziva moved back when she realised he was serious about staying silent for now.

Chandler's stomach chose that moment to growl in hunger. She sighed and tucked into some roasted peppers. They were perfectly crisp and her tongue salivated at the flavours.

Every so often Ziva would tap her arm to get her to glance out the window at a moving cloud she thought had a different shape and Quinton would tell them both how close they were to their destination. Chandler wondered what their stories were. Ziva seemed to be as excited and nervous as Chandler, but less concerned. Quinton just looked like he was at home. Hopefully she'd learn them in time. But she also worried about that too. It meant more ties in her life. Ties she might one day have to cut or have them cut on her.

She ate more and cracked her knuckles with every new mouthful to keep her growing anxiety under control.

The rest of the journey was calm. The pilot of the air-shuttle spoke over the inner-voice that they were coming in to land earlier than expected, having bypassed the snowstorm as it had changed course in their favour.

Landing, Chandler decided, was her least favourite part of flight. Even in normal shuttles stopping made her awkward and nervous; the carriages wobbled like they were going too fast to ever stop. An air-shuttle felt *worse*, like it would land through the ground, not on it.

With shaky legs, she climbed out of her seat. Quinton helped get their bags down from the overhead storage first, and they climbed out of the air-shuttle. Chandler felt much better once her feet were on tarmac again. The world was solid beneath her.

Once outside the front of the port, the air bit like a rogue snake. Ziva shivered beside her as they hailed a cab. They piled inside the warm cab once one stopped for them, and Quinton gave the driver the instructions to go their hotel.

As they drove away from the port, Chandler caught sight of snow beginning to fall. She couldn't hide her smile.

"Something good out there?" Quinton asked. His knees were brushed against Ziva's, who sat in the middle. They were a little crammed in with all their luggage, but it wasn't *bad*.

"Snow," she answered.

"Back home has snow?"

"It does," she agreed. "But it doesn't come down often."

Ziva bumped their shoulders and smiled when Chandler looked at her. While "home" had snow, it wasn't ever that grand and hardly ever sat on the ground to matter – people just called it a problem when it did, and life went on. But Chandler had a connection to it with how close it was to her Abnormality, and it enraptured her.

"I think we need a nap when we get in," Ziva said, yawning. Chandler knew she'd changed the subject on purpose, and dipped her head to hide her smile.

Quinton nodded. "I'm not against that idea."

"What time's the museum open until?"

"Are you travellers on about the Grand Snowdonne Museum?" the driver asked.

The three passengers blinked at each other. A divider separated them from the driver up front, but they'd heard anyway.

"We came for a tour," Quinton answered easily. Technically it wasn't a lie, but the effort, or lack thereof that it took for him to school his face to neutrality troubled Chandler. She cracked her knuckles.

"Lucky," the driver said. He spoke in English, but his accent was thickly Snowdonnian. "The whole place is open until midnight this week. Part of a special exhibition."

"Special exhibition?" Ziva questioned.

"We'd come for the regular stuff," Quinton jumped in. "This just makes our trip even better!" He flashed a grin.

"It's a special exhibition of all Abnormal artefacts," the diver confirmed. The three looked at each other again. "I wouldn't trust any of that stuff though. If those Abnormals had anything to do with anything, it's never good." The section separating them lowered, just enough so the driver could peer back at them all using a mirror. "I should've asked before, but you're not Abnormals, are you?"

"No," Quinton said. "They have to declare that kind of thing upfront, right? Isn't it kind of law?"

"Right, right. Good." The driver said no more, drawing the divider back up.

The three sat quietly with the silence only being broken by Ziva or Quinton pointing out where else they would like to visit. How much was for show was uncertain. Chandler couldn't join in. She sat stiffly, as if her ice had been used against her.

It was alright for Quinton and Ziva to lie about their Abnormalities, they could hide them easier. They didn't have powers that so obviously showed or outted them. But Chandler's was a little more at the forefront, a little more present. It might not be elemental, but it wasn't far off. Elemental powers were easy to grasp and hard to hide because of natural factors in life, and every normal saw those powers as a threat that very life.

Ever since her Abnormality had surfaced, she'd had nothing but shame. She'd been kicked out of schools and a few jobs, and had nearly ended up in jail just because she'd been in a place where there'd been a fight – she was the only Abnormal around, so who else was to blame?

She cast her sights out the window. The snow was falling heavier now. As she stared at the clear flakes, she wondered if this job really could be a way for her to run *and* have her Abnormality been seen and used as a good thing. Even if some people truly didn't deserve her help. Even with all the secrets she would now have to keep.

Eventually, the cab dropped them off at the hotel. Stepping outside into the storm, tiny flecks caught in Chandler's hair and stuck to her clothes. Her insides warmed. Her dull mood ebbed slightly.

A shifting noise reverberated nearby and soon a huge wedge of snow slid off the slanted roof by the entrance, smacking down right on top of her head. Quinton and Ziva laughed, and Chandler laughed along with them.

Maybe hiding could be running. Maybe secrecy could be telling. Maybe, *just maybe*, she'd get to have a life that she could control and would be hers alone. At long last.

CHAPTER ELEVEN
ZIVA

24th Day of Autumn 2406

The hotel room they were staying in was bigger than the entire layout of Ziva's family home.

There was a living room with red sofas and a cabinet full of drinks and glasses. Two different bedrooms that were stacked full of furniture in gold and white. One oversized bathroom with a bathing tub big enough to swim in. There was even a balcony that overlooked the snowy city with enough room to hold a large table and a wood fire.

Night was drawing in fast. The cold crept closer, too, but inside the room, someone had preset the temperature to cosy.

"How did we even get this place?" Ziva asked, staring out at the view.

Quinton dumped his bags and jumped onto the nearest sofa, tucking his hands behind his head. "I pulled a few strings," he told them casually.

"A few strings?" Chandler scooted round the room and dropped down on the floor between the sofas. "I didn't know you had strings to pull."

He turned his head to smile at her. "Our kind are everywhere. If you know where to look, you can find them."

Cautiously, Ziva manoeuvred around to the free sofa and sat, placing her hands in her lap, and bit her lip. She didn't know if she liked the implication of being part of a "kind".

"How about some grub?" Quinton suggested, changing the subject.

Chandler shrugged. "Or we could nap now and get food later, when were already out?"

"I would *love* a nap," Ziva said.

"You did say that in the cab," Quinton nodded.

"And I meant it."

Truly, Ziva was drained. Between arriving at Redwing yesterday, then her midnight stroll with Abel in the gardens to arriving here, at this plush hotel in the middle of a beautifully snowy country, it felt like a whole week had passed. In reality, barely twenty-four hours had gone by from start to finish.

Ziva laid down awkwardly on the sofa, the pillows too lumpy and the cushions too plump, and grabbed the Star of David necklace she wore. Though she didn't personally believe in God, her grandmother did. Holding the necklace she'd given Ziva made her feel closer to her family despite being hundreds of miles away.

No one spoke but the lights eventually switched off. Even though the curtains were still open and the scene beyond them was lit with nightlife, the room grew dark. In her mind, Ziva could hear a faint crackling of a fire and wished to be sat around it. She just couldn't pick who she wanted to be there with her.

The museum was well lit, burning white lights igniting the space and fighting back the darkness of night.

Ziva rubbed her eyes against them.

Whatever crowds had been here during the day were gone now. Their trash had been collected, though a few stray cups and tissues had been stuffed under benches inside different areas.

"What do you think?" Chandler asked, walking up to her side.

"Of what?" Ziva asked back.

Chandler motioned to Ziva's food. She looked down at her chilli-topped cheesy chips. "Not as spicy as I thought they'd be."

"Is that good or bad?" Ziva held out a chip and basically fed it to Chandler, who accepted it with grace. After a minute, Chandler nodded. "Not spicy, but there's a kick," she decided.

In repayment, Chandler held out her steaming bowl of soup. It was apparently a delicate dish in Snowdonne made of vegetables and salmon. Ziva was dubious about trying it. Though she didn't follow religion like her grandmother, it had been easier for the entire family to eat as she had. But fish had always been ok to eat.

After a moment, Ziva sighed and they swapped foods. What was the harm in trying something new? She tried the soup with two decently small mouthfuls. It wasn't bad. Mostly it was warming. The fish broth was a little strong, but otherwise decent. The vegetables were cut into small chunks and cooked through.

They'd woken from their naps about an hour ago to a cold room. The chill had sunk right through to their bones as if an ice storm had whirled through. They'd all bundled into more layers immediately, and Quinton had found a way to turn the heating back on.

The quick nap had turned into a nearly two hour slumber. Ziva had woken wrapped in a blanket – who'd put it over her, she didn't know – but she'd climbed out from beneath it and had made them all hot drinks. They'd put on their shoes as they'd drank and discussed ideas, and had left the comfort of the hotel room in search of food and the museum they were really here for.

Quinton sidled up next to them, holding his own bag of plain chips. "All grubbed up, *abbies*?"

Chandler sipped from her spoon as loudly as possible, letting that be her answer. Ziva nodded and bit into another chip, relishing in the spice and heat.

In a silent and collective decision, they all stepped away from the cafeteria part and into the main museum.

Old and new collided inside. Suits of armour were posed next to animals long extinct and new ones recently discovered. Delicate artwork was framed above sculptures that appeared half-finished. Ziva didn't know where to look or what to focus on. There seemed to be no order here, only chaos. History and the present were folded into one moment. And it wasn't specifically dedicated to this or that, just *everything*.

They had ten days to solve a mystery. Ten days to find a Mask.

Ten days didn't sound like a lot of time.

And this place was going to make it difficult.

Ziva couldn't deny how cool the power of the Mask and its original owner sounded. The power to gift a power? The Mask could grant freedom to a wearer? It all sounded better than the ability to change colour.

Nervously, she glanced over at Quinton. His hair was now exceptionally stark white. Back in the hotel, they'd picked out names for their cover identities – Ziva was Shira, Quinton was Kaleb, and Chandler now Josephine – and Quinton had asked for a new hair colour at the same time.

At least her gift seemed to be holding up. The red hadn't come back through screaming, but it was only a matter of time before it did. Her grip wasn't strong and she hadn't had much practise to strengthen it.

They walked through the museum like tourists, as if they really were here to see every exhibit. Chandler, Ziva noticed, seemed to *actually* be as impressed as she was. Quinton, less so.

Soon they found the "artefact" exhibit the cab driver had mentioned. Ziva's heart-rate spiked as she read the introductory welcome board.

Most of the world still hated, or at best disliked, Abnormals. To have a whole collection of their things in one room was like lighting a fire in a fireworks factory and expecting nothing to go wrong.

Several of the displays were broken or hidden beneath raggedy curtains. Whole display units were missing, open spaces in the floor indicating that something had once stood there but no longer did. It seemed strange, like the museum was displaying the artefacts *and* the Abnormals themselves in one room by keeping the damage and destruction present. It was almost like the curators were saying "see, we can't have anything nice because they ruin it, even when we're doing them a favour." Ziva turned away as her eyes welled.

"Over here!" Chandler called thankfully a moment later.

Ziva trudged over to Chandler, nibbling at the remaining scraps of her chips. The plaque stamped on the display case before her read: "*The Mask of Iris*". Plain as day and *empty*.

"Coming here was a waste of time," Quinton commented as he joined them. Ziva couldn't have agreed more.

A security guard wandered past, wearing a tough vest and carrying a gun in hand, and Chandler signalled to him. Quinton glared at her, hard. Ziva backed up a step. She disliked Officials and Arrestors, like most Abnormals did, and didn't want to attract any sort of their attention.

"Excuse me, Sir?" Chandler asked, drawing him closer to the empty unit. "The Mask? When was it last here?"

The guard had a speckled, balding head but refused to chop off the sides that melted into a scraggly beard. His belly hung over his trousers and his shirt button looked like they might pop at any second.

He eyed Chandler suspiciously. "Why d'ya wan'o know?"

"Because we came all the way to see it!" Chandler flashed a dazzling smile, and Ziva blinked at the brilliance of it. "We wanted to see *all* the Abnormal artefacts. We're doing a group project on them for school. On the Abnormals, I mean, and how they've managed to press themselves into an otherwise organised and upstanding society, slowly turning our good place into one of crime."

The guard nodded furiously. "Nothing good has 'ome of those Abnormals."

"We're hoping the project can get us into Canton University."

"You three came all the way from New London?" The guard studied them each in turn, and Ziva tried to flash a dazzling smile of her own. If her mother saw or heard her right now... "I'm impressed."

"It's dedication to our craft and beliefs," Quinton said.

The guard nodded again, but set his eyes on Chandler with a crazed and fixated gleam to them. Ziva shivered and took a minimal step towards Quinton. "This place was broken in'o a few weeks back," the guard said. "Bloody Abnormals, ruining and stealing things they think belong to 'em. Bet they're now running a riot with those missin' things, stealin' cars, breaking in'o 'ouses."

Quinton shivered dramatically. "I hate to even think about it."

"Sorry to disappoint you lot," the guard said, mostly to Chandler. "Comin' all this way for somethin' that isn' here no more.

"Was it all stolen in one robbery?" Chandler asked, gazing at the case forlornly.

The guard sighed, looking defeated. "We're not exactly sure," he admitted. "The whole room had been trashed and all cameras had been shut off for 'bout three days before."

"Three days?" Quinton questioned. "So some little bastard had planned it?"

"Seems to. The crew who didn' notice were fired 'cause of it."

Chandler turned to him. "But you didn't," she said. "And that's good, because you've been ever-so helpful." She flashed another smile.

The guard licked his lips and bobbed his head before walking off. Ziva caught him taking one final look back at them, at Chandler, before he dipped out of sight.

Chandler shivered. "I feel like I need a shower."

"He wasn't even watching me and I feel the same," Quinton complained. "The way he was basically screwing you with his eyes and licked his mouth like you were his next meal..." He fake gagged.

Chandler grew slightly pale. "I don't want to think about it. If I do... No, I don't want to think about it."

Bile rose up in Ziva's mouth and she fought it back down. She changed the subject to combat the icky feelings. "What are we going to do now?" she whispered, careful in case the cameras were working again. "We don't even know if the one thing we're after was stolen at the same time as the rest!"

Quinton grimaced, looking between the empty case, Chandler, and Ziva. "It was called the lost Mask for a reason," he whispered back. "It had been missing for years, and then miraculously turned up here. Someone *had* to have had it before it appeared again."

"Yes, but *who*?" Chandler asked.

He shook his head. "That's up to us to figure out."

Panic began to build in Ziva's core as she started counting on her fingers. "We're meant to find a Mask, one that grants freedom to the wearer, that was lost before it was found and is now lost again. Then we're meant to take it. And *then* we're meant to hand deliver it to the maker's family."

Chandler threw her bowl and spoon into the nearby trash receptacle, and cracked her knuckles. "I bet finding the family who are alive today is going to be the easy bit here."

Quinton grinned devilishly. "Don't start making bets around here."

Ziva looked around but they were still alone. "What do we do?" she repeated.

Turning his smile to her, Quinton said, "How about we stop whispering in a near-empty museum and talk somewhere we can be loud?"

Ziva rubbed her temples with her fingers, the pressure of her core having risen to her head. "I think I'm going to need a bit more sleep before we discuss strategy."

Chandler nodded. "I'm with you."

"But we've only got ten days."

The large bell-tower they'd passed on the way in began to chime, twelve times in total.

The three of them glanced at one another and, spookily, whispered in unison, "Nine."

CHAPTER ELEVEN

QUINTON

25th Day of Autumn 2406

Plenty of places were open and other things were around to keep Quinton interested, but there was a very *specific* patch on the wall that was just *more*-interesting.

Right in the middle between two doorways, above the alcohol cabinet and bar – only gross to Quinton because he'd seen his parents pretend to be people they weren't around their fair share of those kinds of things – was a hole. It was so tiny, he'd almost missed it. Probably from a screw removed long ago.

He groaned, pressing the heel of his palms to his eyes. He wanted his notebook; he'd left it in his room to keep it safe and hadn't brought it out yet. He still hadn't managed to draw the last vision he'd seen of himself and Chandler. The image rubbed around inside his brain, stretching out, taking root because he hadn't taken the time to see it with his eyes, too.

He still hadn't told *her* what he'd seen either, and it was her possible future.

Depending on how it was looked at, it didn't appear to be a bad future. They'd been together, Chandler wearing a marriage ring. *That* was interesting. So was the fact that in all his years with his gift, Quinton had never seen himself.

Gretchen had messaged him back, yelling in text that he needed to tell Chandler. And he would. He wasn't planning on keeping it a secret, that went against his own code, and especially since it probably had something to do with this mission.

But Gretchen had also warned him.

If he was seeing himself in futures, were his powers manipulating and growing? He knew it was possible. There were some people who had gifts that could adapt and become *bigger* than what they once were over time, like they matured. Some had buds of a power that bloomed into a flower. Others started with a full garden to hand. Others had only a seed and it would never sprout.

With every Abnormal, with every *person*, everything was different and nothing was the same.

But what did it mean? He could already see ahead in time, into all the possibilities there. What would he eventually be able to do if this wasn't the end for his power?

He groaned again.

"If you keep making noises like that, people are going to get suspicious of what's happening in this room."

Quinton removed his hands from his eyes and stared at Ziva. "Let people think they hear whatever they want," he said. "People in hotels hear many things all the time anyway. They see them, too. A little groaning isn't going to ruin *their* moods."

Ziva smiled. "Mind if I join you?"

"Be my guest. You can stare at this wall with me."

"Is that was you were doing?" she asked.

"Something like that," he said. He shuffled over, allowing enough room for Ziva to slip onto the floor beside him.

Their backs touched the sofas, knees bent, arms at their sides. If anyone could see them, they looked like two people that had just had the worst day of their lives and were wallowing together. The fact that only one light in the room was on added to the moody ambiance.

"Can't sleep?" she asked him.

He laughed humourlessly. "I was about to ask you that."

"I can answer first? Obviously it's a no."

"Neither of us would be on the floor if we could." He sighed and released his legs, letting them unfold. "What's on your mind?"

"A few things," she answered. "You?"

"A few things," he mimicked.

His eyes wandered around the room, to the laptop that was open, to the TV that was on but silent, to the window that was covered. He hadn't talked to his parents in weeks, but that was normal – they used to go longer. His best friend was away on mission, but she'd return in time. He was now part of a mission with two new recruits, but they'd figure it out.

"What are we going to do?" Ziva mumbled, more to herself than him.

Quinton answered anyway. "We're going to complete this mission."

She turned her head towards him and he tried to keep his face straight, which was hard when he saw the state of her hair. "How?" she asked. "You've completely missions before. What was your first one like?"

"Yes, tell us."

Quinton looked up with a raised eyebrow. Chandler crept further into the room as if afraid to disturb them too much. She dropped onto the opposite sofa and tucked her legs beneath her.

"There isn't much to tell," Quinton said truthfully.

"So share what little there is?" Chandler pushed. "And what are we all awake for?"

"Because we're about to be arrested and we wanted to be prepared?" He grinned.

"About fucking time. How dare they let us Abnormals run wild."

Ziva snorted, turning her gaze to Quinton. "We're serious though about knowing about your first mission."

"I'll answer that," he said, "*if* you both answer something for me?"

Chandler scowled. It was hard to see in the faint light, but still noticeable once he focused on her. "Technically, the mission question was Ziva's, not mine," she said. "I get to ask something else."

Quinton reached up to the nearby light switch, illuminating the room in a sudden yellow glow.

This hotel wasn't as flashy as the places he usually stayed, but he kind of preferred that. These rooms were cosy and felt like life happened here. Usually the places he stayed in felt cold and almost too large to exist in, like a maze he was trapped within.

"My first mission was boring," Quinton told them. "All I had to do was make sure a private personal Abnormal got off a plane and into a car. They did and went on to the Summit Talks of the new century."

Chandler sat forwards. "*You* were part of the Summit Talks?"

"If you count playing a bodyguard for like ten minutes, yeah."

"I remember watching them on TV back home," Ziva said. "We were all gathered around, my whole family. We sat in that room for hours, glued to the screens."

Summit Talks were a way for the leaders of all countries to come together to talk about progress in society in the ways of health, culture, environmental impact, and Abnormal integration. Everything was spoken about back in the Year 2400. All except Abnormal integration. Once again, they'd been overlooked. Mainly because no government had a single Abnormal on board.

"Oh, I never said." Quinton shuffled to face Ziva properly. "Thanks for the hair change." He touched the lengths of what had once been his red hair. Now, it was shocking white. "Is it permanent?"

She shook her head. "It doesn't have to be?"

"And if I want it to be? Is that possible?"

This time, she nodded. "I just let go of the gift and it sort of just sticks. I don't know how else to describe it." She bit her bottom lip in concentration, her eyes roaming over his head inch by inch carefully. "If I don't let it go, it will slowly slip back anyway."

"Does it hurt to keep the façade up?"

"No. Just tiring."

"Then let go. I can always dye it again, right?" She nodded.

"You want to be a ghost?" Chandler chimed in. She'd sat back in the chair again and a sly grin slid across her lips. "And I think you've asked *way more* than your fair share of questions to Z now."

"*Z*?" Ziva questioned. "I have a nickname?" She looked utterly surprised by the open way her mouth hung. Chandler shrugged, her smile turning softer.

"Fine," Quinton pouted, making it sound worse than it really was.

Ziva tapped his shoulder and he turned to her. Her eyes creased in the corners and suddenly it was like a band snapped against his forehead. Quinton flinched, but the sensation was gone in a breath. He touched his hair; the ends were clear white as if he'd bathed in pure snow that would never melt.

Ziva sighed. "That's better. Just let me rest a couple of hours, and if you hate it by then, we can change it again."

He rested his hand on her knee awkwardly, but she didn't

brush him away. "I'll use dye next time," he said. "You save yourself."

"And, on this day, we remember the *darling* Quinton that was, for he gave his luscious red locks of Hell over to become a ghost of Earth," Chandler mocked, small grin returning.

"You think I'm darling, do you, *precious*?" he teased back. "And you liked my red hair, I know you did."

Chandler never answered but did roll her eyes.

Quinton smiled and grabbed his thick, tying his hair at the nape of his neck. Ziva reached up and flicked the little ponytail. Chandler tilted her head slightly at him. He honestly didn't know which reaction was funnier, but both were pretty laughable. Being in this kind of situation reminded him of what would happen if Gretchen was here, or even the Grittal brothers.

The sentiments and mocking gestures sounded friendly despite them having not known each other long. They didn't dislike each other, nor did they have enough opinion on the other – Quinton certainly didn't – but it was nice to find someone who matched some of his energy.

"Actually I don't think you *could* come back from being a ghost," Chandler decided.

"Why, would you know?" he asked, eyebrows rising.

She smiled but it didn't reach her eyes. "No."

"Then what *would* you know about?"

"Ice."

With the drop of just one word, the room's temperature plummeted. Flakes glided from the air and landed, melting on impact.

"That's what you were going to ask me," Chandler said confidently. "Wasn't it?"

"Don't start making bets you don't know you can win."

"This would've been the only one I would ever place money on."

Quinton raised a hand and caught a falling flake. It turned to a droplet in his palm. "You're right. It's not an element," he mused.

Chandler cracked her knuckles and all the cold was sucked away. Quinton felt the air pull like a whirlwind towards her.

For most of his adult life, Quinton had been around Abnormals. He'd been there to witness many different Abnormalities at many different times. They all felt new and powerful. This was no exception. The way Ziva could change colours and Chandler controlled ice was invigorating, *intriguing*.

Suddenly he didn't feel so overwhelmed. His heart calmed its thumping in his chest and the racing heat of his body dropped back to normal. While he still couldn't quite see how they were going to complete this mission, he understood that, at least on some base level, they now trusted each other.

For sharing the knowledge of a gift was no easy thing. It meant letting someone else *see them*, see their entire soul. Quinton had done so, so many times, with many people. His power was one of the easier ones to explain after using. And though he was used to it all now, he had never really feared it to begin with.

"Your question," he abruptly said. His mind ticked and he somehow knew he was going to be right. "It's about what I saw, isn't it?"

"What you saw?" Ziva asked, just as she had on the air-shuttle.

Chandler didn't move, and that was answer enough for him.

Quinton angled himself to face both girls. He lifted his necklace and the crystal that was attached. "I can't remember what I've told you, if anything. But my gift is one where I can see into the future. I don't ever know how far I see, and nor do I know if what I see is set in stone. Futures have been known to warp and shift. Some don't at all. It all depends on the universe and how it feels it wants to move."

"And someone just has to touch the crystal?" Ziva said.

He nodded. "I hold it after and it shows me what I need to see."

"Can't you just hold someone's hand or something though?"

"Do you want to hold my hand?" he joked. Ziva laughed but didn't disagree. "I need the crystal to channel my power. Another crystal has never worked, only this one. I don't even remember how I acquired it. One day, I just did, then my power kicked in. It's been attached to me ever since, helping me with my sight."

"None of that sounds bad!"

"It isn't. But there are downfalls to my power, and it *can* be bad. Only because I can never be certain if the vision will stay or change, and if it does, how much by."

"And I touched the crystal," Chandler admitted. Her gaze settled on Quinton's face, a scowl etched into her eyebrows.

Ziva whistled beside him. "What did you see?"

Quinton looked at Chandler since it was her future. She shrugged. "As long as it's not *bad* bad, I have no issue with Ziva hearing it."

"Define *bad* bad?"

"I don't know!" She flung her arms up slightly. "You seem to have had a lot of practise, so you should know."

Quinton took a deep breath. "The only thing I need you to understand first is that I've never seen myself in a vision. I could hold the crystal for hours and *nothing*."

"Ok..." Ziva drew the word out.

"But I did." His stared locked onto Chandler's, and a bolt of something sharp passed between them.

"You saw yourself?" she asked, sitting further upright. "In my future?"

"Are you sure you want Ziva to hear?"

"Why? Did what you see make you uncomfortable?"

Ziva and Quinton laughed, and he noted how the corner of Chandler's mouth quirked up too. It simmered back until the room was quiet. "Are you sure you want to know?" he asked.

"Is there something *that* seriously wrong?" Chandler challenged. He shook his head, because it wasn't necessarily *seriously wrong*, but...

"It's a little personal, maybe."

"As long as it's not weird or overly personal, though why you'd see that..." She glared at him with a fierceness backing it. "Whatever, it's fine. You can say it. I asked for your power as much as you asked my mine."

"Alright." He took in a deep breath and felt his heart leap. "I saw us together. I don't know how close we were or what we were doing, but it was only us, and you were wearing an emerald and silver marriage band on your correct finger."

Chandler blinked. When Quinton thought she might yell or scream, she simply climbed off the sofa and padded across to the balcony. The freezing air rushed in as she stepped outside.

Yelling, screaming, crying... They were all reactions he understood and knew to expect when someone learned of their future. Walking out... He knew people didn't always like the truth, but this something else entirely. It was almost like confusion, like Chandler herself didn't know what else to do.

It utterly baffled him.

Ziva put a hand on Quinton's knee. "You didn't do anything wrong," she whispered. "But I think you should talk to her."

"I don't think she wants to talk to me of all people right now."

"I don't think this is about me. Or even you."

"Feels *a lot* like it's about me."

"I'm not sure."

"I just happened to tell her what I saw, a vision that included me *and* her, and she walked off. Tell me again how that doesn't seem personal." His heart stuttered.

"Just, talk to her." Ziva climbed to her feet. "I'll make the teas for when you're both ready to come back inside." She walked to the kitchen segment of the room and looked back over her shoulder. "Take a blanket with you."

Quinton watched Ziva go.

Groaning once more, he climbed to his feet, snatched a blanket, and opened the balcony door to face the ice and the girl he now knew could control it.

CHAPTER THIRTEEN

CHANDLER

25th Day of Autumn 2406

A heavy yet fluffy blanket fell over Chandler's shoulders. She looked up and saw Quinton. He avoided her glare, only releasing his grip on the blanket when she grabbed the edges to secure it in place around herself.

Chandler turned her attention back to the sleeping city. "Don't you have one?" she asked quietly.

"I'm quite warm-blooded," he replied.

She pulled the blanket tighter around her body despite not feeling the cold. "Thank you, for mine, even if I don't need it."

Out the corner of her eye, she saw him not. "A better thanks would be sharing with me when I nearly freeze in a couple of minutes because I'm too stubborn to go back inside and get my own."

An unexpected laugh jumped from between her lips.

He fully turned to face her and she did the same. He wore an easy smile. Chandler wasn't used to seeing someone so carefree, or how disarming it was.

The sky above them captured her attention quickly as she looked away from him. Various blues shifted to lighter tones. Clouds drifted, appearing soft and full though they were probably just full of more snow. Running a hand over the burning cold railing, she attempted to settle the rhythm of her heart so it wasn't the only thing she could hear.

Quinton shifted closer at her side, like the space they shared was closing in on them. "I didn't mean to upset you," he whispered. "I live by a code, some rules I set myself, when it comes to my gift." He leant on the railing, peering out across the city, looking just as he had the first time Chandler had seen him, just no longer from afar. "It might not always be pleasant or what you want to hear, but I refuse to lie about what I see. Whether it's good or bad. That's not up for me to pick and choose what everyone knows and what they can be prepared for."

Balancing the blanket on her shoulders, she managed to crack her knuckles. "I appreciate that."

"People tend to forget that while I'm *telling* what happens or might happen, I have to *see* it. I almost live that future in the moment I see it."

"So the moment you saw with us," she looked up at him and he turned his gaze towards her, "you lived that when you touched the crystal after me?"

"I stopped existing in the real moment and entered the future moment for as long as it lasted."

"Have you never seen yourself before? Really?"

"Never." He reached up and slid a hand through his hair. The band that kept it tucked fell to the floor by their feet. "Gretchen will tell you when you meet her. She's in Egypt right now."

Chandler shivered under her blanket. "I think she got a better mission."

"Digging up dusty bones?" Quinton laughed. "I'm not sure. I'm not great with bones and their names, or their breaks. She's in her element there."

Bending down, she picked up his hair-band and held it out like a peace offering. "Meeting her would also mean staying."

"Or waving goodbye on the way out."

Chandler dumped the band in his outstretched hand and pulled back quickly, grasping for her blanket. "What made *you* decide to stay?"

"Several things," he admitted. "My parents and what they'd chosen for my life was the main reason. What they wanted wasn't what I did. But this job, while intense as fuck, can be fun. And the people aren't so bad."

"I don't believe that for a second."

"Which bit?"

"That all the people here aren't so bad."

"Want to place a bet?"

Chandler scowled. "On what?"

Quinton grinned like he could see right through her scowl to the interest behind her eyes she was trying to lock up. But he couldn't. He could see into the future, not through people. She turned her gaze away in case her façade slipped.

"On you," he answered.

"Not this again." She rolled her eyes.

"I don't need to bet on your powers anymore," he reminded her. "I know you're not an elemental now, remember?"

"Then, what?"

He moved, shifting round to lean back on his arms, his head tilted in her direction. "Even if it's a one-sided bet," he smiled, "I bet you'll say."

She couldn't help the scoff. "What makes you think that?"

"I don't know. I just think you will."

"Can't deny that I love the confidence."

He laughed, bright and carefree and *honest*. It was genuine joy. Chandler scowled at it. As much as she'd never been so free herself, she didn't think she'd ever experienced enough happiness to be how Quinton was.

They stood in silence as the city around them started to wake.

Lights in windows began to turn on and a few car-horns started beeping. From their balcony perch, Chandler could see how even a cart ran up the side of the streets, following along a line all the way to the faraway mountains.

"It wasn't you," she blurted.

She saw Quinton's head snap towards her. "What wasn't me?"

"I didn't come out here because of you."

"There was me thinking I smelt bad or something."

Chandler shook her head. "You smell fine. It wasn't even what you'd said either."

"Then—"

"Why?" He nodded at her question and she sighed heavily. "I've never fit in well with people. I know you asked me to touch the crystal and I did, that was my choice, and I don't regret it. I will admit it stunned me, what you saw. But it was weirder to hear you speak about me, and how you said it. It made me panic. It made me think and wonder if I might be able to fit in." She slipped the blanket off her shoulders when Quinton shivered and walked to him, draping it over him, careful not to touch him with more than the material. "The marriage ring though? That *completely* blind-sided me."

He grabbed the blanket with both hands, swaddling himself. "Yeah, I don't know what that's about either. You were just wearing it. But I'm convinced it's about the case somehow. Neither of us looked older, not even a year. I need to properly draw it to see it clearer, but..." He trailed off.

Curiosity overtook Chandler's brain. "You draw?"

"You saw me with my notepad and pens." He smiled down at her. "Whatever I see, I draw. It's what I was doing when you stumbled into the drawing room the other night."

Chandler wondered if she'd ever see the drawing he must've made of her and even considered asking, but bit her tongue to stop herself. They didn't know each other, not really. She had no right to ask for anything.

Guilt swam through her blood. It was a familiar feeling, one she'd been plagued with her whole life, mostly for things that weren't her fault. However, this time, it was.

Quinton had said he would never lie to a person about what he saw, would never keep it away from them. Chandler commended that. But she couldn't say the same. Though, it wasn't quite about what she saw. It was more about what she felt. And it wasn't really lying if she'd partly told the truth.

Because truthfully, while she didn't fit in with others and never really had, she didn't trust them. Her mother had taught her not to trust her own family, so why should she ever believe in strangers? She had a complete disconnect with people. Most of them, she'd put the distance in place before they could do it to her. If only to protect herself from disappointment. She slid through life like a constantly wounded animal, wrapping herself up before the injury ever came.

Chandler was trying to save herself from any more hurt, but she also didn't want to be lonely.

Existing without people was an isolating thing. No one could get close and nor would she. She supposed now she did have Ziva. She'd let the girl in almost right away. There had been something about her that had told Chandler she was incapable of betrayal.

Maybe one person, for once, would be ok.

Chandler sighed and caught Quinton shivering. The blanket had slipped slightly from his shoulders and she went to push it back up. But he stole her out-stretched hand and pulled her body to his, grinning down at her.

"Comfy," he teased, wrapping them both up.

"I didn't ask for this."

"Maybe not. But you can take the cold out of the air as much as you can give, right?"

"Yes," she sighed. "And before you ask, I'm not planning on sharing body heat. I'll take the cold and leave it at that."

"I wouldn't *dream* of asking." His grin widened, illuminating his stormy-coloured eyes. Though Chandler could feel no difference, she drew the cold to her. Quinton's smile shrank at the same time. "How do you feel?"

She felt his breath on the top of her head, but her sigh was definitely because of the question. "Tired," she admitted. "Maybe we should go back inside?"

Ziva's head suddenly peaked round the door, a cheeky little smile on her face. "I think you should," she agreed.

Chandler glared and sent a current of cold she leeched from Quinton to Ziva, who spluttered almost instantly. Her power wasn't *just* about ice. Taking the cold and displacing it was a minor side-effect to her gift but helpful all the same.

"Have you been spying on us?" she asked.

"I swear, I was about to come and get you!" Ziva rubbed her face as if that could block out the cold. "But I saw you get closer and left you alone."

"And stood at the door."

Ziva bit her bottom lip. "Maybe."

Chandler rolled her eyes and pulled back the current. "It's a good job I like you."

Quinton opened up the blanket fort barely an inch. "Come on, icy."

She blasted him with the cold, sending slivers of ice that peeled off the roof too. He made the mistake of opening his mouth, probably to complain, so a few drops stabbed at the end of his tongue. His lips sealed shut rather quickly. Chandler raised her eyebrow in challenge, and when he said nothing, she pulled her power back and the ice-fall stopped.

They walked side-by-side back into the room. Only once they were back in the warmth did Chandler realise she'd wrapped an arm behind Quinton and he'd draped an arm over her shoulders.

To share a blanket, she thought, not feeling the lie.

She slid from Quinton, leaving him the blanket, knowing he needed it and she didn't. Ziva offered her a cup of tea and she held it like it contained magic. It tasted as herbally as it smelt.

"It should help us sleep," Ziva said, sipping from her own cup.

Quinton made a 'cheers' motion. "You've been named the official tea maker of this group."

Ziva positively beamed. "Some things don't change. I was the tea girl back home too."

"They always say you should do what you're good at."

They all sat on the sofas, switching the TV on.

Ziva and Quinton continued to talk about tea and home, but Chandler sat in silence with her thoughts. The vision troubled her. Quinton assumed it was case related, and she thought so too, but she hadn't been lying when she'd said it had blindsided her. She'd *never* even dreamt of being thought of in that way, as a loved partner, even if it was fake.

But she also knew she'd do it if she had too. If it meant completing this mission, or any, she'd do what it took. She'd do almost anything to get away from her old life.

She was tired. Tired of not having friends or family. Tired of not being able to be herself. Tried or not being able to *trust*.

She was tired of not having a life.

"Wait!"

Quinton burst free of his blanket and nearly threw his cup

in the process. Chandler watched as he scurried for the remote to turn up the TV volume. Some news anchor was talking and shuffling papers, discussing the day's events. A smaller picture was presented on the screen beside him.

"I know that guy," Quinton announced as the small picture overtook the other.

"You know him?" Ziva asked, voicing Chandler's next question.

The person Quinton was referring to was a head banker at one of the top firms in the world.

"Well, I *did*," he said.

Chandler put her empty mug down. "And?"

"I knew him once, but I'm pretty sure he died."

Ziva gasped. "*Died*? Are there any powers of resurrection?"

Quinton narrowed his gaze. "Probably." He stared at the screen. The head banker shook someone's hand. "Something's off."

"Maybe he didn't die?" Chandler suggested.

Quinton shot her an unimpressed glare. "He was dead. The buried and very gone kind."

"The Mask!" Ziva suddenly chirped. "Couldn't the Mask give freedom to whoever wore it?"

Chandler glanced at her. "Yes?"

"He's hosting a party tomorrow," Quinton told them.

Rolling across the bottom of the screen were the words "LOUIS MAYFAIRER HOSTING GRAND PARTY TO ELIT GOLD GUESTS". The banker, Louis, grinned in a way that wasn't entirely nice to look at.

"Are you really saying it's not the real him?" Chandler looked between the screen and Quinton.

"No," he answered, not taking his eyes away for a second. If anything, he squinted harder. "But I'm also not, not saying that."

Ziva sighed. "Because that's easy to understand."

"I'm not saying he hasn't been brought back from the dead, and I'm also not saying someone isn't wearing the Mask," he clarified. "But it's worth a look, right? It could be a lead?"

"It's more than what we had," Chandler agreed. What they'd had was nothing.

"This might also be nothing and we waste more time looking in the wrong direction." Quinton turned his scrutiny towards them. "But it's oddly convenient someone who I'm sure was dead is now suddenly very much alive *and* the Mask that can transform people has gone missing, all at the same time."

Ziva wiped a hand in the air as if it were a board to clean the space of previous thoughts. "How are we going to get in? What are the Elite Gold Guests?"

Quinton seemed to shrink; it was barely perceptible but Chandler noticed. "They're the banks favourite clients, or the friends of the man who run it. So only the 'elite' members of society will be invited for cocktails, small talk, judgement, and hors d'oeuvres."

"But how are *we* getting in?" Ziva repeated. "If we want to snoop, we've got to figure out a way."

Quinton grimaced. "My family will be invited. Which means I will be too."

"Your family are *elite*?"

"They are."

"So you can play yourself and actually get inside?"

"Yes."

"Quinton?" Chandler called.

He faced her, and she didn't dare ask about the smile in his expression as she swallowed the thick lump that had formed in her throat. For a sense of calm, she sought out the air's water, twisting some of the droplets into flakes. She crackled her knuckles for good measure.

It was scary to know of something that happened before it came to the present.

But equally as scary to know that the time for the events to play out had arrived.

"I'm going to need a ring."

CHAPTER FOURTEEN
QUINTON

26th Day of Autumn 2406

"It's not going to fall off," Quinton whispered.

Chandler's head snapped up. "It's my size, right?"

"I didn't cut your finger off to get it measured! You were with me."

The news announcement of the banker's party had been yesterday morning. Nearly a full day had passed since then. It'd been easy to agree that it had needed investigating.

The majority of yesterday had been spent gathering things for the event. Quinton hadn't minded much. His new suit fit like a glove, even if it would become uncomfortable as time went on. His crystal was concealed underneath his new shirt.

All at the expense of his parents. Well, from the loaded credit card his parents had thrusted at him years ago and never checked the statements for, just paid it off in full whenever they needed to.

They had also helped to pay for Chandler's dress, a rich emerald velvet number that had long sleeves to cover her tattoo – he was *dying* to ask about it – and her new ring.

The ring itself was a square emerald encased in silver, the band engraved on the inside with the words "my sweetest blessing". It was *exactly* as he'd seen it vision and had known the second he'd laid eyes on it in the jewellers that it was the one.

"Are you ready?" Chandler asked him discreetly.

"Are *you* ready?" he asked back. "We'll be entering a whole new world here."

"You won't be."

He glanced away for a second. "No, not me."

"As long as you're prepared to explain me, then it's fine." He looked back at her and her gaze softened, the hazel in her eyes sharp. "How do I look?"

"Blonde." He let out a half laugh.

Ziva had changed Chandler's hair to a honey-blonde before they'd left, hiding her more-so. Quinton's hair was still stark-white but the people he was about to mingle with knew him to change his hair often – it was his way of outwardly rebelling.

"People like blondes," she commented and stomped her foot, her heel clicking.

Quinton crooked his elbow. "Shall we, Josephine?"

She accepted the arm and her cover name with ease. "Into the pit of vipers we go."

He barely had to push on the doors before they swung open. Chandler rolled her shoulders back and stood taller. She was a foot shorter than him but exuded all the confidence he'd seen when she'd first arrived at Redwing. And even if it was false, that she was terrified out of her mind, it was impressive.

He hated to admit it but he still didn't know what to make of her. She appeared as confident here, at least to look at, as she'd been then. But out on the hotel balcony, he'd seen a whole other side to her. Most people came in many dimensions. He looked at the small smile on Chandler's face and thought how he'd probably barely scratched the outer layers of hers.

Making an effort to flash the ring on her finger, Quinton led them into the jaws of the beast.

They were instantly met by a waiter passing out gold flutes of champagne. Quinton picked one, handing it to Chandler, then took one for himself. The waiter moved on as Chandler sipped, and then grimaced. He did the same. Champagne had never been his favourite drink.

"I hope Ziva's got a good view," Chandler whispered, using the loud music to muffle her voice.

Quinton laughed and sipped again. "Oh, I'm sure she does. Smile. All our best angles are on display."

Ziva was back at the hotel. Yesterday, they'd called home to get Dalton's help in hacking into the cameras of this building. With the help, they'd managed to access this part of Louis' home perfectly. Dalton had even given Ziva the access codes just in case she got locked out at any point and couldn't call him.

There was also no guarantee Dalton had closed off his link and that people at Redwing weren't watching like it was some damn movie. It'd happened in the past to other people on other missions.

Letting his sights linger on the cameras, he dipped his head so his lips were a bite away from Chandler's ear. "We can turn back if you want," he said. "We can join Ziva and come up with another route through this."

"And miss a chance to meet your parents?" She angled her face so they were looking at each other, barely a breath between them. He could smell the rose on her skin and see the shimmer on her cheeks. "I don't think so, *sweetie*."

Quinton laughed, probably a little too loudly. "Sweetie?"

"We *are* to be married." She wiggled her fingers that were still on his arm, letting the ring shine.

"Lovely, *precious*." He took her hand, holding it gently, and stroked his thumb over the back. "We are to be married," he mimicked. He looked up just in time to see his parents crossing the room towards them over Chandler's shoulder. "Speaking of..."

Quinton straightened up, a formality he'd never dropped in all the years – even when he didn't have to play the part of Quinton Eichner the eighth, he held himself up. Gretchen made no end of jokes about it. No matter how much he slumped, when faced with authority, he stood tall.

The two bodies walking his way were half each of what made Quinton whole. His father, Quinton Eichner the seventh, had soft grey hair that had once been light brown, cut short at the sides and neatly combed. His mother had a gentle smile and stormy bluey-grey eyes. They strode arm in arm, a drink each in their free hands. Both wore matching black, just as Quinton's velvet jacket matched the velvet emerald of Chandler's dress.

"My son, is that you?" his father asked despite being clearly able to identify him.

Quinton's parents stopped before him and his heart kicked out, hard.

His mother passed her glass to his father. "My son," she cooed, and reached to straighten his bow-tie. Her eyes passed by him to the woman beside him. A sly smile entered her blush-red lips. "Are you going to introduce us?"

"Mother, father," Quinton bowed his head. He realised then that he still held Chandler's hand, was still drawing circles into the skin, and neither of them had moved away from the other. He put on a smile. "I would like you to meet my fiancée, Josephine Houst."

His mother beamed. "It's lovely to meet you, honey!"

"It's so lovely to finally get to meet you too!" Chandler slipped out of Quinton's grasp and he let her go so she could place a kiss to both of his mother's cheeks. She then went to his father and he lifted her hand to kiss before allowing her to kiss his face.

Quinton had to admit it, he was impressed. Chandler had fully embraced the role and the way of this world easily. And all without much guidance. He wondered how she did it. To greet the family with kisses and make small-talk to the "elite" wasn't easy. But she made it look simple, delicate. He knew this was her first time doing this, and now he was interested to see what else she could do.

His father caught Chandler's hand as she went to pull away. He ran his scrutinising eyes over the ring that lay heavy on her finger. "Emerald," he commented. "How delicate."

"It's her favourite colour," Quinton said, just as Chandler said, "It's my favourite."

Quinton stole a sideways glance at her. She wasn't looking at him but he noted the small smile on her mouth. He wondered how true, how *real*, her answer was because this wasn't something they'd discussed having an answer on beforehand.

His mother broke the moment by clapping her hands together. "We simply *must* have dinner together."

"Maybe another time, dear," her husband said. Quinton tried not to sneer at his father. "We are here to celebrate a friend's birthday, not to organise a family gathering."

"There will be a time!" his mother cheered.

"Sounds wonderful," Quinton said, smiling at his mother.

Dinner with his parents didn't sound wonderful at all. And if he went, he'd have to bring Chandler. He didn't want to subject her to that.

He glanced at her again, finding her smiling politely and not appearing uncomfortable at all. She was *definitely* a woman of two sides: the one she showed and the one she kept to herself.

"Tell me, dear," his mother beamed at Chandler, "how did you meet?"

"Actually, it was an accident," Chandler said, keeping up with the smile. "A friend had set me up with someone else, but I happened to bump into Quinton." She looked up at Quinton adoringly and he tried to ignore the single stutter inside his chest because it was a *fake* look. He genuinely smiled back, wondering if she was thinking of *just* how they'd met like he was. "He'd been in his own little world at the back of the tea room."

Quinton laughed, hoping it sounded believable, hoping their *whole story* sounded believable. "I think I startled you more than you startled me."

"Oh, I can agree with you on that."

"You caught my attention and made me stop drawing."

"All I did was walk in." Her smile softened at the edges and he blinked.

"You still do that?" his father cut in.

Quinton swallowed and looked at his father. "It's how I concentrate," he said. "It's focuses my mind."

"It's sweet," his mother said, taking verbal scissors to cut the tension between father and son. Quinton had always been grateful for his mother's ability to do that. "And I cannot wait to hear more, but your father's correct. I'm being too nosey—"

"You're not nosey!" Quinton cut in.

His mother gave him a wink. "And we're here to celebrate a friend."

"I'm glad you accepted your invitation and the responsibility," his father commented.

Quinton's smile soured. "It's a public gathering. One I'm obligated to go to still." Chandler slowly slid her arm through his and it melted some of the tension in him, though he could feel a coldness radiate from her slightly.

"Did you know our host, Mister Mayfairer himself, was resurrected?" his mother chimed, changing directions in conversation again.

Chandler gasped lowly and Quinton knew *that* wasn't fake. "Resurrected? Is that even possible?"

Quinton's father's eyes turned to Chandler again, and softened, but only slightly, and much like an animal's. "Tell me, how much do you know about Abnormals?"

The music and chatter seemed to grow in pitch around them, but not volume. Quinton had ignored it mostly until then, but now he could hear useless noise. He had to strain to hear anything anyone was saying around it.

"Not much." Chandler lied as if she wasn't lying at all. She lied like all her words were truth. And she said it all crystal clear.

"What about my son?" his father pressed.

"Sir?" Chandler slowly shifted to look at Quinton's face straight on. "Are you asking if your son knows or if I know about you son?"

His father's thick eyebrows rose. "She has a tongue!"

His wife slipped her hand over his chest. "Just like I did, and you loved me for it."

He visibly calmed and Quinton felt himself breathe. "To answer you, I wondered if you knew about my son since you claim not to know much about Abnormals."

"I know about him," Chandler said, a little harshly. "I know everything I need to know about him. I might not know about Abnormals in general but I know about my fiancé and the love I have for *all* of him."

Quinton was glad he hadn't drunk anything in the last minute or it would've all been coming out again; he could barely swallow his dry choke. He looked at Chandler, hoping he appeared like he was sharing his "love" back. Honestly, he was just astounded. If things were different and they weren't practically strangers, the words would've sounded lovely. That didn't disqualify the way they made him feel warm and the jump his heart did.

"Very well." His father nodded. "To go back to resurrection, our host was indeed brought back. It wasn't in the papers for privacy reasons. But most of us here know."

Chandler nodded once. "I appreciate being informed."

"Don't we all, dear," Quinton's mother said.

"An Abnormal brought him back," Quinton's father continued. "Man's been living for the past few days and decides he needs a party." He rolled his eyes. Quinton knew he objected to the idea. "It was part of a plan to see if their so-called gifts worked."

"Darling," Quinton's mother said. "We must be going. I've just spotted DeLuca!" She turned to Chandler and reached out to hug her. "It was lovely to meet you, and now that you're in our son's life, I'm sure we will be seeing a lot of you."

Chandler smiled politely. "I'm sure we'll share a glass of wine in no time."

His mother melted and looked to Quinton. "She seems like a lovely woman and you better look after her."

"I will, Mother," Quinton agreed.

"Goodbye for now," his father said curtly. "Keep your back straight and make sure you look at that offer." He gave a pointed look.

Together Quinton's parents walked off and the music and noise of the party peeled away with them.

A waiter stopped by and Chandler quickly swapped their empty glasses for full ones. She downed hers in one gulp. The waiter paused and then gave her a new one before scurrying off.

"Your mother's nice," she said once they were alone. "You father could do with some work."

Now Quinton *did* choke on his drink. "You're certainly not wrong."

Chandler swallowed her next drink again and put her glass on a nearby cabinet. "Come on."

Without warning, she stole his drink, put it down, and then took his hand to drag him onto the dance-floor. The volume of the music vibrated his chest, but at least it now sounded like music. Chandler waved their joined hands and arms, and made them move together semi-decently until they blended into the crowd of other dancers.

But all too soon the music changed and a slow song came on.

Quinton watched as Chandler stood perfectly still for a moment before she interlocked their fingers and drew herself close. Quinton, being a perfect gentleman put his free hand to the small of her back, and touched their locked hands between their bodies in an intimate embrace.

Lowering his head, he whispered into her ear, "This is unexpected."

"If we tried to whisper in a corner, we'd be noticed," she muttered.

"So you didn't bring me here just for a sneaky dance?"

"I'm not even going to dignify that with an answer." She untucked herself to stare up at him. "Are you alright?"

Chandler's question sounded earnest and he smiled. "I'm fine," he answered honestly. Meeting and being around his parents was always a struggle, but having Chandler around had somehow made it easier. "Are *you* alright?"

"Yes." She sighed against him, and anyone looking would see it as contentment. He dropped his head on top of hers so he could hear what she was saying. "What are we going to do? You were right. The man we came here for isn't who we're after. He doesn't have the Mask. He was just resurrected."

Quinton laughed. "You say that like it's an easy thing."

"But it's what we didn't want."

"I know. The only thing we *can* do is go back to the start."

"We had nothing at the start."

"There's nothing for us here, either."

She peered up at him again, her face inches from his. "We're running out of time already."

He grinned down at her. "There's always time."

"You sound confident."

"Oh, I'm nowhere close to confident." He wouldn't lie, not to Chandler. He didn't know why he thought it, but he knew he would keep that promise. "We have nothing, but we have a little time, and we'll work with it."

She sighed again. "I hope this works."

"I do too."

"We're trusting you, me and Ziva."

"A truly dreadful decision."

They laughed and danced and laughed and danced.

It was hard to say who complained about having enough first – Chandler about being tired or Quinton about his shoes – but someone did and so they gradually slipped away from the party when others begun to, sneaking out a bottle of bubbly with them.

CHAPTER FIFTEEN
ZIVA

27th Day of Autumn 2406

Every time a blueberry burst or the buttery pancake mix touched her tongue, Ziva savoured the sweet taste. The sweetness was a stark contrast to the bitter news that'd come in this morning.

Somehow, the press had gotten into the party and now it was known worldwide; Louis Mayfairer was a man brought back from the dead. To Ziva, Chandler, and Quinton, it just proved what they'd suspected. There were even images coming through of Louis and the man who'd resurrected him side by side. He was a man reborn and not someone hiding.

"That's that then," Ziva said, taking another large bite.

Ziva had viewed the party from the comfort of the hotel room. Parties weren't her kind of thing and thanks to Quinton's vision, she hadn't been a contender to go anyway. She'd sat eating cheese puffs and drinking tea while her friends had danced and made small-talk.

The free entertainment she'd been given had made sure she never looked away once. People had gossiped about their lovers and affairs. Others had gone to take drugs in a secluded bathroom together.

But it had also been interesting to see Quinton and Chandler act as partners. They'd done well, convincing enough to fool his parents at least. Even Ziva could admit she'd been tricked by their act, if only for a few minutes.

And it had all been for nought.

Chandler pinched a blueberry from her half of the plate – the girls were sharing a breakfast, neither with enough appetite for one each. "Seems so," she said, passing the newspaper over to Quinton who sat beside Ziva.

He flicked the paper open and read. When he looked up again, his face was tight and his mouth matched a straight line. "Sorry," he said.

Ziva rested her fork. "What are you apologising for?"

"I don't know," he shook his head, "but I thought I was onto something with him." He nodded at the paper.

The little café beside their hotel wasn't bustling yet. The day had barely begun. Light was still struggling to rise. Noises from the street barely flowed in through the glass, and only once did Ziva hear a distant car-horn. It seemed everyone was sleeping in this morning or they were working from home. Either that or the news had kept them glued to screens.

"Would've been nice," Chandler said after a moment. "But I don't figure anything to be that easy. It was a good shot though, even if it didn't work out." She gave Quinton a small smile.

Ziva put her hand over Quinton's, squeezing slightly. "It doesn't matter. We had a false start. So what? We just reset, like you said. Haven't you had to do that before?"

Quinton flipped their hands so his was on top, and he squeezed back. "I have."

"So, what do we do?"

No one answered. No one *had* an answer.

Last night, Quinton and Chandler had returned home in silence. Ziva had spied them giving each other a nod before separating off to their rooms as if they hadn't been dancing and laughing minutes before.

Since Ziva shared a room with Chandler, she'd waited a good while before following. Chandler had been quiet but Ziva hadn't been sure if she'd been asleep. She'd climbed into bed anyway. When she'd woken, she'd noticed Chandler had rolled over in her sleep. Not wanting to disturb her, figuring she needed some peace, Ziva had gotten up despite the early hour.

The silence from then continued on now. They ate their food with distance. None of them looked to the other, nor did they look up when the server refilled their mugs with tea and coffee. The servers then walked away, their shuffling feet easily heard.

"We need to investigate the break in," Chandler said suddenly, throwing the words from her mouth quietly.

"The break in?" Ziva asked. She pushed the plate away, done with it.

Chandler nodded. "We need to see who walked in and out of the museum that day."

"Couldn't that be hundreds of people?"

"Probably, yeah."

Ziva looked at her. "Do you think it'll help?"

Ziva's eyes passed to Quinton whose own gaze had risen, as had his eyebrow. "It could," he answered. "We have to start somewhere, right?"

"But what if we don't find anything?" Ziva barely had the stomach to say the words but someone had to. They'd already seen failure once, and she didn't think she could handle it again, not on her first mission, a mission that could mean *everything* on her path to owning something.

Quinton sighed, tucking his white hair into a band. "We'll worry about that if we're smacked by a brick wall, but not before we know if there is one."

The brick wall came.

It took many hours, many video tapes and replays of them, and quite a few food containers filled by the local dessert place and their goods, but they eventually hit the dead-end they were convinced was following them.

Chandler physically threw her papers down and they landed with a *thump*. "What now?"

Ziva could clearly see the frustration lines between Chandler's eyebrows and was sure she had ones to match. Even Quinton's normally smooth face was wrinkled. Ziva nearly suggested a pamper night of face-Masks and nail polish but didn't think it would be appreciated, so stopped herself.

They were all wound up too tightly. The only way they'd come undone would be by resolution or explosion. Ziva hoped for the former but feared the latter.

"Should I make up some tea?" she suggested.

Quinton smiled at her kindly. "That's a lovely idea. I'll help."

They clambered into the little kitchen area and began to work around one another.

He got down the mugs and Ziva prepared to fill them. As she rested against the counter, waiting for the kettle to boil, she peered over. Chandler sat with her legs wide open, laptop between them and at full volume, with stacks of papers in both hands.

Ziva looked back over her shoulder. "Quinton?"

"Mm?" He leant against the furthest counter, slouching, but looked uncomfortable, like he had to fight to stay that way.

"When you've hit a wall before, how did you climb over it?"

"In all my years at Redwing, I've only ever been on four missions. This one is my fifth."

"*Four*? That's it?"

"That's it," he nodded. "I told you about my first."

"What about the others?"

He sighed, untying his hair and letting the white strands fall to his shoulders. "I can only remember one time where we were backed into a corner."

"And?" Ziva pressed.

"We got out of it by looking at it from a different angle."

"But, we've done that?" Ziva scowled.

The kettle clicked off, the water boiled. She moved to it and poured the water into the mugs, and Quinton was ready with the milk seconds later. She reached past him for the stash of snacks she'd brought with her – a huge bag of savoury walnut biscuits. Tipping the biscuits on a plate, she lifted it and her mug. Quinton grabbed the other two and they went back to Chandler.

Ziva put her mug down before sitting. Chandler smiled at her tea as Quinton passed it, sipping cautiously. Ziva went to pick hers up again but was glad she hadn't touched the handle when Quinton loudly exclaimed, "A different angle!"

Chandler lowered her papers and mug, scowling. "What did I miss?"

"I'm not sure," Ziva said, looking to Quinton.

"We need a little cheat-sheet boost," he said, talking as if no one else had spoken.

He pulled his crystal out from under his shirt. Ziva diverted her eyes quickly.

Chandler levelled him with a glare. "You want us to touch your crystal?"

Quinton wiggled his eyebrows. "That sounds rather *delicate.*"

She snorted. "The clear quartz you carry around your neck, not the one you carry between your legs and partially think with."

"I'm sure there was an insult in there somewhere?"

Ziva laughed, hard. When she stopped, she asked, "Why do you want us to touch the crystal?"

"We need a different angle," he repeated. "If we look to the future for help, we might find it."

"That's a long shot," Chandler said sceptically. Ziva had to agree. "You said yourself, futures change, and they come to you like flashes."

"You also don't know how far you'll see," Ziva said.

He nodded. "But it's all we've got."

Chandler picked up a biscuit and shoved the whole thing into her mouth. "I'll do it," she mumbled. "I've touched it before."

Once again Quinton wiggled his eyebrows at her, and she flatly stared. He stopped moving but the grin didn't fade.

However, the tension dropped off as Chandler moved the laptop aside and crawled over to Quinton. Ziva bit her lip. But Chandler picked the crystal off Quinton as if she was bored. After a minute, he took it back and secured it in his palm.

Several breaths later, he spoke. "We find the Mask."

The world fell away.

Ziva's heart lept into her throat. She could smell her tea and the biscuits, but no longer wanted them as her stomach flipped. "We find it?" she whispered.

He nodded firmly. "We do."

"That's great and everything, but how does that help us?" Chandler asked. "You've seen we find it, not *how* we do."

He shot her a stare, calculating and direct. "*You* touch it."

Chandler blinked. "I do *what*?"

"It looked like you were carrying it." Quinton drew out his

notepad from where he'd laid it on the table and opened it to a blank page. Many coloured pens were scattered around and he sifted through them for the perfect one. "The Mask seemed to be in a resting state. Like it wasn't being used."

Relieved, Ziva took a deep breath. "What did it look like?"

"It was black, and on someone's face, it would only attach near the eyes."

He began to draw and Ziva leaned closer to see the image take shape. The Mask in the drawing would indeed only fit around someone's eyes, attaching itself by the nose-bridge. Swirls and spikes of gold – Quinton's switched pens for that detailing – curved off the main bulk of the object. It was intricate and *small,* and not what Ziva had been picturing mentally. She'd been thinking of a full-sized carnival Mask, not something that belonged at a masquerade ball.

Chandler shifted. "I touch that?" Her hands stilled at her sides, almost in an effort to keep them there. Ziva watched the struggle. "Will there be any effects?"

Quinton looked up, his artist's focus sifting away. "I don't know," he admitted. "It's a magical object. One blessed with *freedom*, if the stories are to be believed. There could be any number of protections around it. Self-made or otherwise." His attention moved to Ziva who had leaned so close to him, she could smell his aftershave. "You don't have to touch the crystal, I would never make you, but it might give us more to look at?"

Ziva tried to put on a brave front to match Chandler's real one. "I'll do it."

Quinton gently pressed the crystal into her palm and she wrapped her fingers over it. It wasn't warm or cold, just smooth. She waited for a lightning strike or for her heart to plummet through her body like stone, but nothing happened. The quartz didn't even pulse.

Tapping the back of her hand to say time was up, Quinton withdrew the crystal and held it himself.

She swallowed, her bravado sinking the longer Quinton was silent. "What do you see? Anything?"

He opened his hand and the crystal fell against him, back to his chest. "The family," he answered.

"Not ominous at all," Chandler muttered, loud enough.

He searched for a particular piece of paper from the piles surrounding them all. "The family," he repeated. "The ones we're meant to give the Mask back to. I see that we do."

Worry nibbled at Ziva's stomach. "Does that help us now? We're meant to give it back to them, right?"

"What do we know about them?" he asked back.

Chandler drew the papers closest to her up in front of her face. "The man who made the Mask was a creator, a brilliant inventor. He had two children who each in turn had two children. It says he died nearly twenty years ago. He'd lived a long life. *Really* long." She blinked at the paper and shook her head clear of whatever thought had captured her mind. "The Mask had been long gone before that. He'd given it to a museum where it had gone missing from."

"Then it appeared in a new museum."

Ziva didn't understand. "What does that mean?"

"It means that *someone* had it between those two museum appearances," Quinton said. "Between the maker and the museum, and then the museum we visited here, the Mask was somewhere, with someone else."

"Do you think that person stole it a second time?"

"It's possible," Chandler said, lowering her papers. "It had to be somewhere, right?" Her eyes were wide and bright. Ziva noticed how stunning they looked, how much like golden honey they were, even in low light. "I think we should go back to that original museum, the first one the maker gifted his object too, and follow the Masks journey from there."

"But that was from over twenty years ago," Quinton reminded them.

"Maybe if we follow the original path..." Chandler trailed off. "We're missing time in between."

"We might be likely to find out the journey the Mask took if we take it right back to the start," Ziva finished, catching on at last. "Is it likely the two paths cross? Or someone who worked at the first museum maybe got a job at the one here, and when they saw the Mask went after it again?"

"The lines might run parallel." Quinton began to tidy, closing the laptop with a *clink*. "It might give us some answers and some clues. Anything is helpful. If the same person stole it twice, they might've left some marker, something unique for us to identify them by. And if they've committed other crimes, they might be in a database for us to track down."

Ziva nodded. "We might be able to link them. But wouldn't the Arrestors have already tried those kinds of things?"

Chandler started to also pack up, though she scowled. "We're not the Arrestors. We're Abnormals and have Abnormalities on our side to help."

"We have something they don't," Quinton agreed. He looked so different as he talked now, more serious, less playful. It seemed he could split into two different versions of himself. "There's a Mask out there that could turn anyone into anyone else. You can see why that'd be dangerous and why the family wants it back."

"Shouldn't we be looking at crimes then?" Ziva suggested. She picked up nearby printed news articles. "Like, when each crime was committed during the original period the Mask was missing that could've been done by anyone using the Mask?"

Chandler stopped and looked at her. "That's such a big gap we'd have to look at and so many crimes. Too many variables that we can't narrow down."

"But if you take a Mask that changes your entire being, you'd use it for the biggest types of crimes, right?"

"I supposed you would," Chandler agreed.

"How about this," Quinton said. "We go to the first museum and inspect the theft from there. We find out dates and markers, and *then* look at bigger crimes between then and when the Mask was returned to the new museum? It'll hopefully narrow our search."

"I know I suggested it, but would the same people really want it now?" Ziva asked. She looked down, avoiding the eyes of those around. "Would they even be alive still?"

"Depends how old they were at the time. But I don't see why not. We don't know why it was stolen. And we don't know why it was returned, only that it was."

"Then let's pack up," Chandler said. "We have a new museum to marvel at."

Everyone agreed as the path ahead of them opened. Ziva noticed Chandler seemed to be fighting a smile and wanted to smile along. The bricks in their wall were moving aside to let them through, and this time, Ziva's gut told her they were about to walk in the right direction.

CHAPTER SIXTEEN

QUINTON

28th Day of Autumn 2406

A tap jolted Quinton awake. His eyes burst open, his heart-rate spiking, and he searched for what'd woken him. He shouldn't have worried though. Chandler smiled at him as she walked by to sit in the chair opposite his.

"Maybe you should go to bed if you're that tired?" she suggested as she folded her legs beneath her. He noticed that she was wearing her mushroom cardigan and her brown hair had been tied up in a splayed out bun.

"If the beds were comfy, I would," he replied. However, his lack of sleep had nothing to do with comfort and more about the fact that he just didn't sleep well. That, and the way his brain hadn't shut up all day.

She nodded towards his closed notepad. "Drawn anything good?"

He reached for it and the pen, sliding the latter into his hair. "I wouldn't call myself an accomplished artist."

“I bet you’d claim to be better than some though.”

He smiled, but it faltered slightly when his eyes found the clock in the room. “What are you doing awake? Aren’t *you* tired?”

Chandler kept staring, her expression hardening. “Anything good in there you can share?”

He decided to let his last question drop. He was in no place to judge the dodging of questions when he did the same thing so often; it was just different to be on the other side.

They’d taken the night air-shuttle out of Snowdonne to Moscow. Quinton had connections thanks to his family, so had managed to book their travel tickets easy enough – not that it was that hard these days as tickets could be bought on the same day for travel for anyone. They’d taken a private shuttle to the port, also booked by Quinton, and had boarded with plenty of time to go. Gratefully, the flight had been without issue and they’d landed about ten hours later. Bags had been shoved into another private shuttle and they’d walked right into a new hotel suite.

Night still had its clutches in the air of Moscow, along with the cold. Dawn was a few hours off, but it didn’t feel like the sun would make much difference here.

While the girls had slunk off to bed the second they’d entered the suite, Quinton hadn’t found himself relaxing much, even if he had managed to drop off on the sofa for a few minutes.

“I have one I can share.” He flipped through the pages. As he turned the book round, he waited for the reaction. Because it was the image of *them.*

The entire time he’d been drawing the image, something about it had bugged him. Something wasn’t quite right about it. Although he had all the details, from her emerald and silver ring, to their hands against his chest between them, something was *wrong*. The image was how he’d seen it, but it felt like one line was out of place, or a single hair was flicking the wrong way. Something so unnoticeable he couldn't define *what*.

Chandler touched the page with the tips of her fingers, running them down to her own, smaller hand. She traced over the gleam of her ring, the one Quinton noticed suddenly she still wore on the same finger.

Her fingers then traced to their joined hands and then pulled away entirely. "It's brilliant," she whispered, sharing the words like a secret.

"You can keep it," he offered. She blinked in response. "If you want? I can tear it out and you can frame it?"

"I might just do that." She flashed what appeared to be a real, genuine smile and handed the pad back. "Remind me when we're back at the Mansion?"

Quinton closed the notebook, a tad dazed. He hadn't expected Chandler to agree, but he was learning fast that she was full of surprises. And it took a lot to surprise Quinton these days. Yet, she was managing.

"Even if the memento includes me?" he joked.

She shrugged. "I suppose you'll do."

He laughed. "I'll remind you to stare at my face every night before you sleep."

"For what? Nightmares?"

"Well, that's unnecessary."

She shook her head, smiling. "And you called yourself not an artist. I knew I didn't believe it."

"It's still not my best work." He wanted nothing more than to flip back open the page and discover the wrongness of it so he could correct it, could make it perfect.

"You have reminded me though." She slid the emerald ring from her finger and, without looking at it but staring straight at him instead, plopped it on top of the sketchpad. "I think that's yours."

He didn't take it. "What am I going to do with it?"

"Wear it? Sell it?"

"And what if I gave it back to you?"

She shuffled slightly. "Don't you want your money back?"

"Maybe," he admitted. "But money doesn't matter to me."

"Really? Money matters to everyone."

Quinton shook his head; he'd seen how much money controlled people, like his parents, and there were better things to be concerned by and live for. He pushed the sketchpad, and consequently the ring, back towards her. "Consider it a gift," he said.

"A pretty damn expensive one."

"A glittering second memento?"

She laughed but did pick the ring up and slid it onto her right hands' third finger. "Thank you," she whispered, and looked up at him with eyes mostly hidden by the lack of light. "But why?"

He could've cashed it back in but he knew she suited the ring and the ring suited her. It was hers now. Instead of saying that though, he said, "You never know when you might have to play my *precious* fiancé again."

Her laughter faded slowly. "Your parents seemed surprised you had a fiancé."

"Are we getting into the nitty-gritty dirty details of life now?"

She shrugged. "Just an observation."

"Of my life."

"You don't have to tell me anything," she reassured. "The same as you allow me room to say nothing."

There was a moment's pause, a moment for him to breathe and take in the sincerity of her tone. "It's not that I'm not into the dating thing. "But in my life, the way it worked was to have your parents pick your partner, someone of the same current and financial standing as you. You've heard of the term 'power couple' right? That's the *entire idea* in my world. A marriage of convenience and social status. There isn't much for outside of that."

Chandler scowled and cracked her knuckles, the first time, Quinton noticed, since she'd come into the room. "I thought that kind of thing died out centuries ago."

"Not to the elite it didn't. Marriage and money and name server as power."

"And you came from that life."

"I did, yes."

Slowly, his stomach sank.

Back at Redwing, the staff knew who he was, what he'd been, as did the Grittals and Gretchen. Everyone else, all the other recruits, didn't – he didn't think so anyway. Yet, here he was, exposing his real life to someone he'd just met.

"I hated that life," Quinton clarified into the silence. "I left it behind years ago. Or, most of it, at least. I don't think you can fully leave something if your parents are still part of it." He felt his heart pound in his chest and was grateful no one here had super-hearing as a gift. "I've dated quite a few people since leaving that life though, if you wanted to know."

"It's not my business to know," she said, holding her hands up in surrender.

He shrugged. "It's not like I'm ashamed of it not to share."

"Why would you be? I don't see the point in regret like that when it was something you wanted at the time."

"I'm interested in both men and women, too. While we're sharing." He winked dramatically.

She laughed; tonight she seemed free enough to do so, and Quinton was stunned but liked it every time, especially since he was the cause. "Again, hardly my business." She openly looked at him and must've seen something written in his eyes, because, with a teasing grin, asked, "But *dated*? All of them? Took them out to sweet restaurants or the movies or whatever people do? Really?"

"Alright," it was his turn to laugh, "I dated a few and only had sex with others."

"There's the honesty."

"I'm always honest!" His grin slipped into an easy smile. "I'm not ashamed of that either."

"There's no reason for you to be. Everyone's different and everyone wants something different. You're adults and as long as there's consent... Who cares? It's your business."

Quinton picked up his sketchpad again, resting it in his lap. There were many pictures inside, all completed by his hand. Most told of what he'd seen through his crystal. Some, however, were simply memories. The bad ones never lasted long. They had been torn out and burned or thrown in the trash as time came and went.

He settled back in the chair. "Tell me something."

She raised her eyebrows. "Anything specific?"

"Something about you."

Chandler scoffed. "There's not much to tell."

"Doesn't have to be juicy, just... something."

Nodding, she rolled up her sleeves. The markings inked into her skin came clear. Quinton had caught glimpses but now he could see it all clearly. A snake wound itself around her arm, its head at her wrist, covered by vines and roses as a disguise.

"I've seen you looking at it," she said quietly. "My Uncle had the exact same one. He'd always looked after me and I always thought it was cool. When I was old enough, he came with me and I got mine to match."

Something possessed Quinton. The tips of his fingers slid along the snake's body, winding on the skin as it did. Chandler withdrew her arm when he reached the tail, and Quinton sat back again.

"Do you have any others?" he asked, his voice quiet, even to his own ears.

"No." She rolled down her sleeves. "I always wanted more but just haven't gotten them yet."

"What did your parents think?"

"My mother hates that I wasted money on it."

For the first time since coming in, she closed off. Her hazel eyes left his, falling to the table and then away. Her body shrank in size despite not moving. There had been something hidden in her words to explain the change but Quinton couldn't hear them.

It seemed there was a lot recently he couldn't figure out.

"I'm sorry," he said.

"Is your hair another symbol of rebellion?" she asked, clearing the conversation away from herself.

Quinton touched the ends of the white. "It was. Then it just turned into a 'me' thing and I liked it enough to keep."

She tilted her head. "It suits you. But I don't know you with anything different." She grabbed the bits of her hair that'd fallen out of her bun. "I'm glad to be back to brown. I definitely *don't* suit blonde."

"Maybe I'll go blond next?"

"I don't think you'd look bad."

"Was that a compliment?" He grinned as she rolled her eyes. "Bottle blond it is."

Abruptly, Chandler stood but she didn't look at him. "Now that's settled, I think I can get in a few hours' sleep."

"Big day in the morning."

"You should probably go to bed, too."

"Well, I've never been flirted with so well before," he teased, grinning.

She levelled him with a look. "Your *own* bed," she corrected. "And I don't flirt."

Quinton rose and strolled to stand before her. He stole her hands and dragged her towards him, ensnaring her between him and the wall. "You don't?" he argued. "Need I remind you of how well you danced and pretended you did flirt with me?"

Eyes rolling, she ducked around him – he'd left enough room for her to do so, not really trapping her – but he was sure he'd seen a light blush on her cheeks. The dark made it hard to be sure though.

Without a word, she walked off.

He spun round and called to her just as she reached the doorway. Over her shoulder, she looked at him.

"You look better with brown hair."

She left him alone.

Quinton slumped back down, humming the tune he'd had stuck in his head since the party. He opened his book and flipped to the back where he'd drawn the vague image of the Mask they were searching for.

Intricate lines outlined the shape, swirls and dips showing the grandeur. Quinton had seen they'd find and hand it over. It was just a matter of how and providing that future didn't change.

There was barely a week left – time flew too fast. They'd had one false start already. They couldn't afford another.

But he'd seen the end. He hoped it would happen as it'd been shown to him. An unchanged future.

He glanced up at the doorway and smiled to himself.

Both Ziva and Chandler weren't bad people, in fact he quite enjoyed their company, more so as the days passed. This mission didn't seem too bad, either. Even if they didn't get to the end like he hoped they would, if they ran out of time and another team had to step in, maybe it wouldn't be so bad. And if they did run across that finish line together as he foresaw, even better. As long as they crossed together.

Picking the pen from his hair, he flicked to another page and began to draw.

CHAPTER SEVENTEEN

CHANDLER

28th Day of Autumn 2406

Moscow was cold, even for Chandler. She and Ziva had bought large, puffy coats that hung down to their knees. Being as big as they were, the coats looked like they were consuming them, and it was funny enough that Ziva had asked the vendor of the stall selling them take a picture.

Snow, ten inches deep at least, hid the ground. Trudging through was hard work. Icicles hung off roofs everywhere, dripping from their tips when the sunlight touched them. The market tents were huddled close, some only spaced apart by tiny paths that didn't run in a straight line anywhere.

"I can't believe Quinton didn't want breakfast with us," Ziva said, shaking her head as she picked up their mugs of tea from the stall they were stood at.

"I don't think that he didn't want to," Chandler said as she sipped. The warmth swam across her tongue and down her throat. She was built for the cold, could hardly feel it, but some level of warmth was welcome at times.

"Right," Ziva nodded, "he's still asleep."

"I left him a note to tell him where we'd be."

"Do you think he'll come?"

Chandler peered into the next tent and at the old-fashioned ticking clock hanging behind the seller. "It's been nearly an hour."

"Just a few more minutes? He does have to climb through this outdoor market maze to find us. He could be somewhere nearby already? He has to look for us and *I* don't even know where we are. We can't signal to him." Ziva clutched her cup and shrank into her coat, sighing. "If we don't find him in a few minutes, we'll get some food?"

Chandler made no argument and drank her tea. They'd wasted their first hour just perusing the stalls. As well as the coats, Chandler had managed to find herself a deep brown, thick buttoned, cardigan, and Ziva had picked up a little post-card.

In her old life, Chandler had missed plenty of meals. So waiting now for one wasn't anything new. If anything it felt like the most normal thing compared to what she'd done the past few days.

"Wish I'd gotten one in Snowdonne," Ziva mused, looking at her post-card again.

"I'm sure you'll go back one day. You can get one then," Chandler said. She drank the dregs and them put the cup on the vendor's counter for them to take back and wash.

Pocketing her treasure back inside her coat, Ziva said, "I've never travelled before. It all feels so new." They started walking through the rows of stalls again. "I want to remember it all."

"I haven't either," Chandler confessed.

"I always wanted to."

"Then why didn't you?"

"Whatever I did, my siblings had to do." Ziva sighed loudly. "I think my parents were trying to be fair, giving us all the same opportunities, but it became unfair."

"Nothing was sacred and yours."

Ziva nodded and Chandler dodged another shopper in a wild swerve.

She knew a bit about things becoming unfair. Everything she'd had, so did her mother in time. Nothing had been personal by the end. It all was tainted or held no value because she knew she couldn't keep it. But maybe that'd change now.

"Hey, Ziva?" Chandler asked. She touched the other girl's arm and both of them stopped. Ziva wasn't much taller, but it was enough for the angle of her eyes to look down at her. "Can I ask you something?"

"*You* ask *me* something? You don't seem like the kind of person who needs advice."

Chandler laughed sourly. "I can be."

Ziva blinked at her several times. "When I told you we'd be friends, I meant that. Ask away."

Chandler glanced around. No one watched them, vendors too busy serving the customers who were too busy buying. "Have you thought about what you're going to do?" she whispered.

"What we're going to do?" Ziva questioned.

"When we're done with this."

"You're thinking about that already?" Surprise laced Ziva's voice.

"There's only a week left before we have to make our choice."

"I suppose so." Ziva touched her hand to Chandler's, both their fingers overlapping in coldness despite the fact that Ziva wore gloves. "Is this what you spoke to Quinton about last night?"

Chandler fought the urge to pull back. "You listened in again?" She wasn't entirely upset because nothing that'd been said was overly private.

Guilt ran across the girls' expression. "I heard you get up. When you didn't come back, I figured he must've been awake too and you were talking."

Sighing, Chandler stared up at the glassy, blue sky. "He seems to think I'll stay."

"Will you?"

"Will *you*?"

Ziva bit her bottom lip. "I've thought about it," she admitted. "Back home, whatever I had, someone else had too. I had to share *everything*. Nothing was private or solely one person's. Except when my," she dipped her voice even lower, "*power* came. But that's not something you can give away. Oh, they were jealous. For the first time ever I had something they couldn't have. I think they started to hate me for it." Tears threatened to spill suddenly, rising out of nowhere. "But this job? This opportunity? It could be *mine*. All of it here would be mine."

A cord was plucked on Chandler's heartstrings. In one single moment, she understood Ziva completely.

Chandler had had nothing that was entirely hers eithers, and she'd been stuck looking for a better job, for better chances, for an *escape*. Here, she was being offered it all. They both were. They would have to disconnect from their familiars for the most part – contact was allowed, but not a lot – but Chandler didn't have anyone left she cared about to remember. Not with her uncle gone now.

Before she could respond, Ziva said, "I see you've kept the ring." She used her smile to point at Chandler's right hand, where the emerald glistened in broad daylight.

Chandler removed her hands from her friend to crack her knuckles. "I tried to give it back."

Ziva smirked. "Tried *really hard,* I see."

"Quinton wouldn't take it! He said that it was mine."

"It definitely suits you, you know."

She grabbed the ring, just as she had done plenty of times now, still disbelieving she owned something so beautiful. "He also said that I never knew when I had to play his fiancé or wife again, so I'd need it then."

"Don't tell me you didn't enjoy that! Remember, I saw you two together."

"We only danced and drank a little champagne."

"*Only*," Ziva mocked, smiling.

Chandler snorted. "Next time, you can play the part."

Ziva laughed and it bounced throughout the space. Chandler smiled, though her mind was caught watching the glint of her new ring, and how her hand had looked when pressed between her and Quinton. She had to admit – not that she'd ever say so aloud – that dancing *had* been nice, that dancing *with Quinton* had been nice. Even though she'd been playing a role, she'd never felt so free. In fact, since starting this mission, she'd found herself freer than she had been in *years*.

She shook off the thoughts and looked up. As if summoned by those thoughts, Quinton walked towards her and Ziva. His white hair, which he'd left loose, blended in with the snow. His coat was long but not as bulky as the girls'. His smile was bright and wide.

"I found you," he said upon reaching them. "Thank you for letting me sleep in."

"You seemed like you needed it," Chandler said, not meeting his gaze.

"So, what do I win for traversing this maze all alone and without clues on how to find you beautiful dames?"

"How about breakfast?" Ziva suggested, laughing.

Chandler's stomach rumbled. "Anywhere in mind?"

"I passed a few good-smelling places on the way over," he said. Chandler looked up to see him studying them both, grinning. "Nice coats, ladies. I think I need to get myself one to match. Clearly they're high fashion."

Ziva shook her head, smiling. "*Not* high fashion, but definitely warm."

Quinton looped his arm through Ziva's, who in turn roped in Chandler. They started to walk, moving awkwardly as a three-person line.

While Chandler's talk earlier with Quinton had been open and honest, the question on who he really was had been stuck inside her brain. He came from an elite family, but he was reluctant to talk about that side of him, equally as put off by his past as she was her own it seemed. Quinton had said he'd left that life, so Chandler decided to leave it alone. Who was she to judge anyway?

Yet she couldn't stop thinking about him. Of the way his hair swished on his shoulders. Of how it felt to dance with him. Of the kindness in letting her keep a ring she'd worn only for a few hours as a ploy. Of how he talked to her as if he wasn't *more* because of his status. Of his smile.

She shook her head free of him. She didn't know why she was beginning to be wound so tightly and didn't think she liked it. This was just a mission and they were just playing parts. They *did* seem to work well together and he *did* appear to know what he was doing. If she stayed, maybe they could be genuine friends.

That's what her mind was *really* focused on: whether she'd stay at Redwing or not. Everything else was just attached to that question. That was all. Her thinking of Quinton was only because he was attached to a world she was being offered a place within.

The path between market stall tents narrowed so Chandler slipped her arm back, cracked her knuckles, and walked silently behind the other two.

The Moscow Museum of Arts was livelier than the last. It might've been because they'd gone to visit it in the middle of the day. Hundreds of people were walking the halls and corridors. Children screamed and ran up and down the steps with their friends or family. There even seemed to be a group of business people meandering around, and some other people in hardhats.

"What section are we going to?" Ziva asked, flipping open her pamphlet.

Once they'd paid their admittance fees, they'd shed their coats and stuffed them in a secure rented locker. Ziva's bright cobalt turtle-neck was so dazzling in these cream halls, heads were turned towards them when they passed. It made Chandler's mood lift to see her friend shine.

Quinton leaned over Ziva's shoulder from behind to stare at the floor map in the brochure. "The Abnormal section."

Ziva snapped it shut. "What is it with everyone separating our stuff?"

"Be grateful they even keep any of it."

"But why must it be called out by a separate name? Art is art."

"I think part of it comes down to the fact that some things have our magic inside them?"

"But they're not going to blow up!"

"Well they *could*..."

Chandler stopped listening. She shuffled away and stared up at the piece of artwork she recognised.

The Fall of the Rebel Angels had been an interesting piece to read about in her uncle's dusty old art books, but nothing could've prepared her for the magnitude of seeing the piece up close. Chandler knew the artist – Pieter Bruegel – was from the fifteen-hundreds, but his painting had survived to this day. It was one of a few rare paintings that had survived for so long.

"It's a bit of a mess," Quinton said, coming up to her side.

"I think it's beautiful," she told him.

Ziva joined them. "I think I had to study it once in school?"

Quinton shifted closer and leant over the railing that was meant to separate people from the art to stare at the artist tag closely. "I'm pretty sure Bruegel was an Abnormal."

Chandler let her eyes leave the painting to glare at Quinton. "What?"

"Well, he's featured here, at the start of the Abnormal part of the museum." Quinton pointed to the arch next to them and the sign above it, which indeed indicated they were in the Abnormal art space. "And, if I remember right, he was a man who had wings."

"Wait." Ziva threw her hands up. "I thought Abnormals were new? They came about in recent times? Like one hundred and fifty years new."

"Most of us did," Quinton whispered. "We're in existence thanks to the plenty of plagues and viruses, and it's still fought over which one *actually* changed our DNA. But they had plagues throughout history. It's not too much or far-fetched to think one of them lasted."

"You're saying a virus lived for so long and just got *bigger*?"

Quinton nodded. "There have been depictions of people with different genetics and Abnormal *qualities* through the years. But it was minimal then. One or two people at a time. People called them freaks, though, even then." He gazed up at the painting. "The biggest viral outbreak started, for us, nearly two hundred years ago. Most of us changed since then, but something doesn't come from nothing."

"Maybe you should've gone into science," Chandler said. "You seem to be a fountain of knowledge and theories."

Quinton looked at her from the corner of his eye. "I know many things."

Ziva looped her arm through Chandler's as she cracked her knuckles. "Whatever the theories are on mutations, we have them, and we need to move along. We're wasting time," Chandler decided.

"I think it's interesting," Ziva mumbled.

"Why do you have to ruin our fun?" Quinton pouted. "I'm just trying to teach a little history."

"And as exciting and mind-blowing as it is, that an old virus mutated itself and attacked more of us in recent history, it's not relevant right now."

"Well alright then." Quinton held his hands up in mock surrender.

Chandler sighed. "I'm just saying we don't have time to be discussing this."

"So you'll take a history lesson after?"

Ziva reached out and touched Quinton's arm. "I'll definitely take a history lesson."

"See," Quinton beamed. "*Someone* is interested in me." Chandler rolled her eyes.

"Let's move on," Ziva suggested lightly.

Quinton's smile dropped. "Here we go again."

Droplets in the air shivered as Chandler did. She looked for a physical sign of them but there was nothing. She cracked her knuckles again, eradicating the need to reach out to try and make the water freeze.

They went through into the next room, where the displays were wide and expansive. For a world that hated Abnormals, what was displayed before them wasn't what Chandler had been expecting to see. Yes, they kept the items, but never had she seen so many on full display, so close, and without any more than two guards at each doorway.

"Wow." Chandler realised a moment later she'd said it aloud.

"We're definitely in the right place," Quinton whispered.

Chandler followed where Quinton was pointing towards a large display of pictures and scrolls that would've perfectly accompanied the exact artefact they were after. His drawing of the Mask had been nearly spot on. She squinted from a distance at some of the grainy and smudged pictures capturing a black Mask laced with gold.

"They've kept it all here," Ziva whispered in awe. "But this wasn't the last place the Mask even was."

"Maybe we should find out why they've still got a display."

Chandler simply nodded, not trusting her voice enough to talk. Taking a deep breath first, she strolled towards the display case as if her entire body wasn't trembling.

CHAPTER EIGHTEEN
ZIVA

28th Day of Autumn 2406

"We should've bet on how well that was going to go," Quinton mumbled, rubbing his temples. "Not that I place bets."

"You're the one that brings them up all the time," Ziva countered. "Chandler said you even bet on us."

Quinton shot her a look of mock offense. "I did not!"

Ziva was too tired to argue.

During the private shuttle ride back to the hotel, Chandler had nodded off. Ziva couldn't blame her, and let the girl rest her head on her shoulder. The day had been tiring, mentally and physically so. Ziva couldn't wait to slip under a duvet, a fluffy pillow beneath her head.

As the private shuttle slowed to a stop, Ziva nudged Chandler. The girl woke, rubbing her eyes enough to smudge her thin layer of make-up. Ziva offered a smile of encouragement and apology.

“What’d I miss?” Chandler asked groggily, her voice deeper than normal from sleep.

“Nothing much,” Ziva answered.

At the same time Quinton said, “A ride home.”

Ziva reached for the door. “Shall we go inside?”

Ziva piled out of the private shuttle first, Chandler followed, and then Quinton. They entered the lobby and were greeted by a blazing sign. *ECHNEIR HOTELS*. Ziva stared at it, the name familiar somehow. Before she could ask, she was pulled sideways into the nearby lift.

Back inside their suite, she threw her coat off and almost ran for the shower. The day had taken its toll and she wanted to wipe the grime away. The water was scolding but climbed under it with no hesitation. She lathered her body and let it rinse off on its own, the streams running over her skin like a light massage.

Feeling slightly more refreshed, she climbed out and wrapped a towel around herself. She peered out of the door and, seeing the coast was clear, zipped into the bedroom she shared with Chandler.

Drying off, she changed into her pyjamas. If anyone asked her to go anywhere else today, the answer was a firm “no”.

After combing her hair and laying the towels out to dry, she walked back into the living space. With each movement she could smell the cedarwood scent on her clean skin.

She skipped through to the kitchenette area and began making tea. At this point she knew no one would be surprised to find her there. As much as she disliked making tea for the masses back home, here it felt like a privilege. She supposed that was what happened when you did something you wanted and not because you were asked or forced to under the threat of being “*rude*”.

Just as the kettle flicked off, Chandler appeared. She’d tied her hair up, keeping it back from her pale face and out of her hazel eyes.

"How do you feel?" Ziva asked, pouring the water.

"I've been worse," Chandler said, dropping onto the nearby lounger. Ziva passed her a cup a moment later, which she accepted. "How about you?"

Ziva took her mug and sat down on the opposite chair. "Tired. Only tired."

Ziva preferred this hotel suite over the last. It was modern and marble, brightly coloured and up-to-date. There *was* an over-decorative chandelier in each room, but they kind of suited the overall look. At least the place was warm, quiet, and clean.

Chandler sipped her drink and then peered into her mug, scowling. "What flavour is this?"

"Earl Grey," Ziva said. "It's nothing special."

Silence slipped into the air. However, neither of them were in a hurry to override or replace it. They had no need to.

They'd found the information they'd needed at the museum. The scrolls and papers pinned in the case had given them all they'd needed. Quinton had been right. And bloody skies above he'd been smug about it.

The Mask of Iris had originally been in the museum of Moscow for ten months before it had gone missing. People had searched for it to no avail. Just when the people had stopped looking, finally ready to take down the displays, the Mask had reappeared in the new museum.

After its return, the Moscow museum had left up the display, declaring itself to be the original owner of the artefact. More scrolls and writings had been pinned to the display once the two museums had colluded, promising to work together, though the Snowdonne museum kept physical possession of the actual Mask – no one thought it'd be safe to transport since it's fame had begun to grow.

During the Masks "missing" years, it had fallen into the hands of a gang. The only reason the Mask had reappeared was because the gang had been caught doing something illegal.

Articles on the gang were on display in Moscow too, adding more hype to the Mask.

"Are we thinking the gang has the Mask again?" Ziva whispered as if someone from outside might be listening in.

"I wouldn't think so," Quinton said, strolling into the room. His hair was tussled and a pen was forced into it. The top buttons of his shirt were undone and Ziva spied his crystal against his pink flushed skin. He sat beside her, the seat dipping under his weight slightly. "They're locked up and won't be out for years."

"Where have you been?" Chandler asked.

He waved the phone in his hand, raising an eyebrow. "Personal call."

Ziva got up and came back with Quinton's tea. "What did those articles say the gang were locked up for again?"

"Using the Mask to commit fraud in the business sector."

Ziva nearly choked. She lowered her mug before daring to take another sip in case she actually did choke if she took too big a mouthful. She saw Chandler do the same.

"So..." Ziva drew the word out. "We know where the Mask was. We know who had it. And we know who *hasn't* got it now. What do we do?" There was no immediate answer. "Where do we go now?"

This silence was less comfortable than the one before.

Ziva finished her tea in the time it took for her to hear someone audibly breathe. She went and washed her cup, and stood against the counter after. She hated to voice her questions, but where were they meant to go now? They had the answers they'd gone for, but what could they do with that information? What did it mean to this mission?

This mission was becoming a little more impossible as the minutes ticked by.

She pushed off the counter and dropped back down beside Quinton as the questions rattled around in her mind. Had they wasted time? She could answer that one both ways. They'd gathered information but none of it told them how to move forwards.

Quinton carelessly slid his phone onto the table. "We need food."

"How is food going to help?" Chandler asked. She clutched her cup like it was the most important thing around her.

"Because no one can do anything on an empty stomach."

Nearly an hour later, a plethora of food sat spread around their kitchenette. Collectively they'd decided to get take-out from a local place. Bowls and plates and boxes of stuff now littered the counter. Ziva struggled with what to pick.

Quinton came up to her side and said, "The meat is kosher."

She turned and studied him. She'd always eaten how her family had, mostly because it had been easier to follow what her grandmother had started. "How did you—"

"I noticed your necklace," he cut in, smiling.

Instinctively, Ziva touched the star below her throat. "Oh."

He nodded at the food. "I was assured the meat is kosher. It's safe for you. Pick and eat whatever you want."

Ziva turned back to the containers and piled her plate with meat and vegetables. She shoved some steamed broccoli into her mouth on the way back to her seat. "What about recent crimes?" She remembered saying something similar before they'd arrived in Moscow and it seemed like something she needed to repeat.

Chandler pointed to the laptop. "I've looked," she said. There was a plate in front of her, full of noodles and vegetables, but mostly untouched so far. "There doesn't seem to be anything as big as fraud or other problems in the business sector."

"I still feel like this gang has something to do with the Mask."

Ziva chewed a piece of leak and swallowed it as quickly as she could – she hated them, but it was ingrained in her to eat them anyway. The thought made her pause. Her family weren't here to dictate what she ate anymore. She dug around and moved all the pieces of leak she could find to the edge of her plate.

"I have to agree," Quinton announced from where he'd seated himself on the floor.

Together, Chandler and Ziva said, "You do?" They looked at one another in surprise.

Quinton laughed and twirled his fork around some noodles. "Yes, I do. There's something about them. They're the only known people to have stolen the Mask, kept it for a good length of time, and get caught red-handed with it. Plus, if they had that power before, would they really give it up now?"

"You said they were in prison and wouldn't be out for years," Chandler reminded him.

"I did," he agreed. "But they could still be running an operation from prison."

Ziva chewed some meat. "Like what?"

"Their *original* plan was stealing and selling information from inside businesses, hoping for a cash reward."

"You think they're doing that again?"

"There's no news of that kind of thing happening recently. I've looked." Chandler nodded at the laptop for a second time as she finally lifted her plate, taking a bite and chewing slowly.

"Maybe not yet," Quinton said. "Maybe it's still too soon for them to try again."

"The Mask was taken off them when they were captured and has been stolen since their incarceration."

He shrugged. Ziva had to agree with Chandler on this. "That's a long period of time to have passed," she said. "Why would they wait so long?"

"Maybe they're being more cautious this time around?" Quinton suggested. "Making their covers more secure, hiding themselves further inside, wherever they are."

"But the gang is *in prison*," Chandler reiterated, scowling.

"They might have family that picked up on the work?"

Chandler's scowl deepened. "That's still a lot of ifs and buts and potentials and time." She glanced at the laptop and away again. "*If* a family member was hired in a company, it's not going to be known. They might've even changed their name. Who knows what company hired them? None of it's going to be public information."

Quinton sat up straighter; Ziva could almost feel the excitement radiate off him as he grinned. "We're not public people anymore."

"Are you going to call Praxis and ask him?" Ziva questioned. It was the only thing she could think of at this point.

"If they were that well off as a gang, they would've covered their dirt long ago. Playing the long game gives them time. There's always been ways of hiding things. And if they're clever enough to steal the Mask a second time, then I have no doubt they could change their name or lie about who they are to gain access and settle in before pulling the next con."

"Are we *sure* it'll be business sector information theft again? Are we even sure it's *them*?"

"No. But I'm hooked onto the idea now, and an information con pays a high price. Plus for how well they'd played off last time before they were caught on a stupid accident... They had *years* with the Mask. Who knew what exactly they pulled off and what information they sold in those years? Not to mention they'd had a Mask that could transform their faces in their grasp, and yet they got trapped and went down without a fight, and just gave that power up?" Quinton shook his head.

Ziva picked at her plate, pushing food around. She didn't know much about this life of spies and information and societies and how it worked. She doubted any amount of time here would help her to understand. But she was getting a general, basic idea. And it was confusing her even more.

In the market, Chandler had asked her whether she'd thought about staying or going once this mission was complete. She had. She just didn't honestly know what her answer would be. She didn't think even a touch of Quinton's crystal would tell her clearly. It was like she was being pulled in two different directions, her head and heart on two different sides at the same time.

"Then what's the plan?" Ziva put her plate down. "If we think the gangs involved somehow, but they're locked up, what do we do? Someone has to have the Mask. It has to be somewhere."

Ziva saw Quinton grimace. "I just realised. We have someone we can visit who'd know."

"We do?" she asked.

"Because the gang nearly brought *them* down last time by trying to sell their secrets," Quinton said. "They did some digging," he made air-quotes, "to find out exactly who had been involved before even the police had the full picture. We could count people in as suspects or scratch them out with their records."

Ziva pulled a face. "I do not like how this sounds."

Quinton's face morphed sourly. "Neither do I. But I think this might be our only option."

Chandler cracked her knuckles. "What do we do? Who have we got to speak with?"

Ziva shuddered as Quinton's mouth quirked into a wolfish grin. "I'm *so* glad you asked."

CHAPTER NINETEEN

CHANDLER

29th Day of Autumn 2406

How do I look?” Chandler cracked her knuckles and each one made a satisfying *pop*.

Ziva gave her a double thumbs up. “Like you’re ready for a night of fun.”

Chandler rolled her eyes but didn’t fight back the smile, and looked down at herself one last time.

Everything was new. Her black skirt was tight but stretchy, clinging just above her knees. The shirt had maybe a slightly daring neckline considering the circumstances of needing to wear it. Chunky, five inch heeled black boots were sturdy on her feet.

“Remember, you’re only going for information on the gang,” Ziva whispered in the confines of the small hallway. “They know what happened, and it’ll help us.”

Chandler nodded. “It’s just a mission.”

Ziva smiled sweetly. “It’s just a mission,” she agreed, tucking a strand of Chandler’s refreshed blonde hair behind her ear.

"You did *amazingly* last time, and you'll do the same again now."

"The *second* I get a chance to sneak out a window, I'm jumping."

Ziva laughed and spun Chandler round, pushing her towards the door. Chandler sighed and walked out of their hotel suite, holding her head high and hoping the confidence she wanted to embody would flow through her. The lift played tinny music on its way down and she was glad to leave it, swapping it for the outdoor concrete steps that trailed down to the awaiting private shuttle. Quinton, gentlemanly as ever, was waiting by the side and had even opened the door for her without climbing in first. She brushed by and sat, scooting over so he could follow.

The private shuttle took off immediately.

"You look good."

Quinton faced Chandler, his knees pointed towards her. Tonight he wore another suit, though this was more relaxed; a white shirt and a navy waistcoat with navy trousers to match. His white hair was loose around his shoulders, brushing the collar of his coat, though Chandler spied the band he used to tie it back on his wrist.

He didn't look bad himself.

She didn't tell him that, she just smiled, but it seemed like a reply in itself. "Are you sure you want to do this?" he asked quietly. A heavy screen blocked them from the driver, but still they were careful.

Luckily for them, Quinton's parents had a residency in Moscow and were currently there on holiday – they were actually doing a three month tour of this side of the world, starting in Snowdonne and ending in South China in a few weeks' time. Quinton had set up a meeting with his parents as soon as they'd decided what they needed to do to move forwards in their case. They'd have the files they desperately needed, illegally acquired or not.

"Like I told Ziva, I hope your parents leave a door or window unlocked so I can escape," she said.

Quinton grinned. "Trust me when I say I'll race you out."

She smiled again, wider this time, and he seemed delighted at the sight, his own smile growing as his eyebrows shot up. Quickly, her smile faltered.

He reached out for her hand and she snatched it back. He laughed. "No," he said. "Give me your hand."

Reluctantly, she did.

He touched her fingers gently and she suddenly realised what he'd been trying to do. The emerald ring was still on her right hand, and it needed to be back on her left. Carefully, Quinton wiggled it down her finger and picked up her other hand, once again placing the ring on her marriage finger.

"Much better," he commented. His gaze met hers and she could see the storminess despite the darkness of the shuttle.

"I'm getting used to wearing it... on *either* hand."

"I hope this is the last time you'll *need* to, but it will still be yours after. Then you may do with it as you please."

Slowly, Chandler drew her hand back. He paused for a moment before lowering his own hand to his lap. Chandler tried not to look at him, and for some reason zoned in on the bones of his fingers, the redness of his knuckles, the way he tensed the muscles of his hand before resting it.

She glanced back up immediately, heat warming her through. He seemed not to have noticed, peering out the window beside them.

"I never asked you before. Is emerald really your favourite colour?" he asked, drawing his eyes back to her.

"For as long as I can remember," she said.

"I don't think I've ever had a favourite."

"No?"

"I just know I don't like the boring colours."

She went to say that of course he didn't when the private shuttle stopped. Quinton shuffled and opened the door first. Chandler held onto her skirt to make sure it didn't rip or get caught, and hauled herself out too.

Quinton paid the driver and they sped down the street, disappearing back into the city.

He leaned closer to whisper into her ear. "Whatever my parents say to you, unless it's mission related, ignore them." He backed off.

Chandler glanced up at him. "I'm not going to think all their thoughts reflect yours, if that's what you're worried about."

"I hope not."

Without saying anything, Chandler took his hand and they made their way up to the house.

White brick towered up four stories. Golden window frames sat on every level, the lower two stories had plant window-boxes hanging from them. The lush, green front-lawn led right up to the heavy black door with a golden knocker.

Quinton pulled her hand, jolting her slightly and forcing her to stop. "Before we go in, there's something else I want to ask."

She frowned. "Okay?"

"I want to ask your boundaries."

"My boundaries?"

Under the little light of the front door, Quinton's smile seemed soft and almost nervous. "My parents are going to expect us to act like a couple. I'm not planning on sweeping you off your feet and throwing you onto the floor to fuck—"

"As long as you *don't* do that," she cut in quickly, holding back a laugh that was bubbling up inside her chest. "Or pull down my skirt or something, anything else is alright, I promise."

She heard the words leave her mouth and couldn't believe them. But they did. And she couldn't take them back. Plus, Quinton was right. His parents would expect them to act like a couple, even if they weren't really. A peck here and there meant nothing. It was an act, a deceit, to extract information to complete a world-saving mission.

Quinton knocked on the door and Chandler smiled to herself. His asking what she was alright with was sweet, whether they were undercover or not.

The door pulled inwards to reveal Quinton's mother. They shared the same stormy eyes, Chandler realised, and the smile that graced her mouth with his too. She hadn't noticed at the party the other night, but now she could. Tonight, the woman wore a long golden dress fit for an actress at a movie premier, with sweeping bat-sleeves and gemstones stitched throughout.

"Come in!" she said, gesturing to the house with her arms aside. Quinton led the way in and Chandler followed. "What can I get you to drink?"

"Just some wine, mother, please," Quinton answered first.

His mother danced off just as his father came down the stairs. Now *he,* Chandler could be afraid of. With his broad shoulders and hulking height, he had a way about him that demanded attention and he knew it. His suit, oddly, was navy too and Chandler had to restrain herself from jokingly commenting that one of the men needed to change as they'd both turned up in the same thing. If she *did* comment, she could imagine it would be Quinton senior that demanded his son be the one to redress.

"Quinton," Quinton Senior said, nodding once. "Josephine."

Quinton's father, who Quinton had said was the seventh of that name, took her hand and kissed her knuckles. She pushed down the urge to shiver.

He dropped her hand, smiling tightly. "It's nice to see you all dressed up, my boy," he said directly to Quinton. "For the second time in a couple of days, no less! It makes a change to see you outside of jeans." He ran his eyes up and down his son. "Your hair needs work, however."

"I like his hair like that," Chandler blurted. She could feel Quinton's stare turn to her as his father's did, but she focused on his father. "It's one of the first things I noticed about him."

"It's delightful," his mother agreed as she re-entered the hallway with glasses. Chandler took hers and sipped, finding it sweet like summer berries. "Maybe a little trim to tidy the ends, but all the kids are wearing it like that these days."

"My son is not a *kid*!" Quinton Senior's face went a little ruby at the edge. "He is a *man*."

"So I can do whatever I like with myself," Quinton said. Chandler defensively moved closer to him until their sides touched. "And if I like it, and my fiancé does too, I see no reason to change."

His mother waved her hands, the sleeves of her dress flailing. "We didn't invite you here to argue about looks or to have you stand in the hallway. How about we settle down to eat? The food is prepared." She walked off, her heels clacking against the hardwood floor.

Chandler felt the brush of air against her cheek and looked out the corner of her eye to see Quinton's face so close to hers. "I hope you really *do* like my hair," he whispered.

"It was one of the first things I saw of you," she murmured back. "It was just red."

He kissed her cheek, barely a graze of his lips, but she had to fight the heat threatening to rise. She managed to smile up at him. Technically, she hadn't answered him, but she hadn't denied it either.

It was clear the action had been to appease Quinton's father who still lingered in the room, though well out of earshot as he turned and marched out of the room behind his wife.

Quinton's grin remained. Chandler rolled her eyes but took his hand again, and nudged him with her elbow to lead on.

The plates were cleared in a flash.

For the entire span of dinner, Chandler had tried to keep track of conversation. She only answered or spoke when something had been directed at her. Otherwise, she'd looked around like the humble guest she was.

The whole time, Quinton had either held her hand or had his arm draped behind her. His parents kept exchanging looks as if they weren't best pleased by it. But Chandler actually felt a sense of comfort from the gesture, like he was silently telling her that he was there and she wasn't in this alone.

Eventually Quinton Senior led them through to the second living room, not that it looked like lived in. Everything was white. The walls, the sofas, the rug, fireplace, and the shelves and cabinets, all a combination of *white*. It looked clinical; too clean, too *nothing*.

Chandler pressed herself against Quinton as they sat, probably closer than she should have. But when she tried to move to give them both a bit of breathing space, he slipped an arm around her. She fell against him, their hips and legs firmly touching. She scowled up at him, and he grinned, squeezing his hand at her waist where it rested.

His mother clapped her hands together and sat. "I hope the meal was delightful for you both."

Chandler nodded. "It was lovely, thank you."

"Is there anything I can get either of you?" she asked.

"I'm fine, mum," Quinton said, smiling. Chandler noticed how much softer he was with his mother compared to his father. The woman was kind and thoughtful. Chandler liked her.

"Josephine?" his mother asked. "Anything?"

"A glass of water would be lovely please, if it's not too much trouble?" Chandler asked. The urge to crack her knuckles needed to be replaced and holding something would do that.

"I'll have a nice scotch, love," Quinton's father called as his wife went. He settled back in his chair, unbuttoning his jacket and crossing one leg over the other. "So, when do you plan to be married?"

Suddenly Chandler was grateful she didn't have the water. If it had been between her hands, it would've frozen over. Quinton either saw her surprise or sensed it, or even knew what she'd been thinking, because he answered.

"We were thinking next year, early summer," he said casually, as if they were discussing the weather. "Maybe an outdoors lake resort or something?" He smiled at Chandler, and she saw the question in his eyes – was she alright? She gave him a subtle nod.

"Did I hear the magic words '*summer wedding*'?" His mother reappeared, balancing three glasses in two hands. She passed Chandler her water, which she took cautiously – she'd calmed herself enough that it didn't freeze – and then sat and passed her husband his drink while sipping hers. "We were married in winter. There was snow all over the ground and it began to fall as we said our vows."

Chandler gripped her glass tighter, her mind slipping to thoughts of her own parents. Had they ever been married? She didn't know. She didn't know anything about her dad beside his name and the fact he wasn't alive anymore – she didn't even know how he died.

"There's some photographs of it somewhere," Quinton's mother said. "I have snow caught in my veil in quite a few."

"I'm sure it was beautiful," Chandler managed to say.

"It was," the woman mused, smiling like she was indeed remembering it fondly. "Not many people marry in winter, and definitely not outside. But we wanted something special."

"We did," Quinton's father said, sounding as bland as the room looked.

His wife turned to Chandler and Quinton, looking them both over. "Will you need money for your occasion? We can pay for the expenses. Quinton is our son, after all. Though, I'm sure your mother will want to buy your dress, won't she, Josephine?"

Chandler's grip on her drink grew deadly and then Quinton's hand came down over-top of hers, holding and hiding.

Once again, he was the one to answered, and again Chandler let him. She was too busy laughing menacingly in her head at the thought of her mother buying anything, let alone paying from her own purse and for her daughter.

"We wouldn't put want to put you out, mother," Quinton said.

"Nonsense! You are my *son*. My only child. I want to spoil you and this will be how I will do it."

"Mother—"

"There's no point trying to stop her," Quinton's father cut in. "You know once she has her mind set on something, she'll shoot towards it like a rocket." Chandler watched a brief moment of softness lay over the man's face, but it vanished again.

Before Quinton could respond, a quiet ringing echoed from somewhere else in the house. His mother got up and left the room to answer. Silence was left in her wake.

Several moments later, Quinton's father's personal phone began to ring from where he'd stashed it inside his trouser pocket. Without a word, he went to take the call somewhere else. Neither Quinton nor Chandler moved.

Quinton broke the silence. "They'll be back in a minute," he whispered. His brow was furrowed when he faced her. "What happened there? Are you alright?"

"Your concern over my welfare is sweet," she said.

"Not planning on running then?"

"I never said that."

"Tell me if you're uncomfortable. We'll leave."

She shook her head stubbornly, determined to see this through. "I'm fine."

"I mean it," he said. "If you want out, I'll break down the door."

Chandler let out a laugh. "I trust you," she whispered, and truly meant it.

Slowly, he dragged his eyes over her, roaming her from bottom to the top. She shook her head but leaned closer, enough so that she could press a kiss to his cheek.

He blinked for a couple of seconds as Chandler's heart thudded deafeningly. Then his grin turned wolfish and as his gaze drifted back into focus on her face, he seemed to stare at her with a new light. She wanted to say something, *anything*, but his parents returned together at that exact moment.

Just as she looked away, he pecked the side of her face. This time, it was a blanket of safety that fell upon her. A friendly gesture, like he was telling her he trusted her back.

"You two," his mother cooed, clutching her heart. "If I didn't know you were to be married, I would be screaming at you to do it!"

Apparently, their act was working.

Chandler laughed and looked at Quinton, finding him wearing a delighted expression. Their eyes met in a way that shared a common secret only known by the two of them.

He didn't seem bad. Maybe they really *could* get along. They were already working together, and succeeding. As much as it pained to think about, made her insides squirm uncomfortably with nerves, Ziva was already her friend. Why couldn't Quinton be too? She'd thought so before, while they'd been in the market in Moscow. Now that voice in her mind sounded stronger, like it was being louder to try and get to her listen to it. It could work...

Especially if she stayed.

That thought, too, in its own way, was growing bolder.

"I forgot to tell you," his father started, sitting down again. His drink was fuller than before and there was now a smell of smoke on him. Quinton had said before arriving that his father liked an old cigar at dinner, he must have just smoked one.

"Remember all those years ago, when that gang tried to take out the business world as we know it?"

Chandler's left hand reached for Quinton. Unfortunately, because of her shock due to the change of conversation, she'd had no directional control, and Quinton let out a little whimper as her hand latched onto a top part of his thigh. She thought about removing her hand but thought that might somehow be suspicious – like giving away that they were at a point in conversation they desperately needed and had gotten there not by requesting it themselves. So she left her hand but softened her grip.

Quinton gulped beside her. "I remember," he said tightly.

"Well," his father crossed his legs, looking smug, "last week the stocks rumbled briefly and several companies were way ahead on buying or selling just moments beforehand. It looked like that gang were up to their old tricks dealing with insider information."

"They're locked up, aren't they?" Quinton asked.

Chandler couldn't speak. Her heart was bouncing between her throat and her stomach, and her cheeks heated. She told herself the warmth was from the conversation, at how they hadn't been the ones to bring it up, and not at how Quinton had moved his leg so her hand had slid further to the inside of his thigh.

"They are," his father confirmed. "I hired a private investigator to find and follow them when several of us were suspicious last time something underhand was happening. We immediately handed all the evidence to the police once we'd found some, of course." His face only grew smugger. Chandler stiffly removed her hand from Quinton before she hurt him by digging her nails in or let the idea of turning the water in the air around him into ice take root. "But, due to the incident last week, it looks like my *private detective* didn't get them all."

"What makes you say that?" Chandler squeaked out.

"The plan and near execution seemed to be the same."

“So...” Quinton dragged the word out. “What does that mean? What plan? What execution?”

“It appears there may be a bastard still out there.”

“You said that, dear,” Quinton’s mother said lightly.

“Someone tried to hack inside *our* companies’ systems.”

Chandler looked to Quinton, and he stared back.

So freely had his father given up the information, and so freely had they seemingly found what they’d come here for.

CHAPTER TWENTY
QUINTON

29th Day of Autumn 2406

The tension in Quinton's shoulders spread and tightened at his father's words. "How can you be sure?"

"There was a blip."

"A blip? In the system?"

"Something like that, yes," his father nodded.

"And you're sure?"

"I can't be," he said. "Not yet."

"What does that mean?"

"I have someone looking into it."

Quinton sighed, allowing himself to deflate slightly. "Of course you do."

"Do you disapprove, son?" His father sipped from his glass. "This will be your business soon."

"And if I don't want it?" Because Quinton didn't.

"What else are you doing? Still partying and travelling? What is it the kids used to call it? A "gap year". Is that what you're doing? Only you've spread yours out for quite a few years now, haven't you? Left school early and vanished from our house, with our money, living and messing around elsewhere."

Chandler's body shifted beside him and he reached for her hands. He wound their fingers together and she laid her other hand over-top, like she was securing him, grounding him, as if she was saying she would put her whole body in front of his if it came to it. He was glad she was beside him. But he was also sorry he'd subjected her to this.

The phone from before rang once more and again Quinton's mother disappeared to answer it. His father took a long drink and Quinton wished he had the Abnormality to make it the glass explode. He had to cough to hide the rising smile he felt coming onto his lips at the idea. When he was sure it hadn't presented, he spoke.

"I'm trying to live a little," Quinton argued. "That's all."

"Live a little," his father mocked, scoffing. "You can live and work at the same time. It's time you stood on your own two feet and grew into them a bit. Even if you have a job now, which I'm assuming you do since you haven't taken our money for quite some time, you can just leave it. Our business is more important. *Everything* we do is more important. Your new wife can come along, of course. You can both find better value here. Better skills *and* better money."

How could Quinton tell his father that his money was his own, that he loved his job and didn't want to *just leave it*? How could he say he had friends and people he considered better family around him? But none of those things existed to anyone except those who were in it. He couldn't say a damn word. So to anyone else, nothing was real. To his father, there was nothing upon nothing upon nothing.

"And what were *you* doing at his age?" Chandler challenged, a dangerous glint in her eye. "Did you not party and take time to discover yourself?"

"No. I grew up."

"I'm sure." Chandler snorted. "How boring."

Quinton hid his smile by leaning towards her, pressing his lips close to her ear. He saw goosebumps rise along her neck and he could smell the perfume she'd spritz over her skin – sweet, definitely unlike her. "Be careful," he whispered, and pulled back.

"Life isn't about being boring or fun," Quinton's father continued, now slightly redder in the face. "It's about duty, power, and responsibility." He pointed his glare at his son, though Quinton had stopped shrinking under it years ago. "This business of stocks and shares *will* be yours one day. This business of money, of *growing* money, will be yours. Whether you like it or not, you will grow up. And soon. You will have to learn to be in charge and be an adult. I would suggest you start *now*!"

Quinton had never really wished for siblings, but it was times like this he did. Maybe then the business would go to one of them instead. The empire would be handled elsewhere. Because Quinton didn't want it. He'd left it all behind once before because it had been so unfulfilling and stifling. His new life was much better; it gave him everything he'd longed for – the freedom being the best of it all.

It wasn't that he wasn't grown up or an adult. It was that he had a whole other life he actually wanted.

But, sadly, his father was right. One day the business *would* pass down, whether Quinton liked it or not.

He sucked in a breath when his mother returned, cutting off his chance to reply. She passed around slices of a plum meringue. Quinton shoved in spoonful after spoonful to keep his mouth and hands occupied. Out the corner of his eye he watched Chandler do the same.

"I remember you saying that you knew my son had an Abnormality," Quinton's father said, changing the subject. He put his bowl down on the cabinet top beside him.

Quinton swallowed harshly, the meringue scraping down his throat. "I told her, yes."

His father fixed Chandler in his sights. "What did you think?"

She shrugged. "It doesn't bother me," she answered. "His gift sounds interesting."

"*Gift*?" he mocked. "Do *you* have one?"

"No," she lied easily. This time it was like Quinton swallowed sand.

"Has he tested his on you?"

She nodded and bit down on another forkful. "Twice."

"Twice," his father repeated. "He's the only boy in our neighbourhood who grew an Abnormality. No one else in the *family* has one. I had him tested, years back, to determine the strength and the problems his changes may cause."

Quinton found himself speechless. He shivered at the memory of those tests. He'd been wired to machines and tubes. For days his dad had left him at the medical centre until it was decided he had a *mild* Abnormality, one that couldn't be harmful, only potentially truthful.

Afterwards, if anything, his father had chosen to dismiss him forever. Just because he was in some way slightly different. No person with Abnormality could be his son. It was as if Quinton had been gifted the power of a bomb instead of seeing into the future.

Until it had become helpful in predicting the fortunes of shares and stocks.

Quinton's mother discarded the bowls once they were finished. His father told them that they wouldn't be taking a private shuttle back to wherever it was they were staying, nor would he have someone who irresponsibly drank to drive themselves. It didn't matter that they'd only had one glass of anything. Quinton was supposedly a "party animal" to his father, so drank too much whenever, whether it was a sip or a chug.

There was a minute of back and forth before it was eventually settled that he and Chandler would stay the night, and his mother would drop them back off where they needed to be in the morning.

Showing them to their room – just a spare one that was kept for guests – his mother apologised quietly for the fact that they'd have to carry out wearing the clothes they were in now in the morning. Quinton kissed his mother's head, promising it wasn't a problem, and she closed the door for the night with a sweet smile.

He turned in time to see Chandler throw herself onto the double bed and nearly bounce off. When the bed stopped wobbling, she tucked her arms behind her head and looked up at the ceiling, kicking off her shoes.

"I wonder what Ziva's doing," she mused softly. Quinton didn't know how thin the walls were and was glad Chandler was also being cautious.

"Probably having a better evening than we are." He strolled over to the bed and plopped down beside Chandler.

"I wouldn't say I'm having a completely *undelightful* evening."

"Is that even a word?"

"It is now."

He laughed, tilting his head to glance at her. "So, if you're not having a completely *undelightful* time..."

Chandler shrugged. "Your mother's nice."

"Is that all that's saving it?"

"You're not *all* bad."

"I'll take it. You're not all bad either. Keeping your company is rather interesting." He raised a single eyebrow, grinning. "The way you grabbed my leg was interesting too."

Quinton watched the tiniest hint of pink enter her cheeks. "That was an accident," she told him.

"Do I dare ask what you *were* aiming for?" he teased.

Her glare was magnificent. "*Your hand!*"

"Aw, did someone want to hold my hand?" Quinton sat up and stole Chandler's hand, tugging it and forcing her to sit up with him.

As silence filled the air, he realised how close they were. Here, where there was no need to keep up pretences and could have all the distance they wanted, here where they could be themselves and relax.

Quinton smiled and Chandler smiled back.

"Thank you," he said softly.

She frowned. "What for?"

"Trying your luck with my father. I've not seen anyone try and stand up to him in years."

A small laugh left her lips. "I know what it's like to have shitty parents that demand respect but never return the favour."

"I'm sorry about that."

Again, she shrugged. "There's no changing them now, is there."

He let go of her hand and reached out to guide a stray piece of blonde hair from her face. He tucked it behind her ear and trailed his finger down the side of her face, then fell away after.

The room around them seemed to be pushing them closer despite nothing moving. Quinton could almost hear the walls grinding as they shrank towards the centre of the room.

In one movement, Chandler threw her leg over his, and suddenly she rested in his lap. He immediately grabbed her waist. She drew closer, straightening her back and putting her face a breath from his. He was sure her eyes darted to his lips but couldn't be certain as his *definitely* did. He blamed the current circumstances of the mission, of them having to play parts together.

"You're in my way," she whispered, and rolled over the other side.

He laughed when she pulled him from the bed. "What are we doing then? Am I pressing you up against something next or are you folding into me?"

"Would you like that?"

"I'm not confirming or denying anything right now."

Chandler laughed and he grinned. "You said we could run if I asked."

The flirtatious notions faded. "I did."

The grin she manifested grew so big it brightened her entire face. He'd never seen her so alive and his heart thumped. She pulled her shoes back on and went to the window, lifting the latch.

"Then let's run."

Quinton climbed up beside her, and both of them stuck their legs outside.

They looked at one another with a single simultaneous nod, and jumped.

CHAPTER TWENTY-ONE
ZIVA

29th Day of Autumn 2406

Ziva sighed silently. "Mum, I'm fine."

"Where are you? I want you to come home right now!"

She rolled her eyes to the ceiling. If her mother had been there to see it, there would've been consequences. "I can't come home," she said, more than a little exasperated. "I'm in the middle of a job."

"What job?" her mother demanded. "I didn't know you had a job!"

"You didn't know several things, mum. You never realised I didn't like leeks and kept serving them to me just because everyone else enjoyed them."

"*Excuse me?*" her mother's voice was shrill. "Repeat yourself, Ziva Barken."

Safely away from her mother and her fury, Ziva continued. "No," she argued. "You heard perfectly well the first time."

Her mother began to yell but Ziva wasn't willing to be spoken over anymore. "You never let me be my own person, mum! You never even *tried* to let me. Everything was yours or dads, and then that was passed on, too. Nothing was *mine*. My own life wasn't mine! I don't know what I want or who I even am because of you."

"I cannot *believe* I'm hearing this level of blatant disrespect right now! Come home, or—"

Ziva cut her mother off by pressing the "END CALL" button and threw her phone onto the sofa. It bounced off but she didn't try and catch it.

Her hands shook terribly. She touched them to her face, sliding them down to her neck, and crossed her arms to hold her shoulders. A breath made her wobble.

How could her own mother treat her wishes as disrespect? She had to grow up at some point. Just because she wasn't doing it in the exact way her parents had dreamt up for her didn't mean she hated them. It meant she was growing. Evolving. She was an adult now, a woman of twenty-one. Her parents couldn't control her any longer. The space she had in life was hers now to work within. What she wanted, she could have.

If only she could figure out what she wanted.

The walls stopped spinning after a moment, the green fern pattern in them settling. Breath was easier to take in too. The anxiety of disobeying her parents, her mother, and standing up for herself for the first time so boldly slowly ebbed away.

She'd only phoned her mother to let her know she was fine and that her new job seemed to be going well. When her mother had asked what job, admittedly she'd blundered. She'd remembered Praxis saying something about their parents knowing they had to move away for their work, but they couldn't be told what it was they were doing.

Ziva was torn.

For years, her whole life had been presented to her. Her parents had encouraged her to train as an office worker – the company and what type of office work was to be her choice – to eventually rise through the ranks. There'd even been discussions about marriage and children.

But now a new world had opened up before her. She could see the dreamy sand stretching to the cerulean water she wished to run to. On that sea, she could be herself; run her own life, choose what she wanted, which she was damn sure didn't include a marriage or an office. Maybe another job and *maybe* a person in her life of some sort, but it would be *her choice.*

She moved through the third hotel room in so many days and ended up in the kitchen. They were all so expensive looking and she felt so out of place among the separate rooms and high-end tailored furniture that had been placed around vases and glass and plants in corners of the room.

While tea would remain the beverage of her heart, she needed something cold. Drawing herself a cup of water, she heard the door open. She peered through the hall.

Chandler and Quinton trundled through the door, looking slightly rumpled, like they'd been out in the brisk air. Quinton shed his jacket and slung it over the back of the nearby chair. Chandler went off to her room, returning moments later in pyjama bottoms and a thick jumper.

Ziva propped herself on the arm of a chair in the living space. "Did everything go alright? You managed to get away alright?"

"We jumped out of a window," he declared, sounding so unbothered.

Ziva's mouth gaped open and a drip of water dribbled out. She quickly dabbed it on the back of her sleeve. "You did *what*? Are there any injuries? What about blood? Do you need medical assistance?"

A hand pressed into Ziva's shoulder. She glanced behind her

at Chandler, who looked rather uncomfortable, as if passing on comfort didn't come naturally. "We're fine," Chandler promised. "There's no blood and we don't need to be checked for injuries."

"Are you sure?"

"I'm very sure. Though Mr Tough over there," Chandler nodded in Quinton's direction, "got a splinter fence-hopping."

"First you dive out of a window and then you climb fences?" Ziva couldn't believe her ears.

Quinton grinned not so innocently. "There was no window diving," he said. "And we had to escape from the back of my parents' estate somehow."

"Are either of you going to explain what happened that you needed to escape from?" Ziva pressed, putting her glass down.

Chandler removed her hand from Ziva's shoulder and sank into the seat Ziva was perched on the arm of. "Sorry," she said. "I asked to leave, so we did. They wanted us to stay the night and I didn't want that."

"And what happened before that?"

"We got what we needed," Quinton answered.

Ziva looked at him lighter. "You did?"

He nodded, pushing his white hair back. "My father provided the fact, rather willingly, that while he'd had the gang that had tried to take his company's, among others, private information taken down, it seems there may have been one member that escaped. There was a recent attack was reminiscent of the older ones."

"So we're thinking someone got away from the original prison sentence and he's the one that had the Mask?" Ziva asked.

"It's getting more likely the more I think about it, yeah. If they're continuing to take on the business world, trying to infiltrate stocks and shares and secrets, then why wouldn't he take back the Mask to use again? It granted him access before..."

"I still can't see why he'd commit the same crimes," Chandler said. "This is a man who escaped the original capture of his entire group and then restole the Mask that let him cover himself as someone else. Just for him to go back to the original plans that *all* others in the group were taken down for the first time."

"I'm guessing it took the entire group to take the Mask the first time?" Ziva asked.

"We're assuming so," Quinton nodded.

"Yet this person had no one else to help," Chandler said. "This one person who evaded being arrested managed to get it back themselves? That doesn't seem possible."

No one spoke. It was all laid out in the silence. If this person could steal the Mask on their own, what else were they capable of? And why did they need the Mask this second time?

"Do we think them attacking the business world is the end goal?" Ziva asked after a few minutes.

"Does it matter?" Chandler asked. She cracked her knuckles and it sounded like faraway lightning. "We're not having them captured for crimes. We're just having them captured for the *Mask*. *That* is our priority. Our mission is to find the Mask and return it."

"But this person may be committing more crimes with it!"

"They might be," Chandler agreed. "But that'll stop once we have the Mask. All we need is who they are, their location, and the ability and plan to take back the Mask."

Quinton looked between them both and Ziva noticed how his eyes skipped over Chandler quicker than her. "She's right," he said calmly. "Our task is to find and retrieve the Mask. Anything else we stop is a bonus. But, the *why* the Mask is being used is still a worrying thought."

"Yeah," Ziva and Chandler said at the same time.

He sighed and stood. "Well, ladies. I'm sure we will have another weird day ahead of us tomorrow, but I must bid you farewell until then."

"Bid us farewell?" Chandler questioned.

"We don't belong in some long-forgotten novel," Ziva said. "Just say goodnight."

"You will never be able to tear me away from my long-forgotten novels," he said, and then walked away grinning.

Ziva slid off the arm of the chair to sit on Chandler's other side. "I rang my mother before you came back," she confessed quietly.

Chandler turned her head towards her. "What did she say?"

"Nothing good."

"Oh, Z." Chandler sighed. "I'm sorry."

"They can suck on the soles of some muddy shoes for a little while." Ziva glanced at Chandler. "I'll talk to them in a few days, once we've all calmed down."

Ziva reached for her glass and the water turned maroon before she could even touch it. She lurched away as if burned. That had never happened before. Colour changed at her command under the tips of her fingers, not without the guide of a hand.

The water changed back to clear, like no oddity had occurred at all.

"Z?" Chandler asked.

"I'm fine, I'm fine," she waved off.

"You just changed the colour of the water."

"It was an accident."

"I don't doubt that," Chandler said, her smile sad. "But you did it without..."

"Tell me about your night," Ziva cut in quickly. Leaving the glass despite her mouth being dryer than before, she looked at Chandler.

Chandler's face screwed up into a scowl. "It was definitely *interesting*."

"Oh?" Ziva perked up at the words. She did love gossip, just as her mother always had. "Do tell."

Chandler laughed and in doing so her shoulders relaxed. "Quinton's father in particular *really* doesn't like Abnormals."

"But his son is one?"

"He doesn't discriminate."

"And his mother?"

"She's sweet." Chandler fiddled with her emerald ring, twisting it round and round, until it slid from her marriage finger and she returned it to the other hand. "I'm sure I could get along with her quite well if I tried. If I had to."

"What about Quinton?" Knowing she couldn't fight the grin on her face, Ziva let it blossom.

Chandler snorted. "Charming."

"Just charming? You had to really *act* as an engaged couple this time, and in a small, *intimate* space."

"Again, if you think you're missing out, you can go next time instead."

Ziva threw her hands up. "No, no! He's lovely but we'd make a *bad* couple. You can carry on being his fake wife."

Chandler laughed once, shaking her head. "He asked me before we went in what I minded doing and what I didn't."

"What does that mean exactly?"

"He was concerned about how far we might have to go with the act and he wanted to know how ok I was with what we might have to do."

"And what did you say?"

"That as long as he didn't strip me naked, we were good."

Ziva burst out laughing. "You did not!"

"I did!" Chandler's face opened with a smile.

"That's *bad*."

"It was fine."

"You realise that was kind of open?"

"I know you don't have to be naked in any sense to really do anything, but he just kissed my cheek twice and we held hands a little." She shrugged like it was nothing. "Oh, I also climbed onto his lap and grabbed his thigh."

Ziva choked on nothing. "*What*? His lap? His thigh? You climbed him? You *grabbed* him? Did he grab you? What was he like? What did he feel like?"

"It was more of a surprised grab reaction than intentional. I suppose he felt like Quinton would feel, which I don't know much about." Again, Chandler shrugged. "Otherwise, everything was fine and normal."

"Yeah, because having to pretend to be someone's fiancé is normal."

"It's anything but."

Ziva huffed. "Bloody skies above you can say that again."

They laughed together. Their lives on the outside had suddenly, probably irreversibly so, become as Abnormal as they were in themselves.

CHAPTER TWENTY-TWO

QUINTON

30th Day of Autumn 2406

Quinton tossed and turned for what felt like hours. His left hand was just inside the waistband of his boxers while his right was tucked behind his head. Exhaustion wrecked him. He'd even kept his eyes shut to try and help him drift off.

His thoughts, however, were too loud.

They were tangled into webs. He tried to weave his way through them. Thoughts of his family, his current companions, this mission; they were all jumbled inside his brain. He tried to stretch them out, to understand what they really meant and why they were keeping him awake, but they were a knotted mess.

Working through them, or attempting to, tired him out even further.

So eventually, by some grace, sleep finally claimed him for its own.

QUINTON SQUINTED AT THE DESERT. A scarf covered his mouth and nose, and he wore a long jacket that rippled in the wind. Gretchen, with her thick eyeliner, walked alongside him.

It required tremendous effort to shift around the terrain. Their feet skidded backwards with every step. They had to spread their arms to stay upright. Wind threatened to blow them sideways, too, and the blazing sun drenched them in heat.

"I don't like the look of this," Gretchen said, looking out beyond with a hand over her brows to shield her eyes.

"Neither do I," he agreed.

They hunched down at once, using an orange dune to block most of them from sight, only peeking over the top in quick glances one at a time.

Tents upon tents lined the nearby horizon. Some had their entrances flicked open, others remained closed. Flags waved outside nearly every abode and water splashed in the centre from a nearby exposed pipe.

"Why did Praxis send us*?" Gretchen complained lamely. "I'm just the bone girl."*

"You're more like the bone-headed girl," he said back.

Gretchen's punch landed solidly. "Enough of that!"

Quinton grumbled, rubbing his sore arm. "At least I'll win five pieces off Seamus now," he told her. "We bet you'd hit me at some point."

"That was a stupid and easy bet to make. You're very punchable most days."

Someone started yelling in the distance. Quinton and Gretchen turned their attention towards it, just in time to see men bringing in others on cloth stretchers. The injured were placed out by the fountain and medical workers came rushing out from a rough yellow tent, dressed in their heavy cream-coloured uniforms.

"What are we here for again?" Quinton whispered.

"You don't remember?" Gretchen asked. She touched his arm, forcing him to face her.

Slowly, Gretchen's familiar face melted into Ziva's. Her head and ears were covered with cloth but her face was exposed.

His new companion smiled with soft ease. "We're here for the Mask," Ziva answered.

Quinton took a step back in surprise. But his mind seemed to recalibrate, remembering the words and forgetting the past face at the same time. "The Mask of Iris."

"The lost *Mask."*

He scrunched up his face. "How are we supposed to find something that is lost?

Ziva backed away as the face on the body shifted again. With it, the body shrank and the colours around it were manipulated, turning one girl into another.

Chandler.

Her hair was uncovered and waving in the wind like its own flag. A soft blue light made an aura around her, and Quinton could see ice-crystals forming at her feet.

"Nothing is ever truly *lost," she said, her voice close to a whisper. "Not unless it wants to be. Only a person can choose to be lost."*

"But this Mask has power," he heard himself say.

She smiled, her eyes narrowing as she tilted her head. "It has the power of freedom, the power to change.*"*

"It can't just disappear!"

"So the Mask hasn't."

"It's changed." Quinton stared, probably a little harshly, but mostly because the wind and sand around him had picked up. "The Mask has changed shape but it can revert, just as the person underneath will."

Chandler's smile dropped its charm. "Just as I will."

With the wind, Chandler, or whomever it had been, floating away, piece by piece.

QUINTON BURST AWAKE, THROWING HIMSELF from bed in a flurry of panicked motion. When he found his footing again, he padded round the room for something to wipe his sweaty forehead with, and then dove into whatever clothes he could find in the mostly dark room.

He ran into the hallway a moment later.

Ziva and Chandler were already waiting for him in the living room – well, not exactly *waiting* for him, more like they hadn't moved since he'd last seen them. He peered at the clock. Barely midnight. He'd been trying to fall asleep for barely an hour.

Is that it? he asked himself.

"And all the noise was because..." Chandler said aloud.

"Because I had a dream about you," he blurted.

"I'm flattered. I just don't know what to do with that information."

Quinton snorted, finding his heartbeat calming and his brain churning more normally. "You were *both* there."

Ziva raised an eyebrow. "If you think that sounds sweet, then we need to have a little chat."

Laughter bubbled up his throat but he squashed it back down. "No, it wasn't that." He slumped down on the floor before the girls, peering up at them. "You both shape-shifted into one another and then flurried away as sand."

"Charming," Chandler said. She looked at Ziva incredulously. "Now we're interchangeable ghosts."

"Sounds thrilling," Ziva commented. "Could we walk through walls?"

Quinton stared between the two of them. "There were no walls. I was in a sandy place, a sort of desert campground."

"What were we doing there?"

"Talking about the Mask."

Ziva sharply gasped aloud. "The Mask?"

Quinton nodded. "Chandler, in the dream, you said nothing could be truly lost except for a human. I said about the

Mask having power, and you said it is the power of change." He paused for a moment, letting his words sink in properly. "The Mask can't disappear or become lost. It can only change into whatever a human asks of it. *That's* the freedom is grants. But for how long?"

Chandler tilted her head, eerily, like she had in the dream. "What are you saying?"

"What if there's a limit? What if, while it can't be lost and can change, after some time it has to revert? There are limits in all powers. And if the Mask turns back to its original state, then surely so will the human wearing it." He rubbed his face. "We're trying to search for the Mask but we need to find a person. Or *several*. People that have never existed before in certain circumstances. They'd have habits they never had before. They'd say something different they didn't once. They'd even chew new foods differently. We're looking for different people who are the *same*."

"And that's how we find the Mask," Ziva said, a lightness entering her voice. "We find all these people who act the same, *are* the same, and one must be with the Mask. And the Mask person would've made sure not to be in the same place at the same time as the *real* version in case they got caught."

"So, what do we do?" Chandler asked. "How do we do this?"

"We know this person tried something in the business sector last week, right?" Quinton stretched for his laptop and flipped it on. "We need to find a person who looks like they're trying almost *too hard* to fit in somewhere and then we work backwards."

"While you start that adventure," Chandler stood, "I'm going to take a shower." Quinton didn't watch her go, but part of his sleep-addled brain expected to see sand float past his eyes as she departed.

Ziva squatted down beside him. "This is what we're doing now then? Searching for a person who is so obviously unobvious?"

He nodded. "If we can find someone like that in the footage of the business market—"

"How do we do that?" she cut in. "I thought the business market was an online thing, done through phones and computers?"

"It is. But there's an actual communal place people go to. A lot of businesses have a physical set-up in a building and run a lot of their operations from there. There are these massive boards in the main lobbies, more like screens really, and they roll day and night to show stocks and share prices for all kinds of companies. One building does it more than others." He didn't tell her that his father had a stake in that building.

"Companies run the prices of other companies?"

Quinton waved his hands. "It's hard to explain."

"Please, try?"

"It's more like people run the prices of companies. People determine what's important or worth-while investing pieces into, and the companies buy or sell parts of said company. So if the public are buying a lot of crisps, for example, value opens up within the company to invest money in. Your money could grow or shrink like a wave depending on if it's still profitable. Those who invest can earn a part of that profit. So mostly it's about what's 'fashionable', in a sense, in that moment that people can get behind and support, or not, and how much someone can make out of that. It's just a more desired way of gambling, really. At least, that's how I see it."

Ziva gripped her head. "Headache."

A short laugh left him. "It can be," he agreed. "I was brought up around it and still don't know a lot of it."

"You sound like you do though!"

He smiled at her. "I'm a good kidder."

She smiled back and then looked to the laptop. "This person we're looking for probably went into the main business building where a lot of companies buy and sell bits of other companies for money?"

"From what my father said, yeah."

"And you trust his word?"

"*Hell no.*" He sighed, closing his eyes for a second. "But it's all we have."

Gradually, his fingers slid over the keys as the search began, though he had to take a moment to call Dalton back at Redwing again to hack into the main-frame data of the building's security cameras. He thanked him once they were in and hung up.

"My father said the stocks rumbled last week," he told Ziva as he paused the main building's security footage for the beginning of the previous week. "The Mask was originally used for committing fraud or stealing trade secrets."

Ziva shifted, looking like she was trying to get more comfortable. "What kind of fraud or secrets?"

"I don't know," he answered honestly. "I was never told, but I know it could've potentially crippled the markets."

"And you believe that?"

He nodded. "Anything so secret and close kept, though I don't know what kind of secrets there could be... If they got out, it could be severely damaging. Not just to investors but to the stock itself. It could cause collapse."

Ziva audibly gulped. "Shall we play the video and try to stop that from happening then?"

Quinton hit the play button.

At some point, Ziva got up and made tea, Quinton ordered snacks from the local twenty-four-hour bakery, and Chandler returned. They all sat with various documents and scraps of paper surrounding them like sharks in an open ocean, eyes intently watching the laptop as it played hour after hour, day after day, of silent footage. Apparently, even as sophisticated as technology had grown, for some reason sound here didn't record.

Quinton figured it wasn't an accident though. He reckoned people working in the business sector wouldn't want their conversations overhead.

Looking for a person that was trying too hard to blend in sounded easy. Truthfully, it was worse than they anticipated. Throughout that week, it looked like everyone was trying too much. They overenthusiastically grabbed for mugs or ruffled files. Others walked too briskly or cosied up with too many people.

"Where is this?" Ziva asked once they'd reached day four of tape.

"The largest business sector, which is the most likely target, is in New London," Quinton answered.

"Close to home," Chandler mumbled, scowling.

"Very close," he agreed. "Redwing is only a little way out from it."

"Feels like we've chased the horizon all over the world for one Mask," Ziva sighed.

"We *have* chased across the world," Chandler told her. "We came from our homes to go to Redwing, then Snowdonne, now Moscow. That's all half a world away from each other."

Quinton huffed. "It's a lot of distance for one mission. I've never had to bounce around so much before."

"Has anyone? Seems a tad extreme."

"A little travel never hurt anyone I suppose. Just tiring," Ziva replied, smiling. "It's been exciting seeing new sights and I can't be the only one who thinks that."

Chandler shrugged and shrank back. "I won't deny it," she said. "But it will be nice to rest my head on the same pillow for more than two nights in a row."

Quinton examined her blank features. "Where will that bed be?"

That was the question that would lie in wait to be answered

at the end of this mission. Ziva looked more confused than Chandler any time any semblance of the question cropped up, but if Quinton had learnt anything it was that Chandler seemed to be the type of person who would be least likely to share her answer whenever she made it.

For him, it hadn't taken long to decide. But everyone was unique, all wants different.

"I don't want to do morning training if I stay," Chandler grumbled.

Caught off guard, Quinton laughed. "You wouldn't have a choice," he said. "Violette would drag you out by the skin on your ankles." He tasted something sour at the mention of *her* name.

"There's no way!" Ziva disputed.

"She has the ability to move objects with her mind, one of the most highly considered abilities that we know of. And she'd do it. Don't underestimate her."

"Yeah, well, I'll freeze anything she touches me with," Chandler said.

Quinton raised his eyebrows. "That's a fight I'd like to see, even if I think she'd win." He hated saying it, didn't want to bet on *her* at all, but it was a powerful gift she had, and he couldn't deny it. Yet, he hadn't seen Chandler use hers much, so who knew what her full potential could be?

Chandler stared at him. "And that's *if* I stay. I still don't know."

Ziva bit her bottom lip. "We have to complete this mission first."

"Or let the time run out," Quinton reminded them. That had happened on one of his missions before, and the humiliation had stung for weeks – it hadn't been incapability, just time slipping away. He didn't know of anyone who had failed, in any way, their first mission though, so he didn't know what exactly the outcome would be if that happened, if the girls would even get the choice to stay afterwards. He didn't want that to be a potential for them.

Chandler sighed. "We better keep watching."

Ziva scowled at the screen and then paused it a few seconds after Quinton had started it. "What if we stop watching it through a screen?" she suggested. "There are still a few days left. We could always pay a visit to the real place? We might stand a better chance at picking something out in real time there?"

Quinton shut the screen. "That's not bad. We'd have better awareness being *inside*."

"I don't see a problem," Chandler said. "We'd be halfway home, too."

He nodded, grabbing his phone. "I'll book the tickets. You pack."

The girls got up and walked to their shared room, just as they had done plenty of times in the past days. Quinton lifted his phone to his ear as it dialled.

Ziva's plan was solid. Investigating in person might be easier than through a lens. Behaviour they'd encountered so far might only be suspicious because they had no real context of conversation. In person learning might help eradicate any problems like that.

Quinton wanted to cross everything he could for luck to fall on their side. He wanted to stroll in and catch the person wearing the Mask in the act of trying to steal secrets like an old-movie style bank robber – balaclava, bag over the shoulder to carry the loot. That wasn't how things were going to go, but it was a nice thought. Maybe something similar? Maybe they'd bump into someone and the Mask would just fall off their face?

He touched his necklace, holding the stone tightly. He hoped this plan would work and the outcome would be in their favour.

The phone line connected and he smiled to himself.

CHAPTER TWENTY-THREE
ZIVA

32nd Day of Autumn 2406

Legs crossed, newspaper open at her side, sunglasses on the head... Ziva was in the zone.

Over the years, she'd watched plenty of heist and spy type movies with her parents. The people in those films had gone on stake-outs at some point, and Ziva remembered them well, taking inspiration from what she'd seen over the years. So now she was pretending to be a working woman on a break in the local café, which was coincidently across the way from the major Stock Building.

She picked up her chocolate flavoured latte and sipped, finding it *too* sweet. Putting it back down, she bit into the accompanying oat biscuit, finding it much more to her taste. She read some of the notes on her laptop absently while mostly peering over-top of it.

A moment later, her phone rang. She lifted it to her ear.

"You comfortable?" Quinton's voice came through softly.

“I don’t think I can get more comfortable,” she laughed, also trying to keep her voice level minimal.

Today was their second day of staking out. Yesterday, they’d drawn lots for who would be placed where, and they had again today to make it fair. Both days Ziva had won the café draw. Meaning both days she’d gotten to sit with new flavours of coffee and biscuits.

“Keep your eyes peeled, orange,” Quinton said, and hung up. He’d chosen to call her orange and make jokes related to the fruit because she’d chosen to colour her hair a run-down ginger. It didn’t suit her at *all* but it had been too late to change it by the time she’d realised.

Ziva lowered her phone and forced herself to really act interested in the laptop, scrolling down every so often in case someone was watching *her.*

Yesterday had been a dud. No one had come up with anything except sore backs or aching feet. Or in Ziva’s case an aching belly. Though *that* could’ve been a sign of her period since it had come on a few hours back. Chandler had rushed out to get the necessary products she required since Ziva had forgotten to bring any – Quinton had offered, but Chandler had insisted profusely, saying she wanted supplies of things for herself, too.

Once again she drank her sweet coffee, deeply this time, and found the mixture cool enough to soothe instead of burn.

If my mother could see me now, she thought. She shook her head. *She’d hate it. She wouldn’t even look at me if she saw me. I’m no longer what she wanted, even if I’ve barely changed.*

She knew her mother would scream. She would claim that Ziva drinking fancy drinks and tasting sweet goods was unfair on the rest of the family because they didn’t have any. But the whole point of a treat was that it was meant to be special. Not everything was meant to be shared. Not everyone was entitled to the same thing just because one had it, either. Plus, she'd used her own money for such luxuries – Praxis' advancement money had been used for them.

As much thought as she'd given her mother, she hadn't thought much of the rest of them. Guilt gnawed at her, turning the drink sickly in her stomach. But she pushed it down. She'd felt guilty for years, trained herself to believe she had to share whatever life gave her with everyone. So she refused to feel guilty over this; the first time she'd never had to share something. This was hers and hers alone, and it always would be.

Sighing, Ziva looked out the window, just in time to see Chandler sway past as casually as if she really belonged there in her pin-striped suit.

While Ziva had drawn the coffee shop both days, Quinton had switched from being the businessman to the cleaner and Chandler had done the reverse. That meant both of them had the inside of the stock building covered and Ziva had the outside.

Not that there had been much to watch so far.

And they had two days left.

Ziva didn't quite know what fact frightened her more. The thought of failure or how close the end was creeping whatever the outcome may be.

How are there only two days left? She glanced at the laptop's clock. *How can we do all we need to do in two days? We're no closer now than we were at the start.*

She stared back out the window. She had to squint to see, but Ziva watched as Chandler was searched before being allowed into the prestigious building.

For most of this mission, Ziva had been on the side-lines, hung in the background, kept in the shadows. And she didn't mind one single bit.

All her wishing for something that was hers, adventure didn't exactly call to her. She could take or leave those kinds of things, even if it *did*, admittedly, excite her a little. She didn't want to be in the forefront, she simply wanted to be involved and help with things on a smaller scale, so that left the others to do it.

A blaring alarm suddenly cut through the café.

Ziva swivelled her head round to try and spot the origin of the noise. When the owner of the café came running from out back, waving a broom and towel toward the doorway, Ziva was sure she didn't want to be in the kitchen.

"Out!" called the server. "Fire! Out! Leave and run!"

Ziva snapped the laptop closed, gathered her belongings, and ran out of the building along with the other customers.

Out in the square, Ziva clutched her gear for support. There had been nothing in the plan about a fire. She whirled around in several circles but saw no sign of Quinton or Chandler.

She was alone.

The alarm faded the further she was dragged with the crowd until they were in the dead centre between the skyscraper buildings.

Ziva looked back at the café to see smoke rising from where she supposed the kitchen was. The air transformed to become grey and thick, like a fire of a concentrated force had begun and was now trying to engulf anything it could.

Turning round, Ziva could see faces gawking, and wondered if hers was doing the same. But then she realised something. While the café's alarm had grown quiet, another had started. Not only that, but more bodies were joining the café group until she could no longer tell where they were all originating from.

She stopped dead when she spotted plumes of smoke rising from the stock building.

One fire was unfair. *Two* fires? In buildings that faced each other and had a shared patch of land between them...

Ziva's stomach began to tie itself into knots.

She pushed her way through the crowds, not caring as she elbowed a few people. When she got to the edge of the growing group, she pulled out her phone. She tried Quinton and when he didn't answer tried Chandler.

Nothing.

Daring to stare up at the stock building, she tried her phone again. Desperation clawed a path through her heart sending it racing. She had to try several more times before the call finally connected.

"*Where are you?*" she yelled the second she could.

She'd never been one to raise her voice but now seemed like a good time to start. Plus, there was a lot of noise around her that she figured yelling wasn't bad if she wanted to be heard.

"I'm out the back of the building," he answered, talking loudly himself. "It's on fire."

"So's the café!"

"They're *both* on fire?"

Ziva ignored his question. "Where's Chandler?"

"She's not with you?"

"No! She's not outside on your side?"

Ziva stood on her tip-toes, and when she still couldn't see climbed onto the little wall that separated a bricked in flower-bed. She still couldn't see the iconic suit.

"She's not here," she heard herself say in a whimpering voice.

"Then..." Quinton gasped. "*Fuck!* Ziva. She's still in the building!"

"Are you sure?" Ziva didn't want to believe it; she didn't want to think of her friend inside a burning building. "Is there anywhere else she could be?"

"Fuck."

Quinton hung up without saying anything else. Ziva couldn't bring herself to swear back. Instead, she jammed her phone in her pocket and forced the laptop into its bag. Throwing the bag on her back, she grunted and took a deep breath.

Somehow she *knew* what Quinton's lack of answer meant. There was nowhere else Chandler could've been. They would've seen her otherwise.

The smoke grew higher and higher in the sky, a cyclonic mass of heavy grey that blotted out the rest of the normal cloud cover. Ziva clutched at her necklace and whispered a long-forgotten prayer under her breath. She'd never forgotten it and didn't believe, but she wanted safety and would do what it took to get that for her friends. Even if it meant reciting her grandmother's words and having faith in them for one moment.

When she stopped, her stomach lurched. She stuck her hand over her mouth as if that would stop her from vomiting, and ran. She ran as fast as her legs would push, right towards the building that was burning from the inside out.

CHAPTER TWENTY-FOUR
CHANDLER

32nd Day of Autumn 2406

Chandler faced away from the window. She moved with precision, walking the halls as if she had done it every day of her life.

The marble beneath her feet made the clicking of her heels echo and the long hallways made sure the sound lasted. She fiddled with the bottom of her jacket as she went, hoping she looked like a distracted worker worried about her appearance and not someone out of place somewhere she shouldn't be.

Her job today had been to blend in. She'd chosen to walk around in a suit, but mostly went on coffee or photocopier runs so other people didn't have to. She used the excuse that she was a new intern and no one seemed to question her; everyone was too busy giving her a list of things to go get or do to be bothered much about where she'd come from or how her corridor pass didn't quite work. She'd completed a few tasks to blend in well enough, but she was ignoring the rest – until she got caught or questioned – to explore.

A shoulder bumped into hers suddenly, forcing her to glance up.

The woman apologetically waved and dashed off. Chandler sighed. It seemed there was no escape from being walked into, no matter where she was in the world.

She moved on, past the copier and cubicles, past the common area of plush sofas between two different businesses, and past the bathrooms. She'd come to notice each floor had two businesses per level. So far, she'd walked up five flights of stairs and carried on further.

The stairwell door clicked behind her and she began to climb up the next flight. Halfway up, a white noise cut through the unattractive concrete zone. Chandler yelped and clutched her ears. She gritted her teeth and ran the rest of the way, pushing through the door at the end with her hip.

"Fire!" someone called, their voice penetrating the mostly unhelpful barricade Chandler had created for herself. "Fire! We need to get out!"

Chandler edged her way to the wall of windows on the level and peered out. Down below, plenty of people were gathering in the concrete space between the nearby buildings. She scowled. While it seemed most wore suits, Chandler could see people in what looked like aprons too. Squinting, she could just make out a wiggly billow of smoke rising directly across the street.

In a stunned silence, Chandler lowered her arms – the alarm was still yelling but not loud to her anymore. She kept staring. She watched bodies run out of the nearby café.

If there's a fire there, why is the smoke alarm going off in this *building? Could there really be a fire in both? And* where's *Ziva?*

Chandler rooted for her phone, but there was no reception. She cried out several curses but no one was around to hear them.

Everyone was piling outside, pooling on the concrete ground between the two buildings.

She tried searching for Ziva in the mass of people like dots, cracking her knuckles as she went in a sort of count. When she thought she caught signs of her, they vanished in a blink.

It spurred her into action. She needed to get out and find her friend.

Chandler raced down the stairs, skipping several steps each time. The alarm was nearly deafening in the stairwells, and she was glad to leave them as she got to the bottom floor.

She sprinted for the front doors and slammed into them. They wouldn't open. She bashed her hands on the glass until her wrists and palms stung. Nothing budged. They were locked and sealed, probably an automatic result of the fire and alarm – a precaution to keep it contained.

Chandler huffed and ran back the way she'd come. There had to be fire-doors somewhere.

The long corridors began to feel never-ending. She twisted this way and that, running back on herself more than once. But eventually, she dipped round a corner.

She braced herself as her heart thudded, taking deep breaths, and slowed to walk as the smell of strong smoke wafted up her nostrils. She choked, and immediately pulled the edge of her suit up over her mouth and nose.

Peering round the corner, she had to suppress a gasp. A black-cladded figure was bent under a desk. They had a tablet pulled up, screen fully white, and a wire extending from it to the main-frame of a desk computer.

The person tapped on the tablet screen and then pushed some computer buttons. Several seconds went by where they typed commands into both sets of computers, fingers tapping quicker than Chandler had ever seen anyone manage.

After another minute, they pulled the wire free and snatched up the tablet, tucking into a utility looking rucksack. From their pockets they pulled a lighter and threw stacks of nearby paper onto the ground. Combining them, a fire began with a *click*. It glowed orange and then yellow, and it started to caress the underside of a nearby chair.

They spun round, blue eyes wide.

The person's exposed face shimmered.

While Chandler hadn't gotten a good look of the face 'before', her brain was screaming at her that things were different now. She tried to get a better look and realised the eyes were now green.

They changed their face, her brain screamed. *They. Changed. Their. Face.*

The body sprang from the floor and burst, running down the aisles of desks and chairs. Chandler blinked and realised they were running *away* from her. She cursed, dropping the grip of her suit, and chased them.

Her lungs burned and the smell of the smoke followed her everywhere. When she reached the bend in the next corridor, Chandler took a gulping breath. The body was gone.

The ice inside her body and in the air kept her cool, but sweat still dripped down her back from her effort. She stamped her foot in frustration and ran back the way she came.

Halfway back, she crashed into something and stumbled, but hands caught her before she fell. Chandler yanked herself free and looked up, a fist ready to fight. But she stopped short.

Quinton had a faint smile on his lips. Ziva pulled up beside him a second later. Immediately, they all coughed and covered their mouths with their hands.

"How did you get in? The doors were locked," Chandler mumbled. "Actually, never mind." She waved her free hand in the air.

"Are you alright?" Quinton asked, Ziva nodding beside him.

Chandler waved the question away. "Someone was plugged

into the computers. They set a fire once they were done getting whatever they were stealing."

"Someone was here?" Quinton's gaze went over her head.

"They went that way," Chandler pointed behind her, "but I lost them."

"What did they want?" Ziva asked, coughing slightly.

"Doesn't matter right now," Quinton said. "There's fire. Whether the intention is to burn down the building or use it as a distraction, it doesn't matter. We need to get out."

Chandler heard the words but they became a buzzing in her ear. She knew the hotter the fire grew, the more her power would come to her defence naturally. She didn't know how far it would push. She'd never been in a position to make it protect her instinctually before. But heat was her enemy. The fire wasn't big yet, but if it continued to grow, it might just boil her from the inside while draining her at the same time.

She was afraid and her entire body began to shake.

Before she could come up with an answer, a shape caught her attention out the corner of her eye. A vaguely *human* shape.

Against all her brain's protests, she raced after it.

The shape darted away at the same time.

Her friends called for her but Chandler ignored them. The further she got, the harder it became to make out their voices or the still ringing alarm.

Running in heels was never easy, and though she'd had a lot of practise, marble added a new challenge. So did running with a hand over her mouth to block out as much smoke as possible. She only hoped she wasn't being led directly towards the fire.

Chandler's feet skidded on the smooth floor as she stopped. The figure she'd been chasing had spun round on her just head. Chandler took a small step and watched as, once again, their face shimmered, eyes turning to a dark blue. The figure's fists were at their sides, arms tight.

"I don't want to fight you," the person said. It was hard to tell who they were, as if their voice and face were distorted.

"I don't want to fight *you*," Chandler said. She'd never been in a fight before.

"Then let me go."

"Tell me why you're here, why you're setting fires."

The person laughed from the back of their throat. "This building deserves to burn," they said. "Do you know how much money they steal? How many people walk over you daily just for coins and pieces? How much money each company makes and then never pays out?"

Chandler stared. She knew that feeling, what it was like to be beneath someone who never even gave their time, let alone anything else.

They grinned like they'd somehow cornered Chandler despite *them* being in a corner, only a window behind them. The grin shifted Chandler from her mind.

As they went to bolt, Chandler spread her arms. She loaded the water droplets into the air with all her strength. Ice appeared across the floor, cracking towards the criminal in frozen blues.

The criminal tried to back off but the ice reached them, solidifying their feet in place. Chandler inhaled sharply. She'd used her powers before, but never in such an offensive manoeuvring, and never so easily. It was like holding it at bay had finally become too much, and the power just longed to be free.

By being caught up in her own gift, the person was given the chance to break free. They darted forwards with precision, crashing into Chandler, sending them both to the floor. They climbed on top, crushing Chandler's ribcage between their legs. She winced as pain lanced up her upper body but struggled to breathe.

Chandler could feel heat from the fire slinking closer. It must've grown and had begun to tear through the building. Warmth spread over her cheeks and under her skin, beginning to drain her energy as she fought to stay cool against her natural environmental other-half.

In one swoop, the person on top of her punched her squarely on the side of the head.

They shifted and Chandler reached up, aiming for the two blurry noses on their face. She touched their cheek, felt the skin beneath her fingers, and hit the face somewhere near the eye. But then her arm fell away, back to her own body. She could then see flakes of ice climbing to the ceiling above and nothing else. The pressure on her chest released all at once, but she still couldn't breathe.

"Chandler?" a distance voice called. "Chandler? Can you hear me?"

She saw white and grey, but nothing distinct. She could smell heavy smoke, but couldn't remember why. She thought she might have uttered some words about being tired, maybe even yawned.

All she knew was that there was a big, black hole coming for her, and it swallowed her completely.

CHAPTER TWENTY-FIVE

CHANDLER

32nd Day of Autumn 2406

Chandler tried to pry her eyes open but they were too heavy. All she could see was a pale pinkness from the back of her lids. She tried to express her unease but her tongue was too rough and her mouth too dry to work. She felt inside herself to her toes and discovered them cramped and curled.

"Chandler?"

She recognised the airy, soft tone. Ziva. That was her voice. She was the quiet, kind one.

Chandler groaned inwardly. It was hard but she forced against the invisible pressure that was keeping her under some kind of restraint. With a few pushes her eyes broke open. But the blinding light immediately made her shut them again. The cycle of opening and closing them continued until she could keep them cracked for longer than a second.

"There she is."

Quinton. That was his voice. The equally soft yet huskier tone he carried was familiar. He was the jokey one.

Licking her lips, finding them chapped and almost dusty, Chandler tried to swallow. When she choked on scorching air, Ziva appeared in view, blocking out the harsh light of the room with her body. She tipped a cup towards Chandler's mouth. Chandler obediently opened her lips as much as she could and let the girl pour a few drops at a time.

Ziva backed away with the cup after a few seconds. Chandler felt like she could've drunk more, and wanted to argue as the bed dipped at her side. Slowly, she tilted her head to peer around, but her neck was stiff and something covered the top part of her right eye.

Attempting to swallow again, finding it a little easier, she found her voice again. "Where am I?" Talking stung, but it felt good to, like she'd become too stony if she didn't. "What happened to me?"

Quinton shuffled his chair into view, the feet screeching on the floor. His white hair was fading from the bottom, so the tips were a rich ruby. No smile graced his face, though a frown was etched in between his eyebrows. Shadows hung beneath his stormy eyes.

"You're in a medical centre," he answered carefully.

"What?" she asked.

"You were struck across the head," Ziva said. She stood up from the bed and moved to Quinton's side so Chandler could see her. In just the week they'd known each other, her fringe had grown slightly and her hair was more tangled than before. "You passed out. You had to be brought here under blue lights."

"Clearly I'm not *dead*," Chandler said. "So that's something. Unless I did die and this is the start of my hell loop?"

Chandler struggled to focus on Quinton's face as he laughed, but she could see the humour didn't reach his eyes. "See, I told you," he said, glancing up to Ziva. "I told you she'd be fine."

"Bloody skies above, Chandler!" Ziva hissed quietly. "You gave us such a fright!"

Chandler wanted to shuffle to get more comfortable but stopped trying when she found she couldn't move so well. "How bad was the damage? What *day* is it?"

Quinton's frown softened slightly. "Let's start easy," he suggested.

"Alright," Chandler drew out the word.

"You've been resting for a couple of hours. It's still the thirty-second, but only for another hour and twenty or so minutes."

I've spent most of the day asleep, Chandler thought. *Great. The mission is going* brilliantly *right now.*

Because he couldn't hear her brain whirring, Quinton continued. "It's looking likely that the café fire was a distraction to get everyone out, so when the people from the stock building filed out, there would be enough confusion and panic to keep everyone locked together in a single place. Beyond that, we don't know much else. I managed to get into the system with Dalton's help. Some of the files appeared to have been copied in or out, their save dates newer than a lot of others, but also some were *placed* entirely."

"They had a tablet," Chandler said, her voice wobbling. She scowled. "Can I have some more water?"

Ziva smiled, filled up the glass with the water from the jug beside the bed, and helped Chandler to drink. Ziva pulled back and Chandler sighed, a drip of cold water running down the side of her face.

Chandler noticed the room was small yet clean, blue and white. Nothing was hooked into her arms or legs, but there was still a machine beeping somewhere behind her. There was only enough room for a box window – someone had drawn the blue curtains over it – a bed, a small chair that Quinton currently occupied, whatever machine was at her back, and a little screen ahead of her. Chandler assumed the door was round the corner, just past where the wall jutted out, keeping it out of direct sight.

She peered down at the blanket and her left bare leg sticking out from under it. "Can I have my trousers?" Chandler asked, noticing she was laying there without them.

Ziva spun round to her. "You honestly think we're letting you *leave*? That you can just wake up and walk out of here? After what happened to you?"

"I have to leave eventually, right? Why not now?"

Sighing, Ziva threw her folded trousers at her. Chandler groaned as the end of the leg slapped her on the cheek. Ziva looked guilty for a moment before Chandler waved it off.

Reaching inside the pocket, she drew out the item she *really* wanted.

Both Quinton and Ziva gasped loudly, then quickly covered their mouths like they might be discovered because of the noise.

Suddenly, Quinton bolted from the chair and Chandler heard the lock on the door click a second later. Ziva pulled her legs up. Both leant over Chandler as much as they could without physically pressing into her.

"Where did you get that?" Ziva whispered.

Chandler flipped her hand over, inspecting the Mask. "I took it."

"Is that really..." Quinton trailed off, mouth agape.

Chandler half-threw the object in his direction as much as she could. He gasped like she'd committed an atrocity before catching it out of the air.

It was the Lost Mask. Chandler had plucked it right off the criminal's face and shoved it in her trousers. It was the last thing she could remember actively doing.

Turning it over and over, Quinton studied the Mask. Chandler remembered him drawing it as a sketch from a vision and thought now how that image didn't do the real thing enough justice.

The black was an ebony so dark it looked like it could suck

in all the light from the world. The swirls were almost spirals that never quite touched and the dips were full curves. Chandler had no idea how she'd managed to steal the Mask, it appeared like it would mould itself to fit anyone perfectly, but she had. She'd plucked it, literally, right from under his nose.

She had only pretended to punch the criminal to tear it from their face. Aiming for the nose, as it turned out, had been the right point to hit. She'd managed to just graze the skin on the nose and the Mask had peeled away with a claw of her nail. She hadn't even seen it on their face, she'd simply guessed it would be there. She wanted to call it skill, that her fight had been planned, but that was a lie. A happy accident was more apt of a description.

"Wow." Ziva whistled lowly. "We have it. We *actually* have it."

Quinton rose an eyebrow at Chandler. "And you smuggled it out in your trousers?" He sat down, flopping in his seat casually. "Call me impressed."

"Hello impressed, I'm Chandler," she mocked, smiling as much as she could. He laughed.

Ziva beamed too. "Now what do we do?"

"We get out of here," Quinton decided. "We get out and we deliver the Mask to the rightful owners, the family, just as we're meant to."

The machine next to Chandler, which she actually hadn't noticed before, beeped. "What am I hooked up to?" She noticed a line connecting to her right shoulder. "Can I unhook myself?"

"Have you ever seen a movie?" Quinton asked. "You're supposed to tear it out of your own skin aggressively, biting your lip and internally screaming the whole time like a badass."

Chandler stared at him. "I've seen those movies, and those scenes always bother me."

"All you're asking from that is more blood or damage," Ziva added. She turned to face Chandler, smiling sweetly. "I'll help."

Carefully, Ziva lifted Chandler's arm until she could see that the line fed down her arm to a needle that was punctured inside the skin at her shoulder. A slightly blue-tinted liquid was passing through the tube. Chandler stared at it all. She'd never seen a line – in movies or life, not that this moment felt like either – enter at someone's shoulder or for there to be coloured liquid moving inside.

"I think it's just a health solution," Ziva said. She peered closer, squinting. "It doesn't look like anything too heavy. Probably just something to restore you? I don't think it's painkillers. No one said you had any *serious* injuries, just some bruising and a mild concussion."

"A mild concussion? Is that all?"

Ziva ignored her sarcasm. "You only lost consciousness for about twenty minutes but you woke once we got here. They put something in an injection they gave you and you calmed nearly immediately once the needle pierced your skin. You went right back to sleep. They said it was to make you rest so you healed."

Chandler groaned, but not from any pain. "I don't want to know how expensive the medical bills are going to be."

"Not very," Quinton said.

She glanced at him. No matter where anyone lay in the world, everyone had to pay for medical stays once they climbed in price. "What?"

"We all have medical insurance, paid by this company and that, all of which don't exist of course. But we have it, since getting hurt can be quite the occupational hazard. Our bills are paid, unknowingly, by our 'sponsors', just as they pay our wages." Quinton waved a hand in the air. "Praxis and them sort it all out. I barely listen." Chandler somehow doubted Quinton barely listened to anything.

"But I'm not part of that yet," she argued.

"This is still covered, whether you stay or not." He rose and walked to the door, turning back once he reached it. Chandler watched as he tucked the Mask into his pocket with a sly grin.

"I'm not one usually to complain about this, but maybe you really *should* put some trousers on so we can leave now though? If you're feeling as fine as you say." He sauntered off.

Ziva shook her head at the closed door. "You know, he made sure you had a private room?"

Chandler's gaze darted to her. "He did? Why?"

Ziva shrugged. "He said it was for privacy reasons, which I don't doubt."

"But?" She could hear there was something else in her tone.

"No buts. I just think he really was worried about you. I mean, we both were." Ziva took Chandler's hand and stroked the skin gently, carefully, like Chandler might suffer some sort of damage at her touch. "Seeing you lying there..." Ziva shuddered.

"Occupational hazard," Chandler repeated.

"I'm not sure I like how that sounds."

"If we stay in this line of work, I have a feeling *occupational hazard* will be a phrase we become quite familiar with."

"I hope not. I'm aiming for nothing more than minor bumps and bruises. A scraped knee is my limit."

Chandler laughed, and then winced as her head stung.

Ziva skimmed her fingers along Chandler's arm, up to the inside of her elbow. Chandler nodded. In one tug, Ziva pulled the line out. A stinging sensation burst along Chandler's arm and she sucked in a breath between her teeth at its suddenness, but it slowly ebbed.

"Does this mean you're thinking of staying?" Ziva questioned, looking down at the now unconnected line in her hand.

Chandler didn't reply but asked instead, "Can you help me into my..." She looked down and saw she barely had anything on, just some underwear and a borrowed flimsy, see-through cloth t-shirt. "Into my *own* clothes."

Ziva giggled. "I thought you'd never ask."

CHAPTER TWENTY-SIX
QUINTON

33rd Day of Autumn 2406

You look well rested.”

Chandler glared back at Quinton in the mirror, and he smiled. She’d been looking at her face, at the black and blue bruise above her right eye. Red dotting outlined the area, too, but Quinton focused on the actual hazel of her eyes.

“You’ve come into the bathroom to stare at me, why, exactly?” she questioned.

Quinton raised his eyebrows and folded his arms, propping against the doorway. “I wanted to see if you were ok,” he said.

“You’re doing a good job of *seeing*. You’ve stared at my face open-mouthed well enough.”

He chuffed. “Fine. I came to *ask* if you’re ok. The staring was more of an accident upon arrival.”

The sigh that left Chandler’s lips deflated her shoulders.

"I'm alright," she said. "There a small ringing in my ears and I have a minor headache, but I'm otherwise alive."

"Tell me if that headache gets worse."

"Can it be bad?"

"You had concussion."

"Minor."

"It can still develop. There's no nausea or light sensitivity, is there?"

"I feel healthy."

He narrowed his eyes. "Do you?"

She whirled away from the mirror and stalked close to him, having to bend her neck back to glare up at him. "Are you a doctor now? Are you going to make everything all better if I'm unwell?"

Grinning, he lowered his head an inch closer to hers. "If you asked me to."

Chandler snorted and pushed past him, leaving him to laugh and watch her go.

Though he wouldn't admit it aloud, he had been so wound up over Chandler. Ziva had seen how panicked he'd become at finding Chandler as she'd passed out. Once she'd fully blacked out, he'd literally *yelled* for a member of a medical team. Ziva had too, though she'd been more useful in going to do the doors to lead them in. In a single moment, his heart had pinched. They were becoming friends, but he couldn't quite understand *why* it had hurt so much to see her that way.

It was probably because they *were* becoming friends. He remembered being in a similar way after seeing his vision of Gretchen's broken legs come true. It didn't quite feel the same, but it was close.

Ziva appeared in the doorway, a soft smile on her little face. "Are we leaving soon?"

Unfolding his arms, Quinton nodded. "It's only a short ride into the city," he said, starting to walk. "I'll have someone come and pick up our stuff and take it back to the mansion while we finish this job."

"Not a moment too soon, hey?"

He stopped abruptly and peered down at her. "How are you? How do you feel?"

She blinked at him several times. "What?"

They'd both been there with the fires, the chasing, and the medical emergency.

He ran a hand through his loose hair, making him think of dying it again. The ends were turning back to red, Ziva's magic slipping despite her letting her hold over it go. "I've been so distracted," he admitted. "I know you're *physically* ok, but, how are you?"

Quinton was convinced Ziva's smile could make anyone else smile in return. "I'm fine, Quinton," she told him. "I hope you're not about to apologise to me or something? I know you didn't forget I was here. We've all been busy. There's been more important things to think and worry about."

"Doesn't give me an excuse to neglect asking you the important things too."

"You haven't neglected me at all and I won't allow you to think you have." She touched his arm, her hand comforting and warm through his shirt. She walked and acted more confidently now compared to when they'd first met, he could see the difference already despite the short time-span. "Come on. We have a Mask to take home."

Exhaustion was an old friend at this point. Quinton stepped out of the private shuttle yawning. He couldn't wait to just go home, have a bath, and curl up in bed to scroll through his phone for new books and to sleep, only to wake for food.

His boots clomped against the stone steps as he climbed up

towards the house growing closer. Praxis had given the address but Quinton hadn't paid much attention to where in the city they were exactly. Praxis had also, through some means, requested this audience in a way that wouldn't expose Redwing or the group.

At the top of the steps, Quinton slipped his hand into his pocket and pulled it back out again, the Mask inside. Silently, he held it out to Chandler. She took it carefully, tucking it out of sight again in a blink. They withdrew from one another.

"Ready?" he asked.

"Let's do this and go home," Ziva agreed from his other side.

Quinton pressed the buzzer beside the white, grandiose double doors of the lavish apartment complex.

They waited for moments and Quinton started to wonder if anyone would answer.

Just when he was about to ring the bell again, an assistant swung the door open with force. Quinton startled slightly at the abrupt nature of it. But the assistant didn't seem to notice, going on to ask their names. The assistant didn't seem to outwardly react to any of them, moving aside.

Ziva entered first, then Chandler, and then Quinton last. The assistant led them to the golden elevator and clicked the button to the penthouse apartment – it was sixty floors up.

The elevator was towards the back outside of the building, and the entire side facing outwards was glass. They stepped in and it began to rise steadily. Quinton sighed at the city he could begin to see over. He was sure, if he squinted really hard, he could see through the barrier that kept Redwing hidden and find his home in the very far away distance of green.

Quinton left the elevator first once it stopped. He walked right up to the giant double black doors with golden handles and knocked.

Normally, recruits wouldn't take such a personal attachment to a mission. They would just drop their item off discreetly – if an item was part of the task, that was – and make sure it was picked up by hiding nearby. At least, that was what Quinton had heard. He hadn't had an object-based mission before. But he had seen in a vision Chandler handing over the Mask directly. It was one vision he really did want to happen.

Another assistant came and opened this door; this one dressed smartly in black with a little bell-boy hat that had a neat strap tightly clamped under their chin.

"We're here on business," Quinton told the assistant.

"My mistress was expecting you," they said, opening the door to them.

Quinton's stomach shifted – it was just a twisting sensation – but he couldn't explain why. The final stage of *any* mission was nerve-inducing. In all the ones he'd been on, the anticipation had built up along the way, right up until the moment they stepped back inside Redwing. He blamed the twist in him on that.

The assistant led them through the penthouse, not uttering a single word as they went.

Large windows exposed the outside world, and Quinton could still see the outside world through them. He was used to those kinds of sights and the drama of it all. However, Chandler and Ziva didn't appear to be, and took a moment to stop and notice the view. Quinton stomped his foot slightly harder on one step, playing it off as a miss-step, but it was an act to get their attention back on track. He felt horrible for tearing them away from their wonder, but they had a purpose here. They could sight-see all they liked after. And they seemed to realise that, snapping out of their daze together to carry on following.

Around another bend and a curved wall, they came across a woman. She rested against the back of a sofa, arms holding her upright, her ankles crossed. Quinton raised his eyebrow at her.

He'd seen photos of the family before, and she certainly looked to be one of the grand-daughters of the original maker of the famous Mask.

"You requested an audience?" the woman said. The pitch of her voice was a little huskier than expected, but no photo could show a voice.

"We did," Chandler answered.

The woman dragged her eyes over Chandler slowly. "Who might you be? I know the lovely man you're with." She nodded at Quinton without moving her eyes.

"You know me?" Quinton asked, though the woman had already made that clear.

"Who wouldn't?" she replied. "I know your father. You look so much like him, like Lord Eichner."

Quinton tipped his head. "I wouldn't say that to him."

"That you look like him?"

"That you think he's a Lord. His ego is already big enough, there's no need to inflate it further. He might pop."

"So, you're not denying you're his son?"

"I'm not," Quinton confirmed.

He knew money could buy him a way out of this, a way to secrecy, and he had an abundance to use thanks to the very parents he claimed fame and notice from. Praxis would also have a way to fix this, to bury that they were ever here too. Quinton could let this play, let this woman know who he is and use his status to advantage, for now.

The woman turned back to Chandler, her smile like a cat's. "But who are you?"

"I'm Josephine," Chandler lied effortlessly.

"Ah." The woman's smile twisted further. "The famous fiancée herself."

Quinton glanced at Chandler out the side of his eye and spied the emerald ring was back on her marriage-finger. He hadn't seen her slip it back on there. He had to admit he was impressed and wanted to commend her for her forethought in doing so.

"You've heard of me, then," Chandler commented.

"Those of us in high society talk," the woman said. Quinton cursed his parents, not for the first time in his life. The rich and the powerful and the *known* did indeed talk. The woman set her sights on Ziva next. "And you are?"

Ziva smiled to match the woman's; all politeness, no niceness. "Shira," she said. "Friend and personal assistant."

"A friend who tags along to important meetings between important people?"

"A friend who is here because I want her to be," Chandler sniped back. The woman raised her eyebrows. "I will ask you to treat her with as much respect as you do me or Quinton."

"Out my respect for the Eichner's, I will agree," the woman pouted.

"Thank you," Quinton said into the quiet that followed.

She nodded once. "So, shall we discuss why you asked for an audience? I can't be bothered to skirt round the subject any longer. I'm starting to bore."

Quinton caught a flash of movement; Chandler's hands curling into fists, and he reached for the closest one to hide it. "I think we may have found something you have been looking for," he said, taking over.

"Then show me."

Chandler stalled for a moment before dragging her other hand into her pocket and out again. Unfolding her fingers, the Mask uncurled with them.

The woman gasped. Quinton shared the sentiment. It didn't matter how many visions or how many times he'd seen the real thing, he was still beyond impressed. Knowing the power, the power over *freedom*, the Mask had as well, made his insides positively squirm.

"The Mask," the woman whispered. Her eyes snapped up

to all of them in turn. "You found the Mask of Iris. How? And how did you know the family was looking for it?"

"Long story," Chandler said bluntly. She'd styled her hair, with Ziva's help, so it covered the bruises that explained exactly how much trouble they'd had trying to retrieve it.

"We're just happy it's back where it belongs," Ziva said.

Tentatively, the woman reached out, hanging her hands in mid-air. Chandler slipped her hand out of Quinton's and basically dumped the Mask into the woman's outstretched hands unceremoniously. The woman clutched it to her chest immediately, treasuring it like a jewel.

"I cannot thank you enough for finding and giving it back to me," the woman cooed.

Quinton smiled. "Try not to lose it again," he joked.

"I'll certainly keep it closer from now."

Ziva slipped her arm through Chandler's and they walked back the way they'd come. Quinton followed closely. When they reached the door, however, Chandler stopped dead. Her eyes shone in the long mirror beside the door. Then Quinton realised the angle of the mirror was pointing behind them and Chandler was looking past to their backs.

She swung around. "Stop!"

Quinton whirled too and immediately saw what Chandler had. The woman's face shifted and shimmered before a different face revealed itself. The person laughed, high and intensely. "I will *certainly* keep this close this time," they said, waving the Mask carelessly. All pretence vanished. "Thank you ever so much for handing it right back to me!"

Chandler and Quinton darted forwards at the same time.

They were already too late.

The person threw themselves out of the nearest window, laughter ringing in their wake.

CHAPTER TWENTY-SEVEN
ZIVA

33rd Day of Autumn 2406

Fuck!”

Ziva couldn’t quite tell *who* exactly had sworn. It might’ve been Chandler who often said more offensive words. It could’ve been Quinton who kicked his foot into the wall. Or Ziva herself, who shook her head rather vigorously.

A shuttle rail ran right by the building’s exterior, the height quite a few feet below, but the angle would make it possible for someone to reach if they ‘accidentally’ fell out of a window. There would be a bit of staggering, but no major injury if they caught themselves well.

In unison, the trio all backed away from the window. A single, small sigh left Ziva’s mouth.

Chandler flicked her hair back, uncovering the vicious bruise by her eye. “I think,” she scowled, “that was the guy I fought in the stock building for the Mask in the first place.”

"At least we know he's not some kind of magician and can't fly," Ziva commented.

"I wouldn't count him out of being a magician," Chandler said. "I thought his face shimmered before because of the Mask."

"You'd seen that happen before?" Ziva asked.

She nodded. "He'd been wearing the Mask when it'd happened. I stole it from his face minutes later. But I saw him in the mirror, and his face changed when the Mask was in his hand."

"What are you saying? That he already has the ability to change himself?" Quinton threw out. He'd stopped kicking the wall, but the frustration remained plain on his face.

"The amount of Abnormal powers out there... the possibilities are endless. So it would be possible that someone could have the ability to change themselves."

"But then why does he need the Mask?" Ziva untied her hair and immediately redid it again.

Chandler's frown was cut deep. "I don't know."

"Maybe he can't hold the shape?" Quinton suggested. "The power of our Abnormalities isn't always the same. Two people might have the same gift, though I've not heard of any such thing happening, but..." He shook his head, his hair slipping loose so strands hung around his face. "But those two people can also be born with different capabilities. They could have a different ability with their Abnormality. Their limits might be different, or their strengths might vary. And some of us have weaknesses with our gift too. Maybe he can't hold the shift? That's why he needs the Mask. Maybe the Mask, to that man, is a way to solidify the identity change for as long as he wants?"

Attempting to stay positive, Ziva said, "At least we know who has the Mask."

Quinton nodded. "The escaped gang member, right?"

"The problem is, he could be anyone right now," Chandler sighed.

Ziva moved further from the window. She peered down at her hands, and noticed her clothes. Her coat had somehow changed colour despite her not having a single thought about manipulating it. She glanced back up.

"You said his face shifted, even when he wasn't wearing the Mask?" she asked.

Chandler slunk away from the window too. "That's what I thought I saw."

"It's safe to think that you're right at this point," Quinton said.

"We know the Mask is also naturally black, right?" Ziva looked quickly between her companions. "We've established that."

"I think so," Quinton said, beginning to frown himself.

"I didn't touch my coat or even think about it, but the colour's different," Ziva told them, pointing to the material as if they needed encouragement to look. The bubble-gum pink was bright and a little bit of a weird choice for her. "I think, if I can get close enough to him, I might be able to force the Mask to change colour."

"What would that do?"

"I'm not entirely sure," she admitted. "But I have this *feeling*." She didn't want to explain in case her plan didn't work. It was a loose thought at best. But she hoped it was better than the nothing they'd had moments ago. "But if I can force the Mask to change, to give up its *freedom*..."

Quinton tucked his loose strands of hair behind his ears. "How are we going to find this guy?"

"He was stealing files," Chandler said. "Swapping them out for others. If he was at the stock building, would he have been swapping out information of the markets or fiddling the system somehow? But why swap things? Why not just take?"

Ziva shrugged. "Don't ask me."

Quinton shrugged as well. “I don’t know much either, but I’m pretty sure the stocks run on a real-time circuit. They have too. It’s a legal requirement. The companies see the results at the same time we do. Unless they’re cheating and delaying time...” He paused. “But we just said this guy’s ability is that he can change himself, if only for a little while. He’s not a time guy.”

“Maybe we’re looking too much at the stocks themselves?” Ziva let her eyes wander around the room as she thought. “Maybe we don’t need to figure everything out exactly. We just need to know where he’s going and intercept him there.”

“His friends are already in prison,” Quinton reminded.

“Wait.” Chandler’s voice was light. “What were they put away for again?”

“For trying to infiltrate the stocks, mess with the systems, taking trade secrets.”

“What if that person was taking any evidence of that crime happening?”

“Scrubbing their tracks?” Ziva questioned. “Isn’t it too late for that? The crime’s done. The punishment has been served.”

“Not if they’re going to appeal it!” Quinton clicked his fingers and his eyes brightened like he was suddenly seeing the wave Chandler was surfing. “All evidence will have to be retrieved. If they don’t find any...”

“Or it’s been changed...” Ziva added. She was starting to see, too.

“They could get out,” Chandler nodded. “They’d be acquitted. They’d be let out on the fact that either the trial was falsely presented the last time, convicting the opposing side in the process, or a lack of evidence to hold them in any longer at least.”

“I still don’t understand why the Mask,” Ziva said. So many of the same questions were still hanging in the air. “What are they going to do when they’re free? What’s the long-term here?”

“They’d have the Mask and they’d be able to do whatever they wanted,” Quinton said slowly. “I doubt they were just fishing in the computer systems for a way into the stocks. What would be the point? That kind of thing can be done from anywhere, by anyone. It's accessible for anyone."

Chandler tilted her head slightly. "We've got to still be looking at this wrong. It can't be all about the stocks. Money? Probably. But what if it's about what was *behind* the stocks. You said they were trying to access secrets?"

"Like undercut deals?" Ziva looked at Quinton sharply. "Is there a way to manipulate the markets?"

"I already said, with time, yeah," he repeated.

"Anything else?" Chandler pressed.

Quinton threw his arms up, clearly frustrated. "I don't know! I don't work in that life and I never want to. It's my father's business, not mine!"

Chandler edged towards him. "Okay, sorry," she said calmly, and even Ziva felt soothed by the change of her tone.

He sighed. "It's ok."

"We all have our pressure points," Chandler whispered, slightly ominously. Quinton didn't seem to hear but Ziva definitely did. She reached out and touched her hand, squeezing it, and Chandler smiled back. "One last thing?" she asked.

"Hit me with it," Quinton said, seemingly back to his normal self.

"Could someone, theoretically, be able to predict and tip someone else off to invest in a company or thing? Like, they could know or see the prices are rising, or are about to, so they tell someone to put their money in, which hikes the prices up even further, and then the starter of all this sells their shares? They'd make a killing if they bought when it wasn't fashionable too or whatever the fucking term is, and they'd only be making more the more they pushed. It's a cycle of money that's forever climbing in value."

Quinton laughed. Ziva watched as he grasped his necklace. "We know predicting things is possible," he said. "But my

Abnormality isn't always accurate, and it's both general *and* requires people to touch a crystal before I do to see anything."

"But it's possible?" Chandler didn't sound entirely sure.

"I don't know how likely it is for the less than one percent of the population who have the Abnormal genes to have a repeating gift though." Quinton shrugged.

"I'm likely to agree there. But what if instead they managed to create a programme that could work and slow down the stock system from the inside? They'd use *that* to predict and know where to target specifically so it's never miss-guided and looks real enough. They could make their bet and come out winners and cheats. They might fake problems or losses to keep things looking realistic and to avoid suspicion, but it would be *nothing* in the long-term."

"That's..." Ziva trailed off. She didn't know *what* to say. How had Chandler's mind worked so fast? Ziva could barely keep up, and she wasn't the one having to explain the thoughts to others.

"Computer science wrapping itself into a real-world juicy wrap," Chandler said.

"Juicy?" Quinton questioned, eyebrow raised.

"I'm on his side with questioning that word choice," Ziva said, pointing to Quinton with her thumb. "And this is a lot of presumptive work." She began to tick things off on her fingers. "We're assuming this person stole the Mask and was using it as a way of keeping their already acquired body-changing ability stable. We're assuming that they were in the building to gain information and plant more. We're assuming the planted information will be to get their friends free at an upcoming retrial. And then we're assuming the gained information will help them manipulate the stock-markets easier by slowing things down on the inside, leaving them as the only ones who have the real-time working market sheets, when they are all out and at home?"

She grunted, gripping her head. "It's more complicated than we thought."

Quinton offered her a smile. "Nothing's ever easy, not in this life or the one you left, it's just the perspective and thought process on what's 'complicated' that's changed."

Nodding in agreement, Ziva said, "I know. It's just a headache waiting to happen."

"At least we have options of where to look now." Chandler's voice brought Ziva back to their main focal point. "Some things are safe to assume. We took the Mask from him once, and we can do it again. He didn't seem strong enough on his own back in the stock building, and we nearly completely took him down."

Quinton snorted. "*You* nearly took him down."

Chandler ignored him, frowning. "We can also assume that, if he really isn't that strong on his own, and he's setting *something* up, he'll need his friends. So, the end result we can hope for is to either catch this guy as he goes for his friends, which is where I'd say he'd go first, or when the stocks crash and everyone is making losses."

"Or a board-meeting," Quinton added. Ziva must've looked confused because he explained. "If these people are planning on creating a programme, or have made one, they'd want the biggest profit possible. That could come from selling their very own illegal programme. What company wouldn't want the chance to jump ahead of others? The world rotates on money. If that's the case, they'll be hosting meetings with potential buyers."

"Isn't it too soon for that?" Ziva asked. "The programme might not be built yet. Plus, as you said, it's *illegal*."

"People with money don't tend to care about what's legal or not," Chandler quipped. "People with money can pretty much buy their way out of whatever they like, it's just a matter of how much it'll cost them."

"Probably a favour or two," Quinton said.

"Not actual money?" Ziva asked him.

"When everyone has money, it becomes less valuable in comparison to something they can use later on."

Chandler fixed him with a stern stare. "You sound like you know what you're talking about."

Quinton grinned slyly. "I *always* know what I'm talking about." Chandler rolled her eyes, and Quinton turned from her to face Ziva. "You can sell an idea," he said, going back on their conversation slightly. "And we're talking about some clever people here. One person set fire to two buildings for cover, went into private security systems for their computer access, and then *restole* the Mask, anticipating our moves to get here first despite there being no outward advertising on what *we* were doing or over-the-top publicity, if any, I can't remember, that the family want their Mask back."

"I still think they'd wait," Chandler argued. "They know we're onto them now. I wouldn't make any major plans right away."

"But the longer they wait, the more things slip away from them. And, to them, they've already wasted a lot of time."

"All the options we have are major plays," Ziva reminded them. She bit down on her bottom lip. "I think we need a change of scenery."

"What good will that do?" Chandler asked, not unkindly.

"We might be able to calm down? Get some tea to clear our heads?"

"It might help us think a little clearer," Quinton agreed, pointing a kind smile at Ziva, which she returned. "We need a break. We have our options and we can *assume* they won't do anything immediately, so we have at least a little time."

"Speak for yourself," Chandler mumbled. "I barely have elevator music playing inside my mind right now."

Ziva laughed and soon the other two joined, but it was meagre effort from them all. It was easy to see how tired they were.

Not long after they walked out of the apartment and into to a little tearoom Quinton knew of a few streets away. Ziva breathed in the smoky air of the city, but tried not to inhale too deeply – it was still the city.

This mission had nearly been over. Yet now, they had one more hurdle to jump over. How many times would that happen? Unwanted tears suddenly sprang up in her eyes, and she wiped at them furiously.

So maybe it hadn't gone over easy, and maybe it hadn't been all Ziva had initially thought it might be cracked up to be. She didn't really know what she'd been expecting when they'd been given this mission anyway. But she had no doubt now that they'd all see it through to the end. Knowing these people now, wanting to call them friends, Ziva knew they had some unified fight in them to get this job done – both out of pride and spite at this point. It was the will in them to finish what they started.

In that moment, Ziva *knew* what her answer would be when asked whether she would stay or go.

Ziva took a deep breath and the stinging in her eyes subsided. She marched on, and for the first time ever she was leading the way, footsteps echoing behind her. And it felt *good*.

CHAPTER THIRTY-EIGHT

CHANDLER

33rd Day of Autumn 2406

Cream cakes and sandwiches were spread across the table on tiny crystal-white plates. Some cakes were fruity or savoury, crunchy or delicate. Some sandwiches were spicy or plain, smooth or seeded. All of it was mouth-watering, which was curable by the pot of tea each customer had allotted to them.

Chandler reached for another sandwich. Pesto oozed out of the sides, dripping off a thick slice of tomato. She licked it before biting in, chewing to hide her groan of satisfaction. Tastes like this had never been in her life before; she hadn't been able to afford, let alone hide them.

Quinton had done well choosing this place, though Chandler wasn't happy that he was paying. Despite her lack of funds, she would've still preferred to pay her own way. Relying on other people, not just for food, was her least favourite thing.

But the food right now tasted too good to argue over, that and Quinton had already left little room for them to do so.

Ziva poured her tea and chugged it like she was in dehydrated in a desert. Chandler watched the girl's shoulders sink in a silent sigh. She couldn't blame her. They'd both chosen Pink Rose Tea – a speciality to this place, apparently – and Chandler wanted to buy herself enough to fill a tub and bathe in it. It was fruity and full, delicate but not weak. It was said to relieve stress, lessen menstrual cramps, and give a little energy boost.

Towers of canteens filled with all the tea types sat in pyramids behind the main counter. Chandler kept eyeing the Pink Rose Tea ones.

"Stop looking like you're going to rob the place," Quinton whispered, gently elbowing her.

"I'm not going to," she argued. "I'm just interested in purchasing some goods."

"I'd help you rob it," Ziva said, grinning. She lifted a cup to her mouth and sipped the dregs, then ate a bite of her raspberry and peach meringue tart.

Chandler ate the other half of her sandwich. "Maybe I *will* rob it? This tea? It's worth all the problems and prison time."

"I won't have you two dying for it," Quinton said, half hiding his grin behind his own cup. He'd picked a peachy smelling concoction Chandler hadn't heard the name of when he'd ordered. "I'll just buy you both some."

She shook her head. "I don't want charity."

"I'm not treating you as charity. I call it a 'welcome to the club' present."

Chandler looked at him then. "Still convinced I'll join permanently?"

"Not overly," he admitted. He lowered the cup but didn't let go of it. "You're rather hard to pin down. I've learnt that much. I can't tell what you're thinking at any point." He looked over at Ziva. "*Or* you. Right now, I can't tell if either of you want to stay or go."

Ziva laughed. "I like being thought of as mysterious."

Quinton's grin was full of amusement. "A truly mysterious wonder."

Chandler sat back, pulling her hands beneath the table. She clicked each knuckle in turn and then started to fiddle with her emerald ring. She'd already been given a life full of experiences and travel and *gifts*. She knew life at Redwing wouldn't always be the same as this, but she knew it would be different from what she'd had before all this. And she couldn't ask for more than that.

Ever since she'd woken up in that medical room, she'd known her true answer to what she'd do come the end of this mission. She'd probably known before even that, if she was being honest. But something in her ached whenever she wanted to admit it. It wasn't pride though. It was something deeper. Something rooted in complexity.

Wanting to dispel the thoughts, she snatched a cake and shoved it into her mouth whole. She struggled to chew but managed to keep her lips together, even if her cheeks did bulge obscenely. The centre exploded after a few moments, a melting taste of chocolate and raspberry coated her tongue.

'Café au lait' was a quirky place. The literal name meant *'coffee with hot milk'* and yet this place served mainly as a tea-house.

This café sat in the heart of this particular area, literally in the middle of the street. It hovered above the ground on stilts with other posts to keep it in place, allowing people and cars to still whizz around below it. The small elevator up was slightly bumpy, but totally worth it.

From inside, the traffic below couldn't be heard at all. Little round tables were spread about the round room, allowing up to six sets of four guests at once per table. While tablecloths covered the tops and green painted chairs were tucked beneath. The food and drinks had been brought out on old style serving trays by people dressed in jeans and t-shirts.

"If my mum could see me now..." Ziva sighed.

"She'd think you were some rich bitch," Chandler told her, winking. Ziva grinned and filled her cup more, drinking deeply once again. Chandler turned to Quinton. "I'm guessing your parents would be less than impressed to find you here with us scoundrels?"

Quinton leaned over and nicked a thin cake from Chandler's plate, and popped it into his mouth. "I hope so," he said. "And I quite like scoundrels."

"You would," Ziva commented.

He laughed, nearly choking. "I'm serious though about buying you that tea. If you want it, I *will* buy it. To say congratulations on this mission, if you won't take it for any other reason." He smiled again.

"Buy it for us *after* we've completed it?" Ziva suggested. Her brown cheeks flecked with pink. "Would be more meaningful then."

"And that brings us nicely back round to the task at hand," Chandler said. She sat back in her chair, her eyes still flicking to a thick slice of iced carrot cake. "We have to complete this mission somehow."

"Within the next day," Quinton murmured, but Chandler heard and knew that if she had then Ziva had, too.

"So what are we going to do about it?"

Ziva opened and closed her mouth several times, stumbling over whatever she was about to say, and then said nothing in the end. Quinton offered nothing either, only obnoxiously sipping his drink until it was gone and he was forced to put the cup down.

Chandler had nothing to add. Since they'd sat down, she'd thought over the whole mission, from beginning to end, trying to sift through it all in her mind to see what they could do from here and where they went wrong.

Eventually, Ziva broke the silence. "We randomly stumbled into them last time."

"That kind of chance won't come again," Quinton assured them. Chandler agreed.

"They won't be hosting any sort of meeting right now," Ziva said. "In my personal opinion anyway. It's too soon for them to show their faces, so be spotted so publicly."

Chandler nodded slowly. "They'd want to let everything they have fester for a while."

Quinton paused reaching for another cake. "*Fester*?"

Chandler shrugged. "I said what I said."

"So that rules out that option." He grabbed the cake he'd been after, a tiny pink square, and bit into it carefully. "But we'd already established that before we got here."

"What does that leave us with?" Ziva asked, again biting her bottom lip.

"The retrial or going back to the stock-building," Chandler said.

"Why would they go back to the building? You said they'd managed to move files and then set fires to cover their tracks. It seems like they don't need that place anymore. Unless they needed to test something?"

"Or maybe they're lying low?" Quinton popped in the rest of the cake. "They might think we're coming after them—"

"We are," Ziva cut in confidently.

"We are," he agreed. "So they might be hiding up somewhere."

"And we'd never find them," Chandler grumbled. She lowered her voice despite the level of noise in the café being a normal volume that could hide their chatter. "But you saw his face, how he'd *sounded*. He was too happy, too pleased, to have the Mask back. They had *planned* to get it back."

Quinton shook his head, letting a few white and red strands fall free from the band. "That leaves us, once again, with the retrial. And that's a risky move too, since they only just snatched and rearranged the inside files on the case."

Chandler blanched. "Or not." She cracked her knuckles as her companions' eyes turned to her. "They could've arranged for a retrial date months ago because it's never easy to get a date. Plans for this could've been starting *months ago*. We've been thinking of the Mask as the first piece of this puzzle, but what if it's the last?" She shifted in her seat and her gaze connected with Ziva's. "You said you had a plan?"

Ziva nodded and touched the tip of her finger to the cake in front of her, turning its naturally creamy colour to a dark blue. "I *think* so. It's not much..."

Quinton leaned forwards, inserting himself into Chandler's sight. "You're thinking," he commented. She turned to face him fully and found him closer than she thought he'd be. "Do we need to be worried?"

"In here now," Chandler tapped her head, "there's a full orchestra ringing."

"I better be playing the drums."

"*Ziva* is on drums," she said. "*You* are commanding the triangle." Around her, the water in the air shifted. She felt the movement and how minimal it was, but it was enough. "I think I know where they are and where the Mask will be."

Quinton was already moving to stand. "I'll put in an order for two tins of tea." He launched himself towards the counter, too far out of reach to stop by the time Chandler realised what he'd said.

Ziva leaned across the table to touch Chandler's hand, knotting their fingers together. "Are you sure about this?" she whispered.

"No," Chandler said, looking at their hands. She gazed up, smiling half-heartedly. "Are you sure about your plan?"

"Not even a little bit."

"Then we're perfect." She squeezed her new friend's hand. They had no plan, no execution, one day to complete it all, and only a minor hunch to go on. "Whatever happens—"

"We're in this together," Ziva told her, squeezing her hand back. "Stuck in the mud until we pull each other free."

"Together."

Ziva offered the warmest smile yet. "Until the very end."

CHAPTER TWENTY-NINE
ZIVA

33rd Day of Autumn 2406

Ziva tugged on her borrowed suit several times. The jacket fit awkwardly; the shoulders were wide and the arms too long. The matching trousers had been pinned on the inside to allow a straighter line on the leg, and every so often, one caught her skin and she had to bite her lip from crying out.

Her necklace jangled against her neck and moved whenever she breathed. These days it seemed like she was taking air deeper into her lungs.

The arrestor centre's front desk was unoccupied for a while, leaving Ziva to wait awkwardly by it. She tapped the top of it after a minute, clinking her new fake nails against it. Quinton waited at her side, more patient than she thought he would be capable of. She guessed she should've given him more credit for being able to focus, but he just seemed so loose sometimes.

She turned to him. "What's *home* like normally?" she whispered. The thought had plagued her mind for days, and now she was getting closer to having to go back there, she wanted to know the answer. Plus, she wanted to take her mind of the silence for a moment.

He smiled down at her in a way that said he was intrigued by what she'd asked but not surprised at the question. "Busy and quiet," he said. "There are days where all we do is run around the garden, and there are days when we have to come and go completely."

"The down days, what do you do?"

"It depends. There's always *something* happening. The Grittal boys make bets on almost anything to keep everyone entertained, but on a Friday night they host a special games night on the first floor. We play cards or games based on what they choose." He laughed at something. "There was a great Twister incident of about a year ago. The new version had just dropped? Some of us played and it ended in a joint loss situation. It wasn't pretty."

"That sounds like fun," she said honestly.

"It's a classic. Monopoly *is* banned in the house though."

Ziva raised her eyebrows. "What? Why?"

"There was a total hotel and bankruptcy incident two years ago. *I* didn't, but some got into actual physical, powerful fights. Maggie got in between before things got overly dangerous and took the board, burning it in front of us. No one's dared buy another one because no one's seen her act that way before and frankly we're all too scared."

"Maggie did that?"

He nodded. "It was a dark day."

"Because of a boardgame?"

"She's never acted like it since, but no one's forgotten."

Ziva whistled lowly. "What else do you do?"

Quinton laughed. "You're really interested." It wasn't a question.

"I want to know what I might be getting in to."

Raising a brow, Quinton smiled. "Some nights, Aleema plays her piano for us, though we all have to go up to the attic space for that. That's where the piano is and it can't really be moved. Other days we ride the horses out in the long gardens we own. They're called Mouse and Mountain. I don't—"

Ziva giggled. "Who named them?"

"I think it was Violette when she first arrived quite a few years ago." He visibly grimaced.

She could see the distress and back-tracked to alleviate it. "What else?"

"There are also nights where we just order take-out and completely pig out until we physically cannot move. We don't always hang out, but we do when we can. We're our own kind of weird and wonderful family."

"Doesn't sound terrible."

His smile was warm. "Doesn't at all, does it." He opened his mouth like he was about to say something else, but the opening of a door behind the desk silenced him.

A man dressed in a black suit walked through the door from a backroom, tipping his hat off his head to sit behind the reception desk. His head was bald, but his smile made him look younger than he probably was; lines in his skin said he was at least close to middle-age.

"How many I help you today?" he asked politely, his accent local.

"Hi," Ziva flashed her best adult-approved smile. "We're college students from down the road." She gestured to herself and Quinton. "We were wondering if you were open to taking us on for experience."

The man raised his fair eyebrows. "Are you looking to go into arrestor work in the future?"

Quinton nodded firmly, standing up straighter somehow in

the process. "We are. My father was an arrestor, worked all the night shifts, but taught me the importance of protection and safe-keeping."

"And you?" The man stared at Ziva pointedly.

"My dad was in traffic," Ziva added. "I want a little more than that."

Not liking how the lie sounded, she bit down on her lip. It sounded real enough, like her father *could* have been an arrestor, but she wasn't sure she had come across convincing. She wondered if it sounded off because the truth was far less than what she was trying to display it as. Her father was a trash collector, her mother a singer in a local bar, and her grandparents had been teachers. Their real pasts had been why they'd wanted Ziva to take a different root, a higher one.

Ziva didn't want any of it.

She didn't want to be a doctor or nurse or teacher. There was nothing wrong with those professions. It was just that her parents had been the ones to pick them out for her without asking what *she* wanted.

The man behind the desk nodded. "Why don't you have a seat?" He pointed to a selection of ten chairs that were placed in the open-doorway room across from him. He slid over some pamphlets when they turned back to him. "Read through these. When you're done, we'll discuss further. We certainly *do* have some vacancy spots open, and we're always willing to help fellow business families' new generations getting their start." Quinton led off, Ziva following. But then the man called them back and they turned. "One last thing. You're not *Abnormals* are you?"

Ziva hadn't been asked the question in what felt like weeks, so she stumbled slightly despite not moving. Quinton answered for them both.

"Of bloody *course not!*" he spat. "Would the likes of *them* even *think* about joining an establishment like this?" He fake shivered, quite convincingly to Ziva. "What would they even know about law and order?"

The man nodded aggressively with a new gleam in his eye. "You'd be surprised," he chuffed. "We've had a few, granted. Though I suppose, they were just kids, asking about careers. Had to tell them no, of course. And you're right. They know nothing about law and order. All we do is spend most of our precious time rounding them up and shutting their shit down."

Quinton's grin was more like a snarl as he said, "I can't wait."

He put a hand over the small of Ziva's back and led her into the doorless room where they took seats beside one another. They opened their pamphlets and began to 'read' – Ziva actually started to acknowledge the words, but Quinton kept fidgeting.

"I don't like it here," he mumbled.

"Why?" she whispered back. "Is it the fear of being caught or the idea of them actually accepting you into a programme that's making you uncomfortable? Or is it because we are what they hate?"

He gave her an unimpressed look. "I've been close to the law before. Mostly working with them. Before *this*." Ziva knew what he was referring. "Never once have I enjoyed it."

"I think most of us have had a run-in somewhere. It's in their nature to hunt us and for us to run away." Ziva lowered her stinging eyes to the leaflet, the words blurry. "Why do they hate us so much?"

"Because we have gifts they don't. But even if everyone had one, we'd probably still all fight." He wrapped an arm over Ziva's shoulders and pulled her into him. He was comfortable to lay against, so she sank in. "Not that suffering through several world-wide viruses to get a gene mutation was really recommended."

Ziva sniffed against him. "Jealousy?"

Quinton pulled back slightly. He'd fully dyed the strands back to red, the tone more dark cherry than the original crimson. "That's part of it I think," he said. "But there's some kind of rightfulness they all feel, too. Like, they're jealous of our power, but also we're something they can't understand. So what have the humans always done when there's something they don't understand?"

"They push it away," she answered.

"They *lock it* away," he corrected. "The world always hides and hates what it doesn't like or can't become."

Ziva shook her head, sighing. It made sense. Time and time again she'd seen it happen. People would hate others for what they didn't know or didn't have. To be jealous of a gift given through bodily mutation was ridiculous, and then to hate that person was worse.

If the shoe was on the other foot, Ziva just knew she wouldn't hate someone for what they had. If her brother's or sister's had been the ones to be given the power over her, she'd support them and love them in all the ways that made them special. It would just be another thing that made them, *them*.

The differences of the world were what made things so special. But, apparently, not to everyone they didn't. It was just one more thing to fight over.

"Are you alright?" Quinton whispered.

"I will be," Ziva said, smiling. She still felt tense, like she was balancing on the edge between crying and not, but she knew she *would* be ok, in time. There were just some things the world had to accept and so did she.

Quinton bent, wrapping her sideways into him, and kissed the top of her head. Ziva's body warmed at such a tender gesture. "Don't let the rest of the world try to rub you down, Ziva. You are meant to be the way you are. The universe designed you. Believe that you are precious and no less than awesome."

"No less than awesome," she repeated. "You know, you're quite comfy to lean on."

"Anytime you want to lean on me, I'll be free," he laughed.

"How are you getting on?"

The new voice cut through their moment. Ziva peered up at the arrestor from before standing in the doorway. He leaned against the frame, arms folded, eyes watching curiously. Ziva wondered how much he'd seen about their exchange, but he didn't comment, she surmised he just saw that they'd been bent together with Quinton's arm over her. It was a friendly gesture, and that was how Ziva had taken the entire exchange, even if her cheeks felt a little flushed.

Ziva noted the heavily padded vest the man now wore overtop of his clothes, and she smiled. Out the corner of her eye, she watched Quinton smile too, but it was tighter, more reserved.

"We're good," Quinton answered, pulling away from Ziva without moving too far. "I've just finished, anyway."

"I think I've read this one before," Ziva said, waving her pamphlet. "Did some of you come to our college last year for a careers day? I think I picked one up there."

The man nodded. "We visited many colleges last year, so it's possible."

"What kind of vacancies are we looking at being able to fulfil as work experience?" Quinton asked.

Ziva shut her brain off as the man began to drone on. She couldn't keep up with listening to his dull voice.

"Interesting," Quinton said some moments later, dragging Ziva back into the conversation. "I'm definitely interested in the custody receptionist position. I'm not much for fighting or working the streets."

"That kind of work takes a special kind of person," the man

agreed. "Have to have bones of steel and the legs of an athlete to keep up with the law-breakers who run." He laughed, the sound grating, like a back-firing engine of a private shuttle.

Ziva fake yawned and held up a hand to cover it when the man looked at her. "I do apologise," she said, not meaning a single word. "It's been a long day."

"Visiting hours end at midnight." The man glanced at the thick-strapped phone he wore on his right wrist. "But if everyone leaves before, we shut up early. You've got about thirty minutes before it's midnight to ask more questions if you're staying. We have another guest arriving soon, a lawyer."

"A lawyer?" Quinton pressed. "That also sounds like an exciting job!"

"Sounds like too much hard work," the man dismissed. "Too many rules to follow or to work around. It's a stricter way of life."

"I haven't got the grades for that kind of job," Ziva lied. In school, she'd always had the best grades. Until her power had presented. Then her grades had – not so really – mysteriously tumbled.

A door down the hallway opened minutes later as the man droned on again. Quinton listened well, as he had from the start, nodding and answering, but it was faint and distanced to Ziva.

Someone came through. At first, Ziva thought it was another arrestor or receptionist – the dark clothing looked like a giveaway. But when they turned, she could see the suit and the extra pointy shoes. They didn't quite *fit*. Not into their clothes, but their whole self didn't quite fit into the world around it.

The man before Ziva and Quinton apologised and dashed off to greet the newcomer. Ziva swung her entire body to face Quinton, elbowing him just once.

Quinton looked out of the doorway and back in a second. "You sure?"

Ziva shook her head but she trusted in Chandler.

Chandler who was back at the hotel and not here because having three Abnormals come along to a police station was three to many and looked like a guilty confessional. Chandler whose idea and thought this moment had brewed from.

Soundlessly, Ziva stood and shuffled to the open doorway. Both the man who'd spoken to her and Quinton before, and the visitor turned as if sensing her there.

Ziva smiled overly sweetly and walked down the hall, past them, to the bathrooms. She slipped inside but left the door cracked open. Her breaths came out in unsteady huffs, her heart racing inside her chest. Her blood drove around her body and her hands grew clammy.

If my mother could see me now.

She tucked the hand that wasn't propping the door open at her side. Toilets weren't the best place to hide, but there was nowhere else she could gain access to at short noticed, and this room at least smelt clean and bleached.

As her heartrate began to slowly normalise, a figure stepped into the thin crack of vision she had. She could see enough and focused for extra measure.

In one swoop, Ziva yanked the door open. It didn't crash into the wall behind her like she wanted but it had the desired effect. The figure turned.

Ziva saw swirls of black and dives of gold in her mind. The colours especially. It was a plan on a whim, a last-ditch attempt to make something work. Her reasoning was that if she could take the freedom of the Mask away, how it chose to present itself, it would then take the freedom it offered to others away, taking away how others wanted to be presented.

With the image of the black and gold Mask solid in her memory, she pushed it from her mind, her fingers twitching at her sides.

And the unfitting figure's face began to morph.

The Mask of Iris became stunning white and silver on their face, and as crystal clear as day.

Ziva didn't give them a single chance. She didn't even smile. Just yelled, "Abnormal!"

CHAPTER THIRTY
QUINTON

34th Day of Autumn 2406

Yells and shouts of warnings flew through the halls.

The arrestors physically threw themselves at the false lawyer, restraining and pinning him to the ground with their own bodies. The man's face was a picture-perfect example of shock and horror combined.

Ziva didn't stop crying for help until a female arrestor came to console her. Then she'd winked behind the woman's back to Quinton.

Quinton had to watch it all with a hand over his mouth to stop from laughing.

The false lawyer was dragged away and it took another hour of paperwork and people scuttling about like beetles before Quinton and Ziva were free to leave the arrestor centre.

Stepping outside into the brisk night's air, Quinton grabbed Ziva's arm and had pulled her into a thin alleyway. There, they laughed. Laughed and screamed and bounced up and down on their feet with joy. Because they were free from the entire mission.

Chandler had been right. She'd suggested that, with the Mask back in his possession, the man would try and see his friends to possibly finalise *their* plan on this retrial. That meant he would have to visit them in the arrestor centre. Of course, he wouldn't have shown up as himself, so, alongside Ziva's half thought through plan, Chandler had had the idea to trap the man where he would be caught no question and seen for what he was. They were using an Abnormal against himself.

And Quinton's father had done the rest of the dirty work – by initially trapping the group and keeping tabs on the one missing from the collection – himself without knowing it.

After Ziva had nearly screamed the bricks off the building, the arrestors had come. They'd each taken one look at the false lawyer in the Mask and had recognised the face beneath it. Quinton's father had distributed the identity of the man to all police stations *before* the incident at the stock building the other day. Quinton hadn't known that his father had discovered the identity of the missing man, but for once, he was glad for his father's secrets. They'd worked in his favour this time.

The Mask itself had been prized off the man's face and seized. Ziva had explained, through magnificently performed tears, that she'd seen the man's face shift and that was why she'd called for immediate help – she'd seen an Abnormal, and that was of course scary to anyone. The arrestors had taken the Mask and it had turned black, and then they'd recognised it for what it was. One had gone to ring the family they knew it belonged to originally, and not the museums it had come to be held by – Quinton's father had distributed that information on the family too, pairing it with the man as a warning that he may move with a disguise. The family had arrived barely five minutes or so before Quinton and Ziva had left. The family hadn't noticed them.

Quinton still hated the fact that he, Ziva, and Chandler had been duped into believing the man before had been of the family. But it didn't matter now. It was done with.

Eventually he and Ziva calmed, and they walked back out to the street. They moved with long, purposeful strides. Around them, the world was asleep, clueless as to what had just happened right below their noses.

This night was theirs.

All of a sudden, Ziva pulled herself free and started running. Quinton glared around wildly to figure out why, and stopped when he spotted Chandler up ahead. He hadn't seen her arrive and step out under a streetlight.

Ziva ran straight for her, launching her body forward so they were wrapped around one another in a tight embrace. Laughter flooded Quinton's ears, and as he approached, he could see how tightly the girls held onto each other.

Before he could protest, Ziva yanked him into the fold. After several gleeful moments, they broke apart, standing as their own selves, but the smiled remained. They were a team now, a unit of three.

"Do I take that hug as a sign that it's over?" Chandler asked. She looked between them, though Quinton noticed how she glanced over his face quicker than Ziva's.

Ziva had been the executor. While it had been Chandler's thoughts that had led them to think the man would turn up to talk to his friends wearing the Mask, it had been Ziva who'd thought of a possible way to combat the Mask's defences to reveal what lay beneath. She'd kept most of her plan to herself – how she would execute it and when exactly kept the tightest to her chest. Quinton had had to trust her and he was glad he had.

Ziva nodded. "It's over," she confirmed.

"You really did it?" Chandler asked, sounding rather unsure, while staring straight at Quinton.

He smiled. "*Ziva* really did it."

Pink graced Ziva's cheeks, made visible by the streetlights. She had used the Mask's gift against itself. That was what he'd realised she'd done afterwards.

It was *genius*. Pure genius.

Ziva tipped her head to the starry sky, smiling. "What do we do now?"

"Yeah," Chandler said, folding her arms. "We've built up to this and now it's just... done."

"Well." Quinton snuck a glance at Chandler, though wondered why he was so unsure about looking at her like he was worried he'd be caught for doing something he shouldn't be. Her face appeared silver under the lights, like pure moonlight resided under her skin. He swallowed thickly and averted his gaze quickly. "Our bags have already gone back, so it's time we did."

"And then food?" Ziva asked, lowering her head.

He laughed. "Then the biggest celebration meal *ever*!"

Ziva walked off with a spring in her step, even swinging around a few light-posts. Quinton followed, Chandler at his side. They were the only three people around.

He looked at his company as they walked down streets in silence. They were *good*. Not just good people, but good at what they could do. With more practise and experience, they could even be some of the *greats*. Quinton had never learnt how Abnormals were chosen to this job – there were groups all around the world, clusters of people doing the same as them, keeping the world turning as one – but they did it somehow. And both Chandler and Ziva really could make it work.

Quinton had been before these doors many times before. So why now did he have a weird pit opening in his stomach?

Chandler pushed open the front doors as if they were nothing but an entryway, yet Quinton felt like they were a barrier he had to cross through. His company went on, arms looped together, and he trailed behind.

The first thing he noticed was that the lights were shut off which was unusual. There was normally nearly always a light somewhere burning into the night. There had to be with so many people in one building.

The second thing was the silence.

Being past midnight, it meant most would be in bed. Strangely though, he couldn't hear the piano. Either Aleema had taken to her room and would come out later, she wouldn't come out at all, or she was playing but the melody was gentle and quiet.

"Who's there?"

Quinton turned at the sound of Maggie's delicate voice. "It's us, Mags," he answered.

A light flicked across his face, burning his eyes and leaving circles in his vision when it dipped away. He groaned and rubbed at them like it would make a difference. The main foyer lights burst into life a breath later.

Quinton stared at Maggie. She carried an old fashioned looking light in her hand – something burning inside a glass and metal cage – and wore a heavy wool dressing-gown. Her feet were shoved into breaking slippers, and her grey hair was wilder than normal. A glass in her other hand said she'd just come from the kitchen.

"You're up late," Maggie complained as a caring mother fawning over her disobeying children would. "Why are you all dressed and running through this house like there's a marathon to be won? You have beds, don't you?"

Quinton sighed but couldn't stop the smile he felt from forming. Nearly everyone at Redwing saw her as a grandmother figure to them, including himself. "Mags?" he said. "We've just returned from a mission."

Maggie's eyes widened and roamed over them all. "Right," she nodded. "Right! I suppose you'll need me and Praxis for a debrief?"

"Let them go to bed." Violette stepped out from the drawing room. Her clothes suggested she hadn't yet gone to bed herself. "They can debrief in the morning, can't they?"

Violette's eyes found Quinton's and he jolted when he saw her sneer lessen. He was suspicious of it, and that suspicion bloomed in his chest like a flower. He tore his gaze away.

"I suppose they can," Maggie decided. She was the original owner and leader of Redwing after all. Her word was final. "As long as the mission *is* complete..."

"It is," Ziva declared, though rather timidly.

Maggie nodded. "Very well then, young ones. Go to bed, but we'll expect you first thing." She turned away and walked right up the stairs, holding onto the banister for support as she climbed.

Violette bumped right into Quinton's shoulder as she passed. She glared, but in a quick change she raised an eyebrow with a slight smirk when he'd expected a hateful glare. Something old and forgotten overtook the suspicion in his body. She was gone before he could think much of it and he cursed at himself, at his body, for remembering what he honestly didn't want anymore.

He *was* confused at why Violette had stepped in and suggested they go to bed, but he wasn't going to let the opportunity slide. Exhaustion could only be held back for a little while.

Turning to his companions, Quinton saw Ziva and Chandler searching around cautiously, like this was their first time seeing this place and they were waiting for a trap to spring.

"Shall we?" he offered, waving an arm forwards.

Their travel-cases and things were bundled up beside the staircase, Quinton realised as he looked over. The helpers of

Redwing must have collected and put them there, ready to sort through later. Maybe in the morning Quinton would come and help put them away?

"We shall," Ziva said. She grabbed Quinton's outstretched hand, dragging him along, with Chandler on her other side in exactly the same dragged state.

They bounded up the stairs as a trio, just as they'd done everything else in the past ten days. Quinton was somewhat sad to see the last step, like it suggested that by reaching it their time as a team was coming to an end.

Though, the meaning of 'end' still depended...

As they reached the girls' rooms, Ziva ran back to Quinton, standing on her toes to kiss him on the cheek. He broke out laughing, even more so when she went and kissed Chandler's cheek, whose face lit up brightly.

"It's been such a pleasure getting to know you both," Ziva whispered in the confines of the corridor. "You really have become my friends."

Quinton bowed his head. "The pleasure and friendship has been all mine."

"Do we have to do the exercise in the morning?" Quinton shook his head – no new recruits had to on their first day and no mission taker had to on the day after arriving back. Ziva sighed, nodding. "I'll see you at the debriefing." She opened her door and slipped inside, the lock shifting with a small yet audible *click*.

Quinton turned to see Chandler watching Ziva's door. "Chandler?" he called to her.

She faced him. "Mm, yeah?"

"Do you have a minute more in you? I have something to show you."

Her eyebrows rose. "Something to show me? We may be fake fiancés but there was a line I drew."

Unexpected laughter burst from his lips.

Quickly, he shoved a hand over his mouth to stop it. Behind him, Flora's door opened. Her head poked out carefully, though her eyes were still half-closed. She gave a small wave and retreated again.

"It's something I've *drawn*," he explained quietly.

Chandler's mouth quirked into a smile. "Alright," she agreed. "I'm probably not going to sleep much anyway."

Quinton wanted to ask why, but didn't. He knew many reasons for why sleep could evade someone or it may want to be avoided. So he led on down the hallway to his room, unlocking the door and ushering Chandler inside.

The room was just as he'd left it, maybe a tad tidier. It smelt odd, however. It could've been his aftershave and the smell of fresh sheets on his bed, but since he hadn't been around any of it for days, it was like his nose was taking it all in anew. He noticed the small bag he'd taken on the mission with him by his bed; it must've been returned earlier than the rest because it was more manageable. He went to it and pried out his sketchbook. There was an unspoken rule around Redwing that no one was to look inside the sketchbook, not unless he was there or had given them permission.

"Here," he said, flipping to the right page.

Chandler crept closer, peering at the image. She made no sound and didn't move. He watched her for a reaction and only saw her eyes glide over the page, taking it all in.

"Is that us?" She slid her eyes up to his.

He nodded slowly, and she went back to staring at the charcoal he'd scribbled on the page. His own eyes slipped to the image, at the lines of their faces, of their hands clasped between their chests.

"When did you draw this?" Her voice was quiet compared to normal.

"I told you to remind me when we came back here so I could give it to you," he said, ignoring her question.

"This isn't the same one. It's not the original."

His mouth parted in a silent gasp. "You can tell?"

Chandler reached out and grazed a finger over the paper, nowhere near the drawing. "Something about it is different," she told him. "I can see that, I just don't know *what*."

"The first version I drew... Something wasn't right about it," he admitted. "This better version... It's yours now."

In one swoop, he grabbed the page and tore it from the bindings. Chandler gasped at his side. The picture remained as whole as it had been and he passed it over into her awaiting hands.

"I'm going to frame it," she told him. "Hang it in my room. Maybe on the ceiling so I can stare up at it."

Quinton smiled and all the words he wanted to say died on his tongue. She was too focused on the picture to notice, but before he could figure something to say, his door opened.

"Honey, I'm home!"

Gretchen stood in the doorway, arms wide, with thick-eyeliner and blonde hair jutting out at all angles. Quinton ran at her, lifting her in to a spinning hug. She felt warm and familiar, and when he put her down he noticed a few burnt patches of skin around her neck and face.

"It's *so* good to see you!" Quinton half-cheered, still cautious that people were sleeping in rooms near him. "When did you get back?"

"Earlier today. Been asleep ever since," Gretchen said, her smile as big as she could make it. She dove round Quinton. "Hello?"

"Gretchen," Quinton turned, "this is Chandler. One of the new abbies."

"Smashin'," Gretchen grinned.

"Hello," Chandler acknowledged with a nod. She slid her gaze back to Quinton directly, leaving him to feel the weight of it as if there was something written in them he couldn't read. "Thanks for the artwork. I meant what I said about framing it."

"It's frame worthy!" Quinton agreed.

"I'll see you at the debrief." Chandler walked to the door, keeping her head down, and let it shut behind her.

Gretchen whirled on him immediately. Her beady eyes dried to dig holes into his face. "Artwork? You *never* give your drawings away."

He shrugged, though his heart skipped once. "I've given you the ones you wanted of yourself."

"I'm your best friend. I have best friend rights!"

"It's one drawing, Gritty."

"But it's not though."

"She had one piece of paper. It definitely *was* one drawing."

"Was it the one of the vision?" She wiggled his eyebrows independently. "The one *you* featured in?" He stayed silent. "And you're lettin' her keep it?" He glanced over and saw how wicked Gretchen's smile was. He groaned while she threw herself onto the bed beside him. "Well, my dear friend. We 'ave a *lot* to catch up on, don' we."

CHAPTER THIRTY-ONE
QUINTON

34th Day of Autumn 2406

A helper knocked on the door before Quinton had even rolled out of bed. He knew he probably should've been downstairs hours ago, but he didn't care.

Gretchen hadn't left his room for hours, wanting updates, sharing her own, and so he'd wanted as much sleep as he could get. If there had been a problem, someone would've come to get him before now. With any luck, Ziva and Chandler would also be late.

He slipped into some trousers and clambered for the door. The helper bowed and entered when granted permission, scurrying to the bathroom first. Quinton snatched up an old jumper, slinging it on, and slipped into some already half-laced boots before leaving.

In the hallway, he could hear all sorts of voices. He groaned. By the amount he could hear, it seemed there was no training this morning, meaning everyone would be everywhere. Quinton huffed, making sure to stomp as loudly as he could. He touched his wrist as he walked, feeling for a band and tying his hair back when he found one. With the red back, he somehow felt more like himself again – not that hair colour made a person – but he had also liked the white while it'd lasted, it just wasn't meant to stay long-term. Gretchen had roared with laughter when he'd told her about it.

Just as he'd suspected, there was no practise. All recruits were gathered at the table at the back of the Mansion behind the stairs. They were eating and laughing and talking as helpers went about replacing plates or refilling teapots.

"Well, if it isn't Queenie." Seamus' voice reached him first, cutting through the other noise. He was sat one seat away from his brother, making sure there was space between them, probably just for Quinton. Quinton took it. "And how has our Queen been? It sounds like you've had an adventure out in the big wide world!"

"Oh, do tell," Doug begged. At some point in Quinton's absence, Doug had shaved his head. He wondered if it'd been a bet.

Quinton glanced at Gretchen who sat opposite them. She gave a noncommittal shrug. He sighed before answering. "It was fine."

"No mission is ever *just fine*," Doug argued.

"Yeah," Seamus backed up. "What about blood? Guts? Gore?"

Doug lent forwards to look at his brother. "I heard there were some sexy times."

Seamus fake gasped. "How sexy are we talking?"

For a split second, Quinton wished that he could shoot lasers out of his eyes or fingertips rather than read the future.

He glared at Gretchen, who shrugged again. He'd shared with her the most important parts of the mission. The small details he hadn't bothered with, they hadn't mattered. This so-called 'rumour' was nothing more than the twins insinuating and trying to stoke a fire for a reaction for no real reason. But there wouldn't be one because, unlike what they implied, nothing sexy had happened. Unless they counted sitting on a bed, talking, while playing fake fiancés, before jumping out of a window sexy? Not that he'd ask them. That would just lead to *more* questions.

As if thinking such things had power, Chandler emerged from somewhere else in the building, arm in arm with Ziva. They both sat next to Gretchen, as they were the only free spaces at the table.

"Sleep well?" Doug asked, turning his short attentions to the newcomers. Quinton inwardly groaned.

"Been better," Chandler answered. Quinton blinked at the lack of a barking retort.

"Maybe I should come up and take a look to see what's stopping you?" Seamus offered. "I could probably fix what ails you, make you relax."

Chandler looked right at him. "Maybe you could."

Seamus elbowed Quinton and leant into him. "You hearing this?"

"We're *all* hearing this," Aleema said form the far left end of the table. She rolled her eyes, clearly unimpressed. "We don't *want* to hear it."

Doug ignored Aleema, leaning in on his elbows. "And what do you think ails you?"

Chandler gave the twins a smile – Quinton had seen it before and his eyes widened. "What's stopping me from sleeping is your god-awful voice which is also, coincidently, what ails me now too."

Doug choked and toppled backwards. Quinton grabbed onto the back of his chair so he didn't crash to the floor in a heap, though he did debate letting him. Seamus spat out his drink on the other side, narrowly missing Wane, his other brother, who sat beside him.

Cheers erupted. Flora climbed from her seat, clapping. Aleema did, too. Dalton laughed so hard he started coughing; he had to thump his own chest. Gretchen whistled into her glass. Wane whooped at his brothers' downfall. Helen, the girl with one eye who was also the youngest at the table at thirteen, thumped her fists over and over. Ziva notably snorted into her tea.

Quinton held his breath for a moment, and Chandler beamed at him before she looked away.

Dough clutched a hand over his chest. "She shot *me*!"

"Powerful," Seamus said, smiling and nodding at Chandler.

"I've never liked someone more from the first second of meeting 'em," Gretchen said. A chorus of agreement started up.

"You lot are *rude*," Doug chided, trying to pout but failing.

"We're fine," Dalton argued. He'd finally stopped choking, but his skin was still flushed.

"Nothing wrong with us at all," Helen agreed.

"There will be if you don't get your arses out of those chairs for training in five minutes."

Everyone stopped, their happy moods evaporating instantly.

Violette stood away from the table, arms folded over her chest. Quinton turned to glare with the rest of them at the table, and noticed how her top exposed a lot of skin. He barely contained his eye-roll.

"Now!" she yelled.

The table erupted. The recruits filed out, taking drinks or stuffing one last mouthful of food in before they ran. Eventually, only Ziva, Chandler, and Quinton remained.

"You three are wanted in Praxis' office," Violette proclaimed, and turned away.

"I guess our party's over," Ziva commented.

Any party's over when she walks in, he thought sourly. Raising he drank the contents in one gulp.

Praxis' office was freezing.

Quinton had felt the cold last night when they'd returned to Redwing, but inside had been warm. Except, apparently, for this room. Either the heating wasn't working or Praxis had switched it off himself.

Praxis sat behind his desk, sipping from a giant mug that had the letter P in bold on the front. Quinton tried not to laugh at the badly rubbed out letters the Grittal twins had added to make it spell out PENIS in big and bold.

Somewhere along the walk, Violette had disappeared, probably either to train with the guards leading the morning's exercise or to screw one of the ones off duty; she had a penchant for that kind of thing. Maggie, however, was at Praxis' side. *She* was always a woman of duty and love.

Maggie smiled. "I see you're awake," she said. "Did you sleep well?" Her eyes surveyed them all.

"Not bad, thank you," Ziva said politely.

"Like a baby," Quinton joked, though it felt like he'd barely slept a moment.

"Yes," Chandler said. "I slept."

Maggie nodded three times, once for each of them. "Then, shall we get down to what we're here for?"

Praxis sat forwards, staring more at Chandler and Ziva than Quinton. "A debrief is a report of the mission that was undertaken, relaying everything that happened, to whatever detail can be managed," Praxis explained. Quinton still remembered the first time he'd heard the explanation. "We simply ask you a load of questions and you respond how you see fit. It's a way to unload, essentially, but it makes a report we keep on file."

"If you want to debrief in private, don't hesitate to ask for that," Maggie added.

"I'm fine," Ziva said, then peered at her company. "Are you two?"

Quinton nodded. "Couldn't be better."

"Sure," Chandler agreed.

"The file is stored away where only I or Maggie may find them," Praxis said. Quinton was surprised to hear that even Violette wasn't welcome to that knowledge, despite being a leader. "We need to take notes in case we have to come back to these points or something mentioned in the future. For example, if you are injured at some point and it may be unrelated or related to the case. We'd be able to count in or count out possibilities."

"It's a record of everything," Chandler said simply. "You meant that."

Praxis sighed. "I sometimes forget you lot aren't *kids*."

"Helen's still a teen," Quinton said aloud. He didn't mention that Helen had been here nearly the longest out of them all, however, brought in as a baby left on the doorstep one night.

Maggie stepped around the desk and leant back against it, the action making her appear younger somehow. "How are you all?"

"Tired," Quinton admitted. "But good." Chandler and Ziva nodded beside him.

Praxis began to take notes.

"The mission is complete?" Maggie asked next.

"It is," Ziva confirmed.

"And the Lost Mask is no longer lost?"

"No," Quinton said. "It's been found and returned."

"What about injuries? Were there any sustained in the process of this mission?"

Chandler touched the side of her head, almost absentmindedly. "I sustained a minor head concussion," she confessed. "I was taken to a medical centre." The bruising around her eye was fading but there was still a splash of green and yellow on the skin.

Maggie leant forwards to study it as if only now noticing. "Interesting." She moved back again. "You said the Mask was returned."

"Twice," Ziva blurted.

"Twice?" Praxis stopped writing to raise an eyebrow at them.

"Yes," Quinton confirmed.

Maggie's grip on the desk seemed to tighten. "Why don't you tell us what happened?"

Between the three of them, they launched into their story, relaying every detail they could.

Ziva told of her hotel vantage point view as Quinton and Chandler had infiltrated a party. Chandler shared about the buildings on fire and all of them running. Quinton spoke of visiting his parents for clues about this bigger-than-they-thought mission. There were words of visions, of tea, of the cold, of shuttle rides, and finally of the police station where it had all ended.

There was so much information that Quinton would never have been able to keep up if he hadn't been a part of it. He was surprised to see Maggie and Praxis still listening so well. In just ten days, they'd done so much. It was easy to forget *how much* had happened in such a small timeframe.

"Eventually he was detained and the Mask was taken off him," Ziva said. "Then the *actual* family was called and brought in for it."

Praxis' pen scratched with finality. "I will type this up in the coming days," he announced. "Congratulations on finishing the mission." He showed off one of his rare smiles and it didn't appear forced. He then settled back, holding his own hands below his chin, and his gaze settled on Quinton. "Quinton, you're free to leave."

Quinton blinked at him. "Free to leave?" he questioned, slightly startled.

Maggie narrowed her eyes. "There are some extra questions we need to ask without you here."

We must ask them if they're going to stay or if they're going to leave.

Those were the real words Maggie hadn't said. But Quinton heard them anyway.

He took a look at Ziva, at Chandler, at his *friends*. Then looked away. What was there to say? While the mission was done, there was still a link in the chain not fully formed or broken, and would remain so until they answered.

And *still*, even now, he couldn't honestly make a bet on what they would choose.

Quinton left his chair and let the door bang behind him with a heavy heart.

CHAPTER THIRTY-TWO
CHANDLER

34th Day of Autumn 2406

Music glided through Redwing. Notes flitted between themselves, tickling the air with their beauty.

Chandler swept up the stairs, trying to remain calm. Her heart was beating so hard it felt like she might collapse at any second. While she listened to that, she ignored the thumping at her sore temple where the bruise still resided.

Helpers passed her, them going down as she went up. She smiled at as many as she could when they looked at her. Most seemed surprised, which was odd.

She followed the music all the way to the top floor. Last night, because she hadn't been able to sleep much, she'd explored more of Redwing. Except she'd never gone into the attic. She'd gotten close, had stood at the door, but had never pressed her hand to it, let alone opened it.

Now she stood outside it again. The music echoed from behind the door accompanied by laughter.

Instead of backing away, she pressed her hand to the door and pushed.

Many other recruits, most of whom she'd seen at breakfast that morning, danced or sat around the edges of the space. Near the centre, a grand black piano was being played by Aleema – Chandler had been told she played mostly at night, but here she was, in the middle of the day.

It felt like there was a party happening and Chandler didn't exactly have an invitation.

She went to turn away when arms encircled her suddenly, dragging her into the fold. Chandler was twirled and then forced to move at a sort of galloping skip. She looked at the face of her partner, and couldn't help the gasp that passed her lips. Gretchen stared down at her.

Chandler had only met Gretchen last night. From first impressions, she didn't have much to go on. She could see the girl's thick eyeliner with wings at the side and neatly drawn eyebrows. Her blonde hair was damp, but had soft waves in it already. There were a few scars around the girl's mouth, tiny and nearly visible, but this close she could see them clearly.

"'ello partner," Gretchen laughed as they continued to dance, not that Chandler had much choice. Gretchen was strong, she'd trapped Chandler in her grasp.

"What are we doing? Is this really a dance?" It felt like they were just galloping with extra energy, turning vigorously as they went, circling around the piano.

"Everyone else is doing it." Gretchen motioned to the other pairs with her head, who were indeed gallop-twist-dancing as well. "I saw you at the door, about to leave. I couldn't 'ave that."

"Why not?" Chandler asked as they made another circle.

"It's a party."

"But you could've let me go."

Gretchen shrugged. "I needed a partner."

"Why is there even a party?"

"We're celebrating the chance that you and the other girl-"

"Ziva," Chandler cut in. Gretchen raised an eyebrow and Chandler realised then just how protective she'd become; how much Ziva had grown on her and how fast they'd really become friends in the past ten days.

"Partner change," Gretchen suddenly exclaimed, grinning.

Without warning, she flung Chandler from her arms. Chandler was sure she'd land on her arse on the hard wooden floorboards. She didn't, though. Something caught her.

"People fall for me all the time."

Scowling at the recognisable voice, Chandler looked up. Quinton grinned down at her. His hair was bright red again, just like it had been when they'd first met. He wore a shirt that was unbuttoned at the top, showing off the crystal that lay several inches below throat. Chandler shivered at being so close to him, at how his body radiated heat like he'd been dancing for days and hadn't stopped.

"I didn't fall," she said back at him.

"Only because I caught you."

"You just love to think the world revolves around you."

His stormy eyes brightened. "Dance around it with me."

They were on the outskirts of the twirling masses, Aleema's music still twinkling from the centre but slightly slower now. Chandler didn't even think, she just grabbed Quinton's outstretched hand.

"I think *you* will be dancing with *me*," she said, and didn't give him a chance to even open his mouth. She yanked him as hard as Gretchen had pulled her and they ended up back in the swirling fray.

"What is this song?" Chandler said over the noise.

"It's one of Aleema's," he answered. "She doesn't just play. She writes, too."

"What's she doing here then? She should be out in the world, bringing her music to everyone."

"You should tell her that, though be wary of how big her head might get."

Chandler managed to shove him slightly. "No one's head will ever be as big as yours."

He laughed and swung her round. "But this place is the safest there is for people like us. For *Abnormals*. You saw the world on our mission. Redwing gives us a chance. *All* of us."

Chandler said nothing else and allowed Quinton to take the lead. He made the movements seems easy as he pulled and pushed her, twisted and twirled. Chandler hadn't done a day of dancing in her life, not even back at the bar she used to work at. But this felt freeing, fun.

Eventually, the music began to drift until tiny notes came from the high end of the keys.

The pairs began to break off to the sides for a rest. Though two pairs did remain – Wane and Flora, and then two girls Chandler didn't know – dancing together under the calmer tone, holding each other close like they were afraid to let go.

Chandler peeled away from Quinton and turned back towards the door. She'd only come up here really to investigate the music, not to get involved in it. Yet she couldn't deny the racing of her heart and how it was beating for fun and not in fear for once.

She lent up against the wall, so close to the door she could back out if she wanted but she made no move to leave. She knew Ziva was in the gardens getting some fresh air. Chandler crossed her arms and propped one foot back up against the wall.

Quinton walked over and joined her. "I believe I owe you this."

Chandler turned and saw what he held out; a tin of the Pink Rose Tea from the café they'd visited. Chandler had almost forgotten about it, but seeing it now tingled her tongue.

"There's one for you and one for Ziva," he announced.

"Why?"

"I said I'd buy it for you. Ziva was the one to suggest giving it once the mission was over, if I remember correctly."

Tentatively, she reached out and took it, then looked up at him. "She was," Chandler agreed. "But what is *your* reason for giving it? Because I remember you saying first that you'd get us both some to "welcome us to the club", I think were your words."

He shook his head. "They don't sound like my words."

"They sound very much like your words." Gretchen appeared at their side. She eyed the tin in Chandler's hands, eyebrows raised. "*Café au lait* tea? I'm impressed. Their peach scones? Incredible."

Chandler shook the tin. "I'm all about the Pink Rose Tea, here." Gretchen smiled.

Quinton looked over Chandler's head, straining to peer round the door. "Where's Ziva?"

"Outside," Chandler said.

"What's she doing out there?" Gretchen asked. "It's hardly a nice day."

Quinton stared sideways at his friend, smiling. "Your version of a nice day is one where there is cloud cover or maybe rain."

"Something wrong with that?"

As loud as he could, Quinton called, "We're moving this party *outside!*"

A flurry of motion all happened at once. Quinton winked at Chandler and dashed off. She looked to Gretchen, a little open-mouthed, who shrugged and followed. Chandler had no choice but to follow as well.

The crowd moved through the house like a tumbling of animals. Some seemed to race, while others took their time.

The doors leading outside were thrown open, and the crowd piled out. Chandler put her tea down on the table and rushed after them. She wished she hadn't. The crowd had already surrounded Ziva, who was chatting to the guard who had first transported them both here; Chandler made a mental note to remember that for later.

Someone in the crowd grabbed Chandler, pushing her towards Ziva as if to create a barrier around them both.

"Now let's *really* get this party started!" called a voice Chandler couldn't place.

Ziva shuddered visibly. "Why is there a party?"

Chandler grimaced. "Something to do with us, *again*."

"What are your final answers?" Quinton stepped into the middle of the circle, and Chandler whirled to face him. She felt Ziva do the same at her side.

"Isn't that something private?" Ziva piped up, somehow finding her voice despite a mass of people around her.

"Not if you're staying!" said someone.

"Not if we have to say goodbye!" said someone else at the same time.

Quinton walked closer. "So?" he pressed.

Ziva stepped forwards and Chandler saw her smile. "I'm staying."

Chandler's heart raced in her chest as she held her hands up. "I guess I'm guilty too."

Quinton's face illuminated but it was quickly swallowed by the crowd as they surged. Before Chandler could even scream, she was being lifted into the air. She looked over to Ziva, and found she too was being raised, and then they were both being carried.

Chandler hadn't looked much at the grounds around Redwing but she wish she had. Beyond the small garden that *could* be seen, lay more land, almost like open space that went on for miles. In the middle of that land, probably closer than it looked, was a lake.

And within minutes, Chandler was thrown into it.

She splashed under the water but found her feet touching the floor. The water was warm, at least, so she stopped her immediate panic. She felt something touch her hand and she knew it was Ziva. Grabbing it, she knew the one way that would get them out of the water fast.

A chill settled around her shoulders a moment later and she clung onto Ziva, pulling her closer. Slowly, but surely, they began to rise.

Cheers on the banks were heard, until they slowly petered out at the sight before them.

The girl rose together, but neither of them were swimming. Once Chandler had calmed, she'd let her powers flow and reach into the water. Below her, the water had begun to solidify into ice and it was pushing them out from the bottom up like rising platforms. Once they reached their full height on top of the surface, with a resounding *crunch,* the lake had frozen over completely beneath Chandler's feet.

Her and Ziva began to walk across the ice together, side by side, just as they'd started here.

It didn't matter that she was sopping wet or exhausted. She grinned. She couldn't help it.

Her grin only widened when she found the pure look of shock on the Grittal twins' faces and as Quinton yelped with cheers of ecstasy, loud enough to be heard over the rest of the recruits they were surrounded by.

EPILOGUE

GRETCHEN

40th Day of Autumn 2406

"You're a *twat*!" she whispered harshly.

Wane rolled his eyes. "Hardly."

"I'm not the idiot who jumped out of the third-floor window!" He shrank at little at that, and she sighed. "I should just leave you with your broken wrists and make them heal at a regular, *humanly normal* pace."

"You should," he said, mouth quirking. "But you won't."

Gretchen grumbled without actually saying anything. Wane was right, after all. She wouldn't leave *anyone* with broken bones if she could fix them, no matter how irritating or stupid they were.

It took several more minutes of mentally stitching and bending bones back into place in the wrists before there was a resounding *crack* from each one. Wane yelped and Gretchen dropped her hold.

"You're done," she announced.

Wane rubbed each wrist in turn. "Is it meant to feel like your bones are being set on fire when you do that?"

She shrugged. "I can't heal myself, so I don't know what it feels like."

"Point."

"Just, promise me no more jumping out any windows?"

Wane stalked right up to her, eyebrow raised. "You know I can't promise you that."

"Not with those brothers of yours."

"This wasn't a bet."

That stumped her. "It wasn't? Then why'd you jump?"

"Quinton had already seen me fall."

Gretchen scrunched up her face. "So you changed your fate by pushing yourself? You're not just a twat, you're a fucking—"

"Ey," he cut in, drawing out the word. "I actually *fell* out of the window. I was up there with Aleema. She'd had some nightmares and I tried to calm her down. We got too close to the window..."

"She pushed you," Gretchen sighed.

"Not on purpose," he argued. "I was just trying to help, but her music sent me. You know what it's like and how powerful she can be."

Gretchen sighed again, this time leaning forwards to press her head into Wane's chest. "I do," she agreed.

Not only did Aleema have nightmares, but the way she played music was incredible. She used one to counter the other. But like the pied piper of old tales, Aleema could use music to make someone do what she wished with notes of any kind at any moment if she willed it. Gretchen had been caught up in many dancing parades, but nothing harmful. But if Aleema had seen Wane as an enemy, not fully out of her nightmares, then of course she would've accidently attacked him.

"What were you doing touching Quinton's crystal?" Gretchen asked next.

"Now *that* was a bet," he answered, laughing, jolting her as he did. "All of us did it."

"And then you get me to fix you right up."

Wane touched under her chin, drawing her face up to look at him. His eyes were soft; the look much kinder than anything his brothers would probably ever wear. He smiled, then whispered, "You didn't have to."

She rolled her eyes. "There are a lot of things I don't have to do. But I do."

"Just for me."

She laughed and stepped out of his grip. "Did someone break a brain-cell in the fall, too? I can't fix those."

Wane's face changed to one of mischief. Gretchen laughed as he reached her, though went deadly silent as she was pressed to the wall, Wane's body pinning her. His hands slipped under her shirt, fingers drawing up her sides, thumb stopping just short of her bralette.

He dipped his head, breathing into her ear. "I think you made me right as rain."

Two could play that game. Gretchen stepped out of his arms and thrust him against the wall. She kept one hand on his chest – not that it would hold him if he didn't want it to.

"Someone's cocky," she teased.

"Someone's honest," he replied.

"Is that so?"

"What's there to lie about?"

Gretchen stepped closer, right between his legs, and slid her hands up to his neck. "Do you want *my* honest answer?"

She stood on tip-toes and he reached under her, looping his arms under her arse to pull her up higher with ease – his gift was strength after all. She kissed him, deep and solidly. He moaned against her mouth and crushed her against him harder.

Wane moved his kisses to her cheeks, her ear, her neck, her throat. Little movements along her skin that had her jittery. She forced him to lower her and then grabbed his collar, guiding him by it to the nearby bed.

Gretchen tipped backwards and Wane crawled overtop of her, pressing his body down on hers. Her hands immediately went to the front of his shirt, and when that was gone, she went for his belt. He equally touched her with fire; one hand cupped her breast while the other fiddled with the button on her jeans until it popped open and he could draw them off with impatience.

Egypt had been the game-changer for them. Staying in one room, discovering ancient bones, and fawning over one mission together had been the kindling. The ever-present tension had been the spark.

Gretchen had been the one to make a move first, and Wane hadn't pulled away. They'd spent the night, and then the ones that followed, with each other in both fast and slow motion.

She would've bet that she'd never have seen any of *this* in her best friend's crystal.

It wasn't that Gretchen hadn't been interested in Wane. He had always seemed good. They'd just never spent *that* much time together, and his brothers were nearly always around to some capacity – they weren't now because they were interested in the newbies and themselves – so they hadn't been given time before. Their close-quarters mission had changed things.

Gretchen had always thought herself interested in women. No man had ever appealed to her in any sort of way, but Wane was different. It made her head fuzzy to think about. It confused her. But she also didn't want to think about it. She just knew this was right for her right now. She'd deal with her thoughts later.

Wane put on the protection he'd need and pressed into her, nipping at her collarbone as he went. Gretchen let out a breath. His pace increased gradually and she felt herself grow more impatient, but in a good way. He bit the bottom of her ear, something she enjoyed, as he let go. Instead of fully pulling away, he dipped his hand and continued his motions, even more intensely focused on her now.

Gretchen came undone with a crashing gasp.

Seconds before the doorbell rang.

The two of them scrambled for their clothes, laughing, pink cheeked. Gretchen was still adjusting her shirt as they reached the first-floor landing, but no one seemed to notice. The door rang again.

"What do you reckon?" Quinton asked, coming to stand beside them.

"Beats me," Wane shrugged casually.

Gretchen pointed at Quinton's necklace. "Can't your magic eight-ball tell you?"

He glared at her. "Ha-ha," he said dryly.

Down below, Violette moved towards the door, her overly-tall heels clicking. Now *she* was someone that seemed to get everyone in this place ticking to some degree, though Gretchen would *never* cross that line – Violette was a snake to look at from afar, nothing more.

Ziva and Chandler came into view from Praxis' office, probably handing in their debrief reports if Gretchen had to guess. They looked up at the same time. Ziva lowered her gaze first, then Chandler.

Gretchen went to say something to Quinton and noticed he was staring in the direction of the girls, at Chandler. She'd seen how they'd danced, how she'd been in his room before. She smirked.

"She's pretty," she whispered.

Quinton scowled directly at her, like he hadn't been thinking that, or hadn't even *seen* the girls until Gretchen had mentioned them. What was he seeing then? What was he thinking? She'd ask. It was her duty as best friend.

"She is," Wane agreed from her other side.

Violette opened the front door and the entire Mansion held its breath. Visitors didn't happen here. The whole place was guarded, so the only people who could come and go were the ones that knew where it was.

Except this person couldn't be one of them.

The doors opened and the collective breath of every person in the room tightened in their chests. Gretchen looked between the visitor and Quinton, and it was like he'd seen a ghost.

On the doorstep was no visitor. It was a wonder she'd even gotten here considering she wasn't even *abnormal*.

"What the fuck?" Gretchen whispered.

Quinton shook his head and made his way to the stairs, and stopped halfway.

Gretchen reached through the air for the visitor's bones, yet couldn't seem to get close. She glared, but the female guest didn't notice. Her eyes were locked on Quinton, confidence oozing out of them.

Frantically, Gretchen looked to Wane, looked to *everyone*, but no one was going to help. No one *could* help. This was no one's business but Quinton's.

And this was his illegitimate sister.

End of Book One

ACKNOWLEDGEMENTS

This project started as a silly little NaNoWriMo thing in 2021. It was meant to be a way for me to clear my head and just be creative without worries or restrictions. It certainly did that, and it wasn't the story I wanted to tell but definitely became something *more*.

So I want to say thank you to Hannah, as always, for coming on this wild ride of masks and mystery with me. Your insight is never dull and I do, somewhat, apologise for the chaotic messages I send you way too early or late in the day. This book really is yours. You are a superhero with the power to control me and my chaos. You deserve all the awards and praise.

And I also want to say thank you to the (mostly) bookish friends I have made. To Alexandria, Natalia, Gennie, Dani, Alexa, Kirsten, Sydney, Hannah, Ashleigh, Jessie, and Tracy. Your continual support and hype never gets old. I could thrive on your kindness for years!

Lastly, I want to thank those that helped me, once again, bring my story to life. To my editor, formatter, cover artist – thank you so much. You all made this book become a real thing. This one is for you too.

ABOUT THE AUTHOR

LAUREN JADE CASE

is a writer from a seaside town in England. She loves writing and reading fantasy, but also sci-fi, dystopia, and occasionally crime/mystery. When she isn't writing, she can be found reading or talking on facetime with her best friend about trips to Scotland or future creative projects.

STARLIGHT is her debut novel and the first in a trilogy, with *STARFALL* as the second book. *BEARER OF MASKS* is a completely new book set in an entirely new universe.

Twitter: @ LaaureenJaadee

Instagram: @ LaaureenJaadee

CPSIA information can be obtained
at www.ICGtesting.com
Printed in the USA
BVHW071005211122
652422BV00005B/188

9 781916 888777